I0619163

SWEET LIFE
A SUGAR RUSH ROMANCE

NINA LANE

SNOW QUEEN
PUBLISHING

Sweet Life
A Sugar Rush Romance

Published by Snow Queen Publishing

This book is a work of fiction. All names, characters, locations, and incidents are products of the author's imagination, or have been used fictitiously. Any resemblance to actual persons living or dead, locales, or events is entirely coincidental.

Cover photography: Sara Eirew
Cover design: Perfect Pear Creative Covers

ISBN: 978-1-954185-02-9

NINA LANE'S SWEET LIFE

❦

He knows if she's been bad or good.

Ice queen Julia Bennett is hot for Sugar Rush CEO Warren
Stone…but will an explosive, sexy night shatter their longtime
friendship?

Warning!
Contains Christmas peppermint martinis, Grinchiness, designer
gowns, red stilettos, mountains, Rubik's Cubes, mulled wine, and
mistletoe sex.

The Sugar Rush books are sexy contemporary romances by New
York Times bestselling author Nina Lane. They can be read as a
standalone or enjoyed as part of the Sugar Rush series.

SWEET DREAMS
SWEET ESCAPE
SWEET SURRENDER
SWEET TIME
SWEET LIFE

Making a list
Checking it twice
Need a good scotch
With a lot of ice.

Julia Bennett checked *Schedule Santa's Elves* off the bullet-point list in her calfskin Montblanc agenda and closed the book. She eyed the remaining action items she still needed to execute for the Deck the Halls show. When she checked off the last bullet point, she would finally be free from the shackles of tinsel and red ribbons.

Not a moment too soon.

Less than two weeks until Christmas, and Julia was sick to death of forced cheer, candy canes, and those blasted holiday ear-worms slithering through her brain. If she heard "Frosty the Snowman" one more time, she'd take a flame-thrower to the fat little creature. And if one more person offered her a stale ginger-bread cookie, she'd grind it beneath the heel of her pointed-toe suede Balenciaga.

Yes, it was a shitty attitude for the woman who was coordinating the extravagant show for the final night of the Indigo Bay Holiday Festival. Every year, the coastal California town hosted a cherished two-week festival involving a gingerbread house contest, arts-and-crafts fairs, musical events, and children's activities—all culminating in Deck the Halls on Christmas Eve, held onstage in front of the town Christmas tree and Santa's Sleigh.

Julia had been more than confident in her ability to coordinate the show of Indigo Bay's resident talent. After all, she owned a successful styling company, organized fashion shows and high-end photo shoots, had worked at top fashion magazines, and hosted numerous events for her late sister's charity foundation. She was experienced, gifted, *skilled*.

But she'd underestimated the festival committee's urge to micro-manage her while knowing perfectly well that Julia Bennett refused to subordinate to anyone. Not to mention the show's lack of budget and the differences between corralling models and corralling thirty acts involving bell ringers, five-year-old tap dancers, poodle acts, a barber shop quartet, amateur magicians, and heaven knew what else.

While the townspeople made up for in enthusiasm what they lacked in actual talent, the whole event had Julia ready to dive into the spiked eggnog and not come out until summer.

She also hadn't considered the fact that all six of her nephews and her adored niece would be in town for the holidays and that they would expect every single family tradition to be carried out to perfection since, of course, Aunt Julia had it all planned. Just like she did every year.

Except every other year she hadn't been reeling from a catastrophic business failure that had her questioning her entire career.

Every other year, she hadn't been facing a milestone birthday looming like a boulder at the top of a cliff, poised to crash down on her like something out of an Indiana Jones movie.

Every other year, Warren Stone—president of the Sugar Rush

Candy Company and the man Julia would have called her *BFF* if she were prone to employing teenage-girl terms—hadn't been hiding something from her.

Every other year, her composure hadn't been fraying at the edges like a badly made pashmina scarf.

Julia turned her attention back to the sketched design and photograph on her desk. She crossed her arms and tapped her French-manicured fingernails on the sleeves of her Chanel suit. Then she sent a lethal glare to the young woman seated across from her.

"Is this a joke?" she snapped.

"Er, no." Her assistant Anisa fidgeted in the chair on the other side of the desk, tugging at the hem of her miniskirt. "Well, I was trying to be fashion-forward."

"This doesn't even qualify as fashion *upside-the-fuck-down.*" Julia placed her fingertip on the photo and pushed it back across the glass desk. "Here's a bit of advice, dear. Pairing faux-fur and sheer chiffon is the visual equivalent of drinking red wine with peppermint schnapps. In other words, it's a vomit-inducing disaster. And even your mother knows that if you look in the mirror and can see your pussy through your dress...*don't wear it.*"

Anisa mumbled an apology, two bright spots of embarrassment appearing on her cheeks as she grabbed the photo. "I'll try again."

"See that you do more than *try.* Now please brighten my day with your absence."

Anisa scurried across the room on her four-inch stilettoes, letting the door slam shut behind her.

Julia made a huffing noise of contempt and skimmed her hands over her skirt. Faux fur and sheer chiffon, for God's sake. It was especially annoying coming from Anisa, who had shown great promise in the months she'd been working at Julia Bennett Style.

Of course, no one knew better than Julia that fashion was subject to varying degrees of criticism from…well, *everyone*.

Her phone rang with a call from Minnie the Pitbull, one of the councilwomen on the Holiday Festival committee. Julia steeled her spine before responding.

"Hello, Julie," Minnie said.

"Jul*ia*."

"Sharon from the Jingle Belles acapella group called me with questions about their costumes for Deck the Halls," Minnie continued. "She claims you haven't responded to her email."

Julia attempted not to grit her teeth. Her email inbox was about to self-implode with messages. "I haven't gotten to it yet."

"I suggest you get to it soon, considering your rehearsals are coming up."

"I am aware. Thank you for the reminder."

"What about the fireworks?" Minnie asked.

"We don't have the budget for fireworks. I have explained that to you."

"Well, everyone will be extremely disappointed if you can't make it happen," Minnie informed her.

"I can't pull money out of thin air, much as I would enjoy that talent."

"I'm just saying that people have expectations for the finale, so I hope you will meet them," Minnie said. "I'm going to email you Howard's rider. He has certain requirements, such as Evian water and Sugar Rush Chocolate Crunchies."

"He's Santa," Julia said. "Not Kanye West."

"Exactly."

Julia hung up the phone with restrained force and took a few cleansing breaths. She was controlled, self-possessed, efficient. She'd always been cool under pressure. All right, not *always*, but her youthful ridiculousness was forgivable.

After moving to London at twenty-two, she'd been determined

to reinvent herself as a woman of poise and sophistication. She'd thrown herself to the task, starting as an intern at *Tatler* and working her way into positions at *Harpers & Queen*, *i-D*, *Look*, and *British Vogue*. She'd done her time under editrixes worse than Anna Wintour and had made more than her fair share of mistakes.

But she'd learned from them, and after returning to Indigo Bay thirteen years ago, she'd started her own successful company. Now she was renowned not only for her expertise and career, which had also included stints at *Vogue* and *Harper's Bazaar*, but also for her position in the wealthy Stone family. Owners of the Sugar Rush Candy Company, the Stones had long dominated the commercial and economic status of Indigo Bay and surrounding towns along the California coast.

As the family matriarch for the past thirteen years, Julia used the position to her advantage. She was aunt to the six Stone brothers and their youngest sister, and she was director of the Rebecca Stone Foundation, which she and Warren had created after Rebecca's death. Julia's many fundraising events had catapulted the foundation to one of the most well-known and funded charitable organizations in the state.

But still...not even that prestige was armor against recent events.

Julia sat in her white leather executive chair and turned to her computer. Her office was usually her sanctuary—a pure, clean space where she could sharpen and focus her mind and creativity. White carpeting, glass and steel étagères, Scandinavian bookshelves. Framed copies of Julia's magazine shoots, awards, photographs, and articles lined the walls.

At the moment, however, the room seemed cold and unforgiving, a direct contrast to the anger that had been ricocheting through her since yesterday.

Her phone's ringtone started playing the song "I Want Candy." The familiar tune made her heart jump. The ringtone was assigned to the man she'd missed during his two-week trip to Switzerland.

She reached for the phone, then stopped. She'd ignored Warren's usual 1:00pm call, and she hadn't responded to his texts since his return yesterday. She couldn't put him off much longer without raising suspicion.

She also couldn't talk to him yet, even though she was accustomed to telling him everything.

Letting the phone go to voicemail, she turned back to the slew of emails in her inbox. The failure of the Evermore deal had hit her hard in multiple places—her company, her reputation, her self-confidence.

What if the Evermore president had been right? What if she *had* lost her design skills? What if she was out of touch with what younger women wanted? Any other time, such criticism would have rolled off her back, but this had exploded through her like a grenade.

Julia blinked against a sting of tears just as a knock came at the door.

"Come in," she called sharply.

Marco appeared with a white china bowl containing a kale salad. Her assistant crossed the room, his elegant, olive-toned features drawn into an expression of mild scolding—which made her remember the horror of faux fur and chiffon.

Julia sighed. "Do *not* tell me she's crying."

"Okay." He set the salad at her elbow and placed a silver fork and cloth napkin beside it. "I won't tell you that."

"Fine." Julia tossed the napkin over her lap and picked up the fork. "Tears build fortitude."

"Then you must have cried a river in your time."

Julia glared at him. Of all her employees, Marco had been working for her the longest and had earned—or taken—the ability to speak to her bluntly without fear of reprisal.

"Did you *see* what she came up with?" Julia stabbed the fork into the kale. "Camel toe isn't even a fashion *don't*. It's a fashion *no-fucking-way-oh-my-bleeding-eyes*."

Marco smirked. "I'll admit it was worse than Lady Gaga's meat dress...okay, maybe not that bad...but cut the girl some slack. She's trying to find her own look, which isn't easy when you're working in the shadow of Julia Bennett."

"Don't be ingratiating. This stuff tastes like grass." Julia set the fork down and pressed a hand to her temple. "Did you get the Deck the Halls fliers done?"

"In your inbox." He nodded toward the computer, his impossibly thick eyelashes and big eyes making him look like the Bambi version of an Italian stallion. "And Lucy of Poodle-O-Doodles called wanting to be sure you'll have Bits-O-Bacon on hand for her performance."

"I told her she needs to bring her own dog treats."

"Apparently she expects the show to provide them."

"Fine. I'll deal with it." Julia waved for him to take the salad away. "And I want your ideas for the Radar fashion shoot on my desk by eight tomorrow morning, or I'll give the project to Enzo."

Marco rolled his eyes, having heard that threat more than once. He picked up the salad and left, letting the door slam none-too-subtly behind him. Julia turned back to her computer. A few seconds later, the door clicked open again.

"If you don't have a brilliant, mind-blowing idea, then go away," she said, her gaze on the screen.

"Let's skip Christmas and go to Seville instead."

Startled, she glanced up. Warren Stone stood in front of her desk as if he'd materialized there by sheer force of will.

"I was about to send out an APB on you." Like a good scotch, his deep voice both soothed her prickly nerves and twisted heat through her.

She rose to her feet, her heart increasing in rhythm as she drank in the sight of him after his two weeks away. Tall and broad-shouldered, with thick, silver-streaked dark hair and a gorgeous, muscular frame, Warren had always appealed to her aesthetic sensibilities. His features were strong and regal—square jaw; wide, firm mouth; those thick-lashed brown eyes that could twinkle with warmth as easily as harden with anger. The boys all resembled him, a line of handsome princes molded in the image of their kingly father.

At the moment, he looked especially distinguished in a tailored Armani suit and a tie patterned with jelly beans—the authoritative corporate president who didn't take himself too seriously.

But though Julia admired Warren's devastating good looks— as did many other women—his physicality was second to his character and the numerous qualities he possessed in abundance. Strength, honor, loyalty, sharp intelligence, confidence, a deep, unending love for his family. *Everything* made Warren Stone the gold standard against which all other men fell painfully short.

Julia tightened her hand on a pen. "What are you doing here?"

"Wondering why you haven't responded to my calls or texts." Warren's gaze skimmed over her. "Where've you been?"

"Just busy." She wasn't ready to tell him about Evermore, though she would eventually. She always ended up telling him everything. Well, almost everything.

"You never take so long to get back to me," he said. "What's going on?"

"Nothing."

His eyes narrowed slightly. "Did you have a migraine yesterday? When I called your office, Enzo said you'd left early."

Julia gripped the pen harder. The effects of the headache still lingered—a dull throb right behind her eyes.

"Warren, I'm fine. I realize you're accustomed to people responding to your messages in three seconds, but sometimes I have better things to do. How was your trip? Your meetings with Alpine Chocolates?"

He shrugged. "Uneventful."

Liar. According to her nephew Luke, Warren had scaled back his work with Alpine Chocolates, the Swiss company that was Sugar Rush's newest acquisition. So whatever the hell he had been doing in Switzerland, it hadn't been business-related.

Which meant it had to be *pleasure*-related. So why wasn't he telling her the truth? She suppressed the urge to push for more information. If he didn't want to tell her, she certainly wouldn't lower herself to finagling him for answers.

They studied each other for a second, like two cats circling, neither of them happy with the other's vague responses. A deep temptation rose in Julia, the urge to tell him what had happened, confess how much it all hurt, and let him help her work through it. That was how she'd dealt with all of her disappointments and failures over the last thirteen years.

Not that there had been *that* many. Certainly not of Evermore's magnitude.

"So have you talked to the boys yet?" she asked quickly, wanting to preempt him before he questioned her further.

"I'm on my way. Detoured here when you didn't answer my call again." He glanced at his watch. "I'll talk to them in about an hour."

"You're really going through with it?"

"It's not a gauntlet." Faint amusement shone in his brown eyes. "It's just early retirement."

"No one, especially none of your sons, have ever expected you to retire at all, much less *early*," Julia pointed out. "So make sure you won't wake up tomorrow morning regretting it."

"I won't. When are you leaving here? I'll meet you at Lotus for dinner."

Much as she longed to commiserate with him over curry and a bottle of wine, he didn't need to hear about the overall shittiness of her week right after telling his sons he planned to retire as Sugar Rush president.

She'd tell him about Evermore later, after she'd had time to figure out what to do. Even though a year's worth of work had been an utter waste, the project itself was still viable and good. *Maybe*. If she hadn't lost all her creativity and sense of innovation.

"I can't go to dinner," she said. "I'm going to see Tyler, then I'm working at home this evening. I need to review the details for the holiday car show."

He frowned. "You told me you were leaving that to him."

"I am, but it's overlapping with some of the festival events, so I told him I'd make sure there's no conflict."

"Julia."

Her name in his stern, disapproving voice sounded like he'd caught a butterfly with his big hands. She bit her lip, suppressing an instinctive flush. He didn't often use that strict voice with her, but it was the *only* thing in the world that made her feel like a girl about to be punished.

He put his hands on the desk and leaned closer, his gaze pulling her attention to him again. Her nose tickled with the familiar scent of him—spicy shaving cream, the aroma of cloves and citrus. She forced herself to meet his eyes, to quell the racing of her heart.

"I'll tell you again," Warren continued evenly. "You're doing too damned much. You did not need to take over Deck the Halls this year in addition to everything else."

Julia expelled a breath of frustration. "If I hadn't, there wouldn't be a festival finale since Jessica overspent last year and got herself fired, which means we have a lousy budget this year. No one else stepped up, so I had to."

"That doesn't mean you have to do it all yourself," Warren said, his features still hard with his *strict schoolmaster* expression. "And you sure as hell don't need to help Tyler with his car show. What you *need* to do is delegate."

"I did." Irritation tightened her neck. "Mia Donovan is handling the Sugar Rush holiday party this year."

"You mean she's helping you because you won't turn it over to her completely." Warren pushed away from the desk, a deep crease appearing between his eyebrows. "If I could ban you from the foundation events, I would."

"You would not," Julia replied curtly. "All the work I do raising money for the foundation comes to fruition during the holidays. You're not taking it from me."

"You need to let something else go."

It was his *command* tone now, not his *gentle suggestion* tone.

The tenuous thread holding Julia's composure together stretched tighter. Warren Stone had been an exemplary leader for years—both of his company and his family—because he knew exactly how to balance control and delegation. He'd trusted his son Luke to take Sugar Rush's reins when he needed to be with his daughter in the hospital, but even then, no one had ever doubted the fact that Warren Stone was still in charge.

In the thirteen years following the car accident that had killed Warren's wife and Julia's sister Rebecca, Warren had achieved a legendary status as the kingmaker, the final authority his sons always consulted before making decisions.

And while Julia was well aware of Warren's mythical reputation, she'd known him since she was fourteen years old. He and Rebecca had started dating at nineteen and were married at twenty. No one more than Julia admired all that Warren had become, but she also remembered the cocky teenager he'd been with a thousand-watt grin and plans to change the world. She remembered the protective brother-in-law, the nervous young father, the dedicated boy working his way up in the family company, the husband devastated over his wife's tragic death.

No one but Julia knew all the complex layers that made up the Sugar Rush kingmaker and president—which was exactly why his criticism of her stung deep.

"You're telling me to delegate when you just spent two weeks in Switzerland working with Sugar Rush's chocolate division," she remarked. "Sounds a bit hypocritical, doesn't it?"

"I'm finalizing projects before I retire."

"And I never take on anything I can't handle," she informed him. "I'll thank you not to believe otherwise."

"I didn't say you couldn't handle it. But if the stress is triggering your headaches, something has to change."

"Thanks, doctor." She sat back down and turned to the computer. "I need to get back to work. Good luck talking to the boys."

She felt him watching her for a second before he turned and strode to the door.

"We're not finished," he said.

The door closed. Regret knotted Julia's chest that his return had been discolored by their bickering. Though she appreciated his concern—he was the only person outside of her doctor who knew about her increasingly severe migraines—she still disliked him pointing out her weaknesses. Maybe because, aside from his children, he'd never seemed to have any of his own. And she never wanted him to discover her biggest weakness of all.

She sent a few emails, then shut off her computer and picked up her satchel and coat. Buttoning it up, she walked out to where Marco was studying a photo layout on the front desk computer.

"I'm taking off early today," Julia told him.

"What about Catherine Markham?" Marco asked. "She'll be here at six for her styling."

The last thing Julia wanted was to face a wealthy, inquisitive socialite who was likely to interrogate her about her projects. While she still handled a great deal of personal styling for Indigo Bay's elite, more and more she'd been wanting to return to her design roots.

"This is me delegating you to handle Catherine Markham." She waved her hand in Marco's direction. "Just don't let her tits pop out of her dress. She'd love to have a wardrobe malfunction, but I'll eat a dozen donuts before I let my name be associated with the public baring of Catherine Markham's surgery-enhanced breasts."

"Let's not get carried away now," Marco muttered dryly. "At most, you'd lick off the powdered sugar."

"Sticking one's tongue out is both crude and visually unappealing."

"That's why we only do it behind your back."

Julia shot him an icy glare, then turned to the door before he could see her crack a smile.

Julia dropped her satchel onto the foyer table and kicked off her shoes. Usually her tension drained the instant she stepped into her house with its pale hardwood floors, white walls, and décor that was a mixture of high-end investments and personal items she had purchased in her travels.

Now, however, not even her own space made her feel better. Nothing could. She was out of wine, it would take too long to make waffles, and her hot water heater was still broken. Her vibrator was charged, but after her shitty week, even masturbation seemed like too much effort. And that was saying something.

Outdated. Tired. Passé.

Vincent Peck's remarks echoed like bullets. She hated that she was letting him get to her—she'd taken plenty of criticism in her time without letting it dent her armor one iota—but this was personal.

She stripped out of her linen suit and changed into black yoga pants and a fitted red Givenchy T-shirt. She splashed water on her face, squinting at her reflection in the mirror.

Despite her approaching milestone birthday, the girl Julia was still evident in her bone structure and the angles of her face. She'd always paid exceptional attention to herself, and her care showed in her smooth, taut skin and tight figure. She'd learned early on that everything about her—from her shoulder-length, honey-blonde hair to her designer clothes and flawless makeup—reflected both her company and her family. Short of actual surgery, she went to great lengths to look her best.

But right now, she both felt and looked every minute of the past fif—no, *forty-fucking-nine* years.

Julia reapplied lipstick and returned to the living room. She had no desire to mope around the house feeling sorry for herself. Since Warren would still be with his sons, she'd go to his house and add her Christmas decorations to his. She never bothered decorating her own house since all the family gatherings took place at Warren's. And he was certain to have a bottle of excellent wine on hand, which she could certainly use right now.

She went into the garage and opened the storage closet. Shelves were stacked with worn cardboard boxes, several labelled *Christmas Decorations*. She set one in the truck of her car and took a second box down from the shelf.

A tattered old shoebox fell to the ground. She bent to pick it up. Her heart suddenly stuttered. She stepped into the garage light and opened the box.

Why had she kept a bunch of mementos? A small dried bouquet of wildflowers. Old photographs of her and Sam—one of Julia wearing a worn patchwork maxi dress and a bandana, of all things—a few trinkets, torn concert tickets. So many years ago, all those memories now distilled to the contents of a shoebox.

A folded, wrinkled piece of paper lay at the bottom. Julia smoothed out the creases to read her own handwriting, still bold and vivacious despite the thirty-year-old faded ink.

Things To Do Before I Turn Fifty

She'd totally forgotten about the list. She'd written it somewhere out in the desert when she and Sam had been on their way back from Vegas. Hot dry air blowing into the car, her bare feet sticking out the side window, her head resting on Sam's shoulder. He'd laughed indulgently at her as she wrote out her list in a notebook and drew little pictures in the margins. Giddy, full of anticipation and hope, she'd detailed all she'd wanted to accomplish before the fifty-year milestone.

She scanned the various numbered items.

27. Learn to say the alphabet backward.
18. Make a working volcano.
43. Memorize all the verses of "It Came Upon a Midnight Clear."
39. Learn the etymology of my name.
21. Color an entire coloring book.

For God's sake. What a silly girl she'd been. She'd have been much better off writing a list of practical, ambitious goals, like *Become senior editor at Style, Travel to Paris, Milan, and Tokyo, Start my own business.*

Or even *Learn how to dress like an adult woman and not an airy-fairy little hippie girl.*

If she'd written a list like that, she could have marked all the items as *completed.*

With a huff of irritation, she crumpled the list and tossed it back into the shoebox. She strode to the trash bin and dumped the box on top of a filled garbage bag.

Just as she was about to slam the lid down, she grabbed the wadded-up list from the shoebox and let the trash lid fall.

What the hell was she doing? She had no interest in an asinine list she'd written thirty years ago. Yet she found herself shoving it into her handbag before loading the other boxes of Christmas decorations into the trunk.

She drove to Warren's house, the tension in her shoulders eased a bit as she navigated the winding, hilly roads and passed the gate leading into his estate. The ten acres of land were a haven of nature and wildlife. The Tuscan-style villa fit beautifully into the landscape, the stone siding and curved windows radiating stately warmth and peace.

She brought the boxes inside. After Thanksgiving, she'd put up lights, candles, Christmas figurines and pillows, but they hadn't yet gotten the tree since the boys and Warren had wanted to wait until Hailey returned this weekend. A stack of fresh boughs, mistletoe, and wreaths sat by the door, waiting to be placed.

Julia opened a box and took out several Christmas candles. She tried not to think about the list crumpled in her purse. The one detailing all the ridiculous things she'd wanted to do before she turned fifty.

How many of them had she actually done? Her birthday was next month.

Not that it mattered. She had no need for a decades-old list that she'd created during the most irresponsible phase of her life. The last thing she needed right now was the unearthing of all her bitter regrets.

Especially the ones involving Warren Stone.

CHAPTER 1

"This is a joke, right?" Luke asked.

Warren Stone turned from the vast windows overlooking the ocean from his eighth floor corner office at Sugar Rush. The noon sunlight spilled into the room. Four of his sons stood in varying stances of surprise and frustration—Luke with his arms crossed, Carson with his hands shoved in his pockets, Evan unconsciously rubbing his chest, Spencer slouched against the desk. Tension stretched the air.

"This is not a joke," Warren said. "You knew I would retire eventually."

"Maybe ten or fifteen years from now," Evan replied. "And we figured you'd give us some notice, too. Like a year or two."

Warren frowned. "I've no intention of giving you a year or two to replace me. I'd be useless within a few months. A lame duck presidency isn't the way I intend to end a thirty-year career at Sugar Rush."

"You don't have to end it at all," Carson pointed out. "If you want to step down from the presidency, fine, but you can take another position. Or work as a consultant. Right?"

"No. My career at Sugar Rush is at an end."

"Dad, you can't just *quit*." Luke paced across the room, his forehead creasing. "You have a *job* here."

"I know that." As president, Warren had overseen the day-to-day Sugar Rush operations and developed strategies to fulfill CEO Luke's vision. He loved the work, he loved Sugar Rush, and God knew he loved his sons. He'd also spent almost his entire lifetime working for his family's historic company. Which was exactly what had made his decision so damned hard.

"Besides, you're way too young to retire," Luke continued.

"Age has nothing to do with it. I've worked for Sugar Rush since I was twenty-five. My first job was on the lollipop production line in the factory. I made my way up like everyone else. But with you boys running operations now, I'm ready to step down. Any one of you can take over as president."

"What if none of us want to?" Evan shook his head. "I'm not leaving the Cocoa Bean Team."

"Then bring in someone else. It might be better if the president was someone from outside the family anyway."

"You want us to headhunt?" Carson spread his hands out in bafflement, like he couldn't imagine an outsider coming in to run the family company.

"If necessary. Or you'd be a great fit for president, Carson, if Evan doesn't want to do it."

Carson and Evan exchanged scowls.

"I've expanded the chocolate division and increased revenue by thirty percent," Carson said.

Warren nodded. "Exactly. Imagine what you could do as Sugar Rush president."

"I don't want to imagine it. *You're* the Sugar Rush president." Carson's scowl deepened, and for an instant he looked like the rebellious ten-year-old boy who had been caught ditching school while his identical twin took a math test in his place.

Affection eased the tightness in Warren's chest. He hadn't

intended to upset his sons with the news, but he hadn't expected their resistance either.

He could understand it, though. Both their family and company had withstood massive trauma and upheaval in the past thirteen years, and it had been through Luke's leadership that Sugar Rush was not only still standing but had flourished into one of the most prestigious companies on a global scale. Warren's retirement meant a major structural change that the whole company would have to navigate, following the lead of his sons.

"I understand your reluctance to restructure," he said. "But if companies...and people...don't change, they stagnate. I won't let that happen to Sugar Rush. I sure as hell won't let it happen to me."

Silence fell. The boys shuffled, casting glances at each other.

"Look." Warren gentled his voice. "I know you've all worried about me over the years. My lack of socializing, the time I spend making these..." He gestured to the model boats and airplanes lining the shelves of his office. He completed the models in his home office/workshop, but had brought some to display at work. "My focus on you and Sugar Rush. So this is a new start."

"But why *now*?" Evan asked. "I mean, this is out of nowhere."

No. Warren didn't tell them he'd been wrestling with the idea of retirement for the past year. Ever since his old college buddy Theo had died after a lengthy battle with cancer. Even in the midst of chemo, Theo had been planning one last "Great Climbing Road Trip" after his treatment was completed. He'd never made it.

And now with Luke happily married, Evan's health prognosis excellent, Tyler successful with his new business, Hailey now graduated from Stanford...Warren had seen more and more the value of letting his children find their own way. He had no intention of becoming irrelevant, but it was time for him to step away from the company that had dominated his entire life.

"Sugar Rush is yours," he told his sons. "It's time for me to leave it in your hands."

Luke frowned. "What'll you even do if you retire?"

Warren shut down his computer. Their reaction to his announcement didn't bode well for their reaction to his post-retirement plans. "Does it matter?"

"Well, yeah," Luke said. "You'll be bored stiff. You know that. How many model airplanes can you make?"

Warren's jaw tightened. He'd taken up making model boats and airplanes after Spencer had brought him a model to work on while he was at Hailey's side in the hospital after the accident. He'd built dozens of models over the years, though his sons saw the hobby as a way for him to isolate himself from the world instead of as a creative pursuit. He didn't like thinking they might have been right.

And he sure as hell didn't want to spend his retirement holed up in his home office, making model airplanes.

"Why don't you start with an extended vacation?" Carson asked. "You're taking a ski trip to Zermatt after Christmas, right? So stay for a few weeks, travel a little, then make your decision when you come back."

"I've already made it." Warren stood, deciding now was not the best time to tell them that his ski trip was much more than that. "I'm announcing my retirement at next week's board meeting. And to the rest of the company at the holiday party. I strongly recommend you start the search now. I'll stay on through the holidays, but on an as-needed basis."

His sons all exchanged glances of exasperation. Warren's shoulders tensed. He neither wanted nor needed them to think he hadn't thought this through. He sure as hell didn't want them to try and talk him out of it—because they might succeed.

"That's my final word," he said. "I leave Sugar Rush to all of you."

He picked up his suit jacket and briefcase, then walked out of the office. Their voices rose in heated conversation behind him. Warren ignored his instinct to return, to mediate the arguments and make things right.

He returned to the parking lot. It was time for his sons to do the work alone. And it was past time for him to get away from a damned desk and to get back into the world again.

Before it was too late.

❧

"Dad, you gotta tell them." Adam handed a pool cue to Warren, his forehead creasing with a frown.

Warren took the cue and positioned his shot. Smoke and the smell of beer hung over the Troll's House bar, and Elvis blasted from the old jukebox in the corner. Clusters of blue-collar workers gathered at the bar, and others hovered around the worn pool tables.

He sank the orange ball and straightened, moving aside to let his friend Henry take his shot. A poker buddy for over twenty years, Henry's craggy face and heavy-lidded eyes belied his sharp mind.

"You haven't told them about retiring yet?" Henry asked.

Warren chalked his cue, ignoring the pointed look from Adam. "Yeah, I told them this afternoon. They didn't take it well."

"Why not?"

"Pushback about restructuring," Warren said. "If they're giving me shit about this, they're not going to like the idea of a climb."

"Isn't that *why* you're retiring?" Henry asked. "So you can do stuff you never had a chance to?"

Warren shrugged. "I also need to make sure the transition goes well. I didn't expect Luke to resist, which means it's not going to be as easy as I'd hoped."

"And that's not going to make it any easier for them to accept the idea of the climb," Adam argued.

"Exactly," Warren agreed. "That's the point."

Adam made a noise of frustration. Henry glanced at them both.

"None of them want to step in as president?"

"They don't want to shake up the company right when it's doing so well."

"What about the others?" Henry asked.

"Tyler won't care." Warren sank the yellow ball. "I don't think Spencer or Hailey will either, but now I don't know."

"They won't care about you retiring." Adam eyed Warren pointedly. "They will care that you want to tackle a climb of this magnitude."

Warren set his cue aside. His son was right—sooner or later, he'd have to tell Luke and the others about his mountaineering plans. They knew he'd been stepping up his rock climbing and bouldering—and they'd seen it as evidence that their father was finally getting back into the world thirteen years after their mother's death.

But Warren hadn't told them he was training to climb the Matterhorn. He'd taken extra time in his business trips to Switzerland so he could perfect his climbing and routing techniques. Adam, who owned a small travel company and had done plenty of adventure expeditions himself, was the only one Warren had told. He'd also sworn Adam to secrecy, although his son wouldn't have broken the confidence regardless.

"I mean, it's not like you're going off on a weekend hike in the redwoods," Adam pointed out. "I want to go with you."

"I won't let you."

"I'll sign up anyway." A belligerent tone edged Adam's voice.

"If you sign up," Warren said, "I won't go."

Adam scowled. "You're a stubborn old bastard, you know that?"

"I've been told."

Affection for his son rose in him. He'd always had a particular soft spot for all his children in different ways. With Adam, it was because of the boy's love for adventure, for seeking out new frontiers and embracing risks. He'd been the ten-year-old who'd convinced his brothers to run away from home and build a camp in the coastal forest. He'd shied away from Sugar Rush in favor of hiking the Inca Trail, leading safaris, climbing volcanos.

Of all the Stone sons, Adam was the only one who wouldn't question Warren's need to complete his own expedition. That, combined with Adam's own experience in rock and mountain climbing, had made it easy for Warren to tell him his plans.

But he'd told Adam from the start he couldn't go. If Adam climbed with him, Warren would be too focused on his son and not his own climb. And this was his trek, something he had to do with the people who had been training alongside him for over a year, friends he'd known much longer than that. The comrades who'd also known Theo and who wanted to do this in his honor.

He had to climb the Matterhorn before it was too late.

"I'll tell them when we get the green light." He hated that he was even partly lying to his son. "MeteoSwiss issued a bulletin about possible storms on the slope, so we're waiting to see if we can even go right after Christmas. No use worrying the others if it's not even going to happen."

"And Aunt Julia?" Adam raised an eyebrow.

Warren's shoulders tensed. Of his entire family, Julia's reaction was the one he was least able to predict—and that made no sense since he knew her better than he knew himself. She wouldn't like the idea of him taking on the iconic mountain, but would she try to stop him? Would she understand when he explained why he had to do this? Would she even listen?

"I'll talk to her," he told his son evasively.

He downed the last of his scotch and lifted his glass toward

Melanie, a curvy bartender about ten years younger than him. She glanced his way and proceeded to ignore him.

Not a surprise. They'd spent one night together a year ago, shortly after he'd become a Troll's House regular. Warren liked the casual anonymity of coming here for a drink and to play some pool. It was a place where he didn't have to be Warren Stone, Sugar Rush president, or even *Dad*.

Which was probably what led him to hook up with Melanie in the first place. A night of forgetting who he was to his family, the company, the town. Unfortunately, Melanie had wanted more than he was willing to give, and though he'd been both straightforward and gentle about their lack of a future together, she hadn't taken the break-up well.

That had been a theme with most women he'd been with over the past thirteen years. Once he'd finally gotten back into the dating scene after Rebecca's death, he'd found it populated by divorcees looking for a husband and younger women looking for a sugar daddy. He'd taken a number of them out, but the dates had been forced and tedious at best and disastrous at worst.

He'd been with genuinely nice women over the years, but a second marriage wasn't in the cards for him, and none of the women had liked the notion that their relationship wasn't leading in that direction.

He set his cue down and nodded toward the bar. "Either one of you want anything else?"

"No, I'm heading out." Adam shrugged into his jacket. "I'll see you this weekend for the tree decorating."

After saying goodbye to his son, Warren shouldered through the crowd. He paused at a table where the four other members of the Matterhorn expedition were drinking pints. Warren had known them for years, having met them through Theo, and they had dozens of hiking excursions and poker games behind them.

"Strike out, boss?" Justin, a tall skinny guy in his mid-forties, grinned and tilted his head toward Melanie. "I always ask a girl to play pool. Works every time."

"Why's that?"

"You can ask her to put her hands in your pockets and tickle your balls."

The others laughed and raised their pints. Warren shook his head, though he liked their ribald banter. Reminded him of his college days—not that he'd tell them that. After him, Justin was the second oldest in the group, with Rick, Peter, and Dave all being ten to fifteen years younger.

But the age differences hadn't affected their tight-knit group, especially during Theo's illness and death. Two months after Theo died, and while Warren was still both grieving his death and reliving the loss of his wife, he'd had the idea to tackle the Matterhorn in his late friend's honor.

He'd brought it up to their climbing and poker buddies, all of whom had agreed without hesitation. Warren had approached the venture like he did business—with methodical planning and research. He'd picked the date because it was the one-year anniversary of Theo's death and also because it coincided with the start of his retirement.

Not that he hadn't doubted the idea over the past year. He had no trouble matching the younger men in bouldering and fitness tests, but the Matterhorn was a relentless, difficult climb requiring superhuman effort. In winter, it would be even worse —a fact he was reminded of every time he considered the fact that he was the oldest member of their group.

He made his way to the bar and told the bartender to put the other men's round on his tab. "I'll have another scotch too."

He settled the tab and picked up his drink. As he turned, a pair of shapely bare legs blocked his exit. He skimmed his gaze down to black heels and red-painted toenails, then back up over a flowered mini-skirt and low-cut T-shirt displaying abundant cleavage.

Well.

"Hi." She smiled and extended a hand. "I'm Laura."

She couldn't have been more than twenty-five, if that, with long dark hair and pretty features layered with makeup.

"Warren." He took her hand, glancing at the drink in front of her. Cosmopolitan. Figured.

"You come here often?" She eyed his chest and shoulders beneath his tailored shirt.

"On occasion."

"Me too." She took hold of his silk tie patterned with jelly-beans and rubbed it between her fingers. "You like sweet stuff, huh?"

"I've been known to indulge."

"Me too, especially with a girly drink." She tilted her head toward her cosmopolitan and twirled a lock of hair around her forefinger. "Usually after work or classes."

Classes. Christ, she was young.

"Where are you a student?" he asked.

"Over at Fordham's Beauty College. I'm learning how to do hair. I work as an assistant at a salon."

"Good for you." Although she was a tempting little thing, Warren's mind shifted to the logistics of that scenario. "Working in the same profession you're studying is a great way to put what you're learning into practice."

She grinned. "You're adorable. What do you do?"

"I work in the corporate environment."

"Of course." She leaned closer, nudging her breasts against his arm. "Hey, if you're getting bored here, I know of another great little pub we can go to. You up for some company?"

He'd have to be a eunuch not to be tempted. And he'd be an asshole if he took her up on her offer. He knew what would happen—they'd get more drinks, go back to her place for the night, and then he'd feel the urge to give her some cash to help her pay for school—which would give the whole night a sleazy vibe. Then she'd want to see him again, and he'd put her off, and she'd take it badly.

Not to mention, she wasn't much older than his daughter. He'd go ballistic if he thought some dickwad his age would ever hit on Hailey.

"Sorry, honey." He put a few more bills on the bar to pay for her drink. "I'm going home alone tonight."

Laura pursed her lips into a pout. "Seriously? I'm a sure thing."

"Don't be a sure thing for any man." He slipped his wallet back into his pocket. "Be the *only* thing for one man."

She blinked, faint consternation rising to her eyes. Warren turned away from her and headed back to the pool table. After saying goodbye to Henry and the others, he pulled his keys from his pocket and walked out to his car.

Not the first time he'd been hit on by a girl half his age, but it was a scenario he found increasingly depressing. Just like the rest of the dating scene.

As he drove home, he couldn't help but wonder if his dating issues hadn't been his fault. No, the women hadn't been the most interesting company, but maybe he wasn't either.

He'd married Rebecca when she'd gotten pregnant at twenty, though they'd been dating for a year. He'd had girlfriends before her, but he'd never played the field like most men did in their twenties. He'd had seven children before he'd turned thirty-two.

And while Warren didn't regret anything about his marriage or children—just the opposite, as nothing could have made him happier—he'd been responsible and an *adult* early on. Focused on his children and work. Set in his ways. Hardly a wonder that he wouldn't be a good companion to another woman, especially after Rebecca.

He drove past the gates of his estate, glad to see Julia's BMW parked near the porch. He'd been more thrown off than he'd liked when she hadn't responded to his call and texts yesterday.

Her vague excuses hadn't worked for him either. Something was going on, and maybe now was the time for him to find out what.

He opened the door, glancing over the decorations she'd started to put up. Julia had been the one to give Christmas back to his children after their mother died. Hailey had only been eleven at the time, and the boys were all in their teens and early twenties. None of them had known what to do about the holidays until Julia stepped in and reminded them that Rebecca would still want them to celebrate.

So they had. First with quiet festivities at home, then later with charity events for both the Rebecca Stone Foundation and Sugar Rush. Over the years, everyone tried to ensure they were home for the holidays, but invariably someone would be missing. Luke was off on Sugar Rush business, Adam was guiding a tour group through Kenya, Tyler was with a girlfriend.

This year, for the first time in a while, they would all be home for the holidays. While that was a welcome event, it also meant that Julia was working overtime to create the perfect Christmas for them all. She'd succeed, but at the expense of her own well-being.

Unless Warren exerted control over her.

He tossed his keys onto the entry table and walked into the great room, expecting to see her fussing with the placement of candles on the mantel. But there were only a few cardboard boxes alongside the wall.

"Jules?" He went into the kitchen. "Julia?"

No answer.

Cold air came through the half-open doors of the breakfast room, which led out to a stone terrace overlooking the valley. Warren pushed open the door and stepped outside. Julia sat at the mosaic patio table, which held a bottle of wine, a half-empty glass, and a creased piece of paper. Her smooth blonde hair concealed her profile, and her usually straight shoulders were slumped.

Warren crossed the terrace in three strides. "Julia, are you all right?"

She startled, turning toward him. Concern flooded his chest when the porch lights glinted off the tear stains on her cheeks.

"Did you take your medicine?" He went behind her chair to rest his hands on the sides of her head, his fingers finding her smooth temples. "How bad is it?"

"It's not that." She waved his hands away irritably. "I'm fine."

Warren moved around the chair to look at her tight expression and reddened eyes. He pushed a lock of hair away from her forehead, letting his fingers rest against her skin.

"You're not fine," he said. "Tell me."

Julia wiped her eyes with a napkin and gave a hiccupping laugh. "I'm being unusually sensitive. Either that or I'm having an existential crisis."

She reached for the wine bottle and poured some into the glass. "At least there's this, thanks to your exceptional wine collection."

Warren pulled a chair up beside hers. "What's going on? Is it work related?"

"Sort of." She gazed at the dark valley. "The Holiday Festival committee is driving me crazy, wanting things that aren't in the budget. And a partnership that I've been working on for a year crashed and burned yesterday. We were less than a week away from closing the deal."

"What was the deal?"

She let out her breath in a long sigh. "I'd approached Vincent Peck, the president of Evermore Associates, to invest in a new clothing line. I've been wanting to get back to design, and as much as I love my clients and styling for photo shoots, I've... rather surprisingly...enjoyed working with girls like Polly and Kate. They're so unaffected and natural. I'd thought I would be transforming them, but it turned out to be more like bringing to the surface what they already had. Like they were little butter-flies. Don't tell them I said that.

"Anyway, they inspired me to create a clothing line for young working women. Vincent was really into the idea and prepared to invest, but…well, things went downhill."

Warren frowned. "Why?"

"A disagreement over the designs." She shook her head, her lips compressing. "He said they were dated and *old*. That clearly I was no longer in touch with what younger women wanted."

Anger boiled in Warren's blood at the idea of anyone, much less a douchebag investor, belittling Julia's creativity because of her age. And because she was a woman. A man would never be subjected to the same kind of criticism.

"You know that's not true," he said. "Peck was making an excuse. More likely it was a budget thing."

"Yeah, but with my fiftieth right around the corner, it stung more than I want to admit." She made a dismissive gesture with her hand. "I shouldn't be so upset, really. Deals fail all the time. He called me yesterday and said it wasn't the *'right project for them at this time.'* So, you know. Fuck him."

Warren smiled. He'd always liked the tough-girl steel beneath her polished beauty.

"Sounds like he's not the right investor for you at any time," he said.

"I know. But it still sucks. I'd been working on it so hard. And I was so close."

"I'll invest in you."

"No." Julia wiped her eyes again. "I never want to mix Sugar Rush business with my company. It just doesn't feel right."

He smothered a rush of frustration. It wasn't the first time she'd rejected his offer. He'd offered to help her multiple times over the years, dating back to when she'd first started her stylist business shortly after returning to Indigo Bay. She'd turned him down every time. And while he admired her need for independence, she and her company were both highly successful. She'd done it all on her own. She had nothing left to prove—either to him or herself. Now her rejection made little sense. Why wouldn't she want them to be partners in business when they were partners in so many other ways?

Especially after a failed deal had left her in tears.

He studied her darkened expression, his insides clenching. She'd had plenty of setbacks in her company, just like he had. None of them before had made her cry.

He picked up the wine and refilled her glass. His gaze fell on the crumpled paper. "What's that?"

"Oh, lord." Julia rolled her eyes with disdain. "I found it in an old box behind the Christmas decorations. I'd forgotten about it."

Warren picked up the paper. *Things To Do Before I Turn Fifty.*

"When did you write this?"

"When I was nineteen. Back when fifty felt like a thousand years into the future."

He scanned the list, which was numbered from one to fifty items.

16. Finish a 1000 piece puzzle.
17. Dye my hair blue.
18. Own a piece of La Perla lingerie.
19. Set a red balloon free.
20. Make mulled wine.

A strange feeling tightened his chest. He set the list down.

"Mulled wine?"

"Some sort of medieval Christmas tradition. I have no idea why I wanted to learn to make it, but there you go. The ambitions of a nineteen-year-old."

"You've done some of these." He tapped his finger on the page. "You must have dyed your hair blue at some point. And there's no way you don't own dozens of pieces of La Perla."

"Well, most of that list contains the musings of a girl who clearly had no direction in life." She shook her head, her lips compressing. "*Bake a perfect carrot cake. Solve a Rubik's Cube. Make vodka gummy bears.* I don't even know what those are. *Buy Wonder Woman underwear.* Clearly I wrote that list when I was high."

"Or when you were a nineteen-year-old who believed that life should be fun and spontaneous."

"Whatever." She pulled in a breath, composure snapping into place around her. "That list just proves how utterly flakey I was. I couldn't even get most of the things done in *thirty years*."

"It's not like this was meant to be a road map for your life," Warren said. "The nineteen-year-old you probably never imagined you'd be as successful and accomplished as you are today."

She acknowledged that with a slight nod. He scanned the second page of the list, his gaze landing on #26, which had a blue checkmark. *Love the right man.*

His jaw tightened. "What does the checkmark mean?"

She looked to where he was pointing and read the item. Regret shone in her eyes. She bit her lip.

"That means it was completed. I wrote the list when I was with Sam. Obviously that one was a mistake."

Old anger cut through him. He took a breath, unsurprised that his dislike of the other man still boiled like acrid smoke. He hadn't liked Sam Craven the first time they met, and his animosity had grown after he'd dumped Julia in an act of pure cowardice.

She set her wineglass on the table. Goosebumps prickled the bare skin of her arms. Warren shed his suit jacket and draped it over her shoulders. She slipped her arms into the sleeves, her gaze still on the valley.

"Even though it's just a silly list, it should have been easy," she said, almost to herself. "Thirty years to accomplish fifty things. It does make me wonder…"

Her voice trailed off. Warren's shoulders tensed even before he asked, "Wonder what?"

"What else I missed out on."

Missed out.

An image of Theo appeared in Warren's mind. His chest knotted. The Matterhorn was the soaring, rough-hewn manifestation of his own urge to not *miss out*. To face challenges now. To push himself as far as he could.

Julia would understand that. Wouldn't she? He was struck with a sudden urge to tell her about the climb. Maybe he wouldn't even need to explain why he had to do it.

"Now I'll stop being so maudlin," she rose to her feet, tossing him a wry half-grin, "and get my shit together. I'll do a little more decorating, then head home. Thanks for the wine."

"There's more."

"Oh, I know."

She went back inside, stripping off his jacket. He watched her go, his mind shifting from the mountain back to the thought of wispy little pieces of La Perla lingerie. *On Julia.* His eyes tracked over the curves of her waist and hips clad in a tight red T-shirt.

He picked up her wineglass and took a swallow. The rim of the glass was still warm from her lips. 2000 Hermitage Syrah. She knew how to choose good wine. She knew how to choose good *everything*—clothes, investments, fundraising sources, furnishings.

He studied the *Before Fifty* list, the big, looping letters and swirls that were so different from Julia's neat, precise penmanship of today. He rarely let himself remember the gypsy girl she'd once been, the wild child who had been the exact opposite of her perfect older sister.

Because if he went down that path…

Warren folded the list in half, tucking it into his pocket before bringing the wine bottle and glass back inside.

CHAPTER 2

"You forgot this." Warren set Julia's wineglass on the coffee table in the great room.

"I never forget wine." She was standing on a stepladder, positioning a fresh wreath over the fireplace. Her raised arms elongated her body and caused her breasts to round the front of her T-shirt.

Not the first time Warren had noticed them. Or imagined what they looked like naked. What *she* looked like naked. Slim, pale curves, long legs, breasts that would fit just right in his hands. Despite his reluctance to date, he hadn't been a monk the past thirteen years, but his affairs had never stopped him from thinking about Julia.

He didn't feel guilty about it either—she was a beautiful woman, and he was a man with a strong sex drive, and one plus one still equaled two. His curiosity about her had become as familiar as their relationship. But he knew—had always known—he'd never discover the reality of what Julia Bennett concealed beneath her flawless appearance.

"I'll help you with that," he said.

"No, I've got it. Stand over there and tell me if it's straight."

"It's a wreath." He moved away from the fireplace. "Any way you hang a circle, it's going to be straight."

"Do you see this bow?" She tapped the red velvet bow. "This needs to be centered at the top."

He cocked his head. "It's centered."

"You're not looking at it."

"How do you know?"

"I can feel you looking at my ass."

"Which is right at my eye level, so who could blame me?"

Julia threw him a derisive scowl over her shoulder. "This is going to take forever unless you cooperate."

"The wreath is straight," he assured her. "And your ass is perfect."

Her eyes narrowed, even as a faint blush rose to her cheeks. Warren winked at her and headed over to open one of the boxes.

"Where did you pick this wreath up?" Julia climbed off the stepladder. "It's nice and fresh."

"From the guy near the place in Santa Cruz where we went that time."

"Oh, the café with the eggs benedict. We should go there again with Hailey."

"Tell me when you want to go, and I'll clear my schedule." Warren held up several glass snowmen from one of the boxes. "Where do you want these?"

"Over there." She waved a hand, and he brought them to an end table in the vicinity of her wave.

They put out Julia's frosted vases, snowflake table linens, and a lighted Dickens' village. On Sunday, as usual, they'd trek into the Santa Cruz Mountains to pick out the tree—an event that would generate a lot of good-natured bickering and end with hot chocolate and a tree-decorating party.

Just one other Stone family tradition that had taken root only because of Julia. Though she could be abrasive and fiercely over-protective where the Stone siblings were concerned, Warren's respect and gratitude toward her knew no bounds. He would never be able to thank her for keeping his family together when they'd all been on the verge of falling apart.

She pulled the stepladder over to the doorway and climbed up to pin a ribbon of mistletoe to the frame. Again he let his gaze skim over her body, lingering on the pale seam of skin exposed at her midriff where her T-shirt rode up slightly.

"I'm thinking one sprig of mistletoe is enough this year," she remarked. "Or Tyler will catch Kate in every doorway just so he can plant one on her."

She tossed Warren a smile and climbed off the ladder.

"She's the best thing that ever happened to him," he said.

"Like Polly is to Luke. And Hannah to Evan."

And you to me.

Julia was unquestionably the best thing that had happened to Warren in the past thirteen years.

She studied the mistletoe hanging right over her head. "Is it centered?"

"Looks great." He was suddenly seized with the desire to close the distance and *plant one on her*. The mistletoe was a great excuse.

He smothered the urge, unsurprised by the strength of it. Knowing she'd been hurt had all his jealous, protective instincts clawing to the surface. Where Julia was concerned, those instincts were always *there*, but usually Warren kept them somewhat contained.

The mention of her ex-husband Sam had also pushed Warren's thoughts in a direction he never let them go—to a Christmas Eve night when he'd had a sudden, shocking taste of Julia Bennett and discovered that she was wild honeysuckle and ripe cherries.

He clamped down on that memory, pushing it back into the box where it needed to stay. Seeking a distraction, he tilted his head toward the kitchen.

"Come on, let's make mulled wine."

"What for?"

"To see what it's like. I'll help you."

Julia gave him a wry smile. "You mean you'll make it while I watch."

"I'm good with you watching."

She raised an eyebrow but picked up her wineglass and followed him into the kitchen. Warren searched on his phone for an "authentic" recipe, then went to the wine cellar to retrieve a few good bottles of cabernet.

"Hot wine with spices sounds rather awful." Julia hitched herself onto a stool at the counter. "If you take it to Sugar Rush, no one will drink it."

"I'm not doing this for Sugar Rush," Warren said. "I'm doing it for you."

She blinked, her cheeks appealingly pink. Warren poured the wine into a clean pot, and added measured amounts of brandy, cinnamon, orange zest, honey, cloves, and ginger. He lowered the heat to a simmer and ladled some of the brew into her glass.

"Try it." He set the glass in front of Julia. "It needs to simmer for a while to reach its full flavor, but this is a start."

She took a sip and lifted her eyebrows. "Not bad. Weird and a waste of excellent wine, but not bad."

"It's called *glögg* in Nordic nations and *Glühwein* in Germany."

"How do you know that?" Julia asked.

"I get around."

"I know you do."

A teasing warmth crackled between them. Warren took the list out of his pocket and handed it to her. "Now you can cross it off your *Before Fifty* list."

"Oh." She looked disconcerted. "I didn't keep the list so I could *finish* it. I don't even know why I didn't just throw it away."

He shrugged. "Then at least you know how to make mulled wine."

"Why would I have ever thought that would be a useful skill?" She gave a humorless laugh. "I mean, thanks for doing it, but it's not as if knowing how to make mulled wine would ever have gotten me anywhere in life."

"You don't always have to do something just because it will get you somewhere," Warren said. "Sometimes it's okay to just *want it*."

"Yes, but the things I wanted at nineteen are very different from the things I want at fif—forty-nine."

"So what do you want at forty-nine?"

She hesitated for half a second before sliding off the stool without a response.

She took the wineglass and list back to the great room. Warren turned off the stove and put the dirty pots in the sink. When he joined her, she was searching on her phone.

"I have to spend most of the week working on Deck the Halls," she said without looking up, "but I can stop by in the evening to finish up the entryway and the other rooms."

"You don't need to do all of this." He sat beside her as she checked her calendar. "Let the kids do it."

"No, I'd like to have it done before Hailey arrives."

Despite his belief that Julia was taking on too much this Christmas, warmth spread through Warren's chest. He appreciated everything she'd done for his sons, but her relationship with Hailey was special. Julia hadn't stepped into Rebecca's maternal role, instead navigating her way between being Hailey's aunt, advisor, and confidante. The fact that his daughter had become such a smart, well-adjusted young woman after what she'd endured was due in no small part to Julia's influence.

"Hailey won't mind if you scale back the decorations," he said.

"I'll get it done. By the way..." She gave him a narrow sideways glance, her nostrils flaring slightly. "You smell like cheap perfume."

"Yeah?" He lifted his sleeve to his nose.

"I guess you didn't go to Lotus after all," Julia said dryly, placing her phone back in her bag.

"I went to the Troll's House. Got hit on by a girl who wasn't born when I graduated from college."

"Nice." Julia sniffed in contempt and reached for her wineglass. "She must have daddy issues."

He grinned at the snide tone to her voice. "Are you jealous?"

"Of course not. I just don't think getting hit on by a girl half your age is anything to brag about."

"Not bragging, just stating a fact. You ever get hit on by younger men?"

She arched an eyebrow. "What do you think?"

A stab of jealousy caught him off guard. He didn't often admit how much he disliked the idea of Julia with another man—younger, older, or her age. He'd avoided the dates she'd brought to social events over the years and never speculated about what she did with them. Because if he did, he might explode with frustration. Not that he needed to think about *that* either.

His jaw clenched. He grabbed the wineglass from her and took a swallow of the warm, spicy wine, deeply regretting having started this line of conversation.

"I *don't* think about it," he said. "Why would I?"

"Well, you asked," Julia reminded him. "And the answer is yes. There's a lot of cougar bait running around out there."

Warren scowled. "You're not a cougar."

"I could be. Just like you could be a sugar daddy."

"Christ." He gave a disparaging snort. "The president of Sugar Rush becomes a sugar daddy. I'd be a caricature. *Hey, baby. You like your sugar raw, powdered, or refined?*"

Julia laughed. "Personally I like it raw, but as long as it's sweet, I'm not fussy."

The husky tone to her voice added fuel to his already hot blood. Against every ounce of his better judgement, he asked, "So do you take the boy toys up on their offers?"

She shrugged and didn't respond—clearly a ploy to make him wait. Time stretched. While they occasionally mentioned their respective dates to each other, their sex lives had never been a topic of conversation. His simmering jealousy rose to a boil. No kid could satisfy a woman like her. No other man could either.

Warren didn't have to wonder how he knew that. He just did. He knew *her*.

"Once," Julia finally admitted. "A few years ago, a...*young man* was an assistant on a photo shoot I was styling."

His neck tightened with irritation. "Young man, huh?"

"He was twenty-two."

"You sure?"

"I asked to see his ID when we went out for drinks with the crew. I ended up going home with him. More out of curiosity than anything else."

Warren swallowed the last of the mulled wine and refilled the glass with Syrah.

Don't ask. Don't ask. Don't fucking—

"And?" he asked.

Dickwad.

"Oh God." She took the glass from him, bringing it to her lips. "He was so nervous and overeager, which I guess was sort of flattering, but I felt like such a *teacher*. It wasn't terribly sexy. Or satisfying. Or...um, long."

He needed a scotch, not another sip of her wine. He rubbed his hands over his face and blocked an unwanted image of Julia naked with a twenty-two-year-old.

"That surprised you?" he asked.

"I might've had some hopeful ideas about youth and stamina." She rolled her eyes with amusement. "I was wrong."

Warren grabbed the glass back from her and drained it. He was having an imaginary pissing contest with an unknown twenty-two-year-old kid. *What the hell was wrong with him?*

"You don't like giving orders, huh?" He tightened his fingers on the glass.

She made a little *hmm* noise in the back of her throat. She'd make the same sound if she were spread out under him, her wrists trapped in his grip, her legs wrapped around his—

His dick twitched. He was usually decent enough to fantasize about her only when he was alone in his bedroom. Except this conversation, *which he'd started*, had fired him with more than he knew what to do with.

"I do enough of that at work," she said, her mouth twisting.

She took the empty glass from him and set it on the table. She had fine-boned features—dark blue eyes, high cheekbones, a straight nose, full rosebud mouth. With her lovely face, long, tapered fingers, and slender figure, she looked like a princess. But she had the heart and soul of a gladiator, one who rarely let others see past her elegant ferocity.

A hard rush of protectiveness and jealousy filled him. He hated the thought of another man, no matter his age, putting his hands on Julia. He hated that she'd been hurt, that someone had blindsided her to the point that she'd cried.

And he hated even more that she felt like she'd failed, that she'd *missed out* on something…because even though she'd lived and worked in London, travelled extensively, built a successful company, had prestige and wealth, if Julia had missed anything in her life, it was all Warren's damned fault.

"So?" Julia shot him a sideways glance. "That was my foray into cougardom. What about you?"

"I've never forayed into cougardom."

She chuckled. "Please. Young Warren never got it on with an older woman?"

He didn't think it necessary to tell her about the VP's wife who'd seduced him at seventeen. "Not recently."

She turned her head to eye him suspiciously. "And you've

never been tempted by those twenty-year-olds in their mini-skirts and moto jackets?"

Ah, hell. She'd told him the truth.

"A few times," he admitted. "But they had to be at least twenty-five."

"And how was it?"

"The sex was great. The rest...not so much. They went on about music and movies I didn't care about, and I kept wanting to advise them on their financial portfolios. Not a dynamic that worked." He refilled the wineglass from the bottle of Syrah. "Not to mention the whole thing had a sleazy vibe I didn't like. Not for me."

"What...or rather, *who* is for you then?" Julia asked. "I mean, besides Rebecca."

Rebecca had been "for him." The perfect complement to his imperfection. She'd been his pillar, the reason he'd become a responsible, hard-working adult at such a young age. His father had insisted that he work outside of Sugar Rush to learn about the "real world" for several years, and after stints at gas stations and restaurants, Warren had started on the production line of Sugar Rush's factory floor. He'd worked his way up in the company, Rebecca steadfastly at his side, her focus on raising the children. He'd never deviated from the path of work and family. Never wanted a woman who could offer him anything different.

Except...

He blocked that thought before it could go any further.

He didn't know what he'd have been if it hadn't been for Rebecca. She'd been a rock. Julia had been like the sea—constantly changing, shifting, moving. Until somewhere along the way, she'd stopped.

Because of him.

Shit. He frowned down at the glass. Who was *for him*? Not the divorcees or sugar babies. Not any of the professional women he'd encountered in his career. Not the Sugar Rush VPs or employees. Not his fellow climbers.

But Julia...he'd wondered often about the possibility over the years. The thought of Rebecca hadn't been the thing stopping him—it had been more Julia herself. The invisible wall she'd put up between them.

He set the glass down and picked up her *Before Fifty* list from the coffee table. A few more blue check marks indicated the items she'd already completed. *Sleep under the stars. Skinny-dip. Go zip-lining. Be there for my next niece or nephew's birth.*

She'd been there when Evan was born. Next to Rebecca on the other side of the bed, holding her left hand while he held his wife's right hand.

"She missed you," he finally said.

Julia didn't respond for a moment before she admitted, "I missed her. Biggest regret of my life, causing a rift between me and my sister. Well, second biggest."

"Sam was the first, huh?"

"No." She ducked her head, the curtain of her smooth blonde hair falling forward to conceal her profile. "You were."

Guilt seized his chest. "I'm sorry."

"Sorry?" She flipped her hair back to look at him. Despite the amount of wine they'd both consumed, her gaze was clear and sharp. "I'm the one who's sorry, Warren. I've been sorry for almost thirty years. What kind of woman hits on her sister's husband?"

The question flared and exploded between them like a long-dormant firework whose fuse had just been lit. Not until this second had either of them ever acknowledged that Christmas Eve night when she'd pressed her hot open mouth against his. His head flooded with memories of her cherry breath, the crush of her sweet, soft body, the tangle of her long hair.

His dick stiffened. He tilted his head back and swallowed the wine. Those memories had taken root deep inside him the instant they happened. Fuck if he hadn't tried his damnedest to smother all of them, to eradicate them from his blood, his consciousness. He'd failed miserably.

"I'm sorry," Julia repeated, her forehead furrowing. "I never stopped thinking that if I hadn't done that, Rebecca and I could have had a much closer relationship. And you never wanted to talk to me after that, did you?"

Shame and guilt knotted in his throat, blocking a response. He stared at her mouth, her lips stained with red wine, the tempting indentation in her upper lip that looked as if it would feel as soft as a flower petal against his finger. Then he made the mistake of moving his gaze lower, over the curves of her breasts.

Christ. Her nipples were hard, poking against the front of her designer T-shirt. She was as affected by memories of their kiss as he was. What was she wearing under her shirt? His mind flashed with an image of her in a transparent black bra that showed off her dark areolae and tight nipples...

He pulled in a breath and tried to rein in his wayward thoughts. "I wanted to forget it ever happened."

Though her expression didn't change, unmistakable hurt flashed in her eyes. She tore her gaze from his and looked down at the floor. A thick, portentous silence filled the air. His heart-beat kicked into gear, heat flooding his veins.

"But I couldn't," he continued. "I couldn't forget anything about you."

"Same here." Her voice was low, contrite. A pulse throbbed at the side of her slender neck. Warren couldn't take his eyes off it, imagining pressing his mouth to the hot vibration, tasting her fine-grained skin. The scent of her wafted to him—no cheap perfume on her, only Chanel No. 5 underscored by the heady smells of red wine and cloves.

"God." Julia pressed her hands to her flushed cheeks and closed her eyes. "You'd think I'd be over it after all these years, but I feel like it happened yesterday. I'm still so ashamed."

He swallowed hard. "Don't be. If there's anything that's changed over the last thirty years, it's that you never need to be ashamed. Not with me. Not about anything."

If his words were any comfort, she gave no indication.

She rose and crossed the room. He locked his gaze to the sway of her hips as she walked to the mantel and removed several family photos. She set them on the coffee table and returned to an opened cardboard box to take out a large snow globe.

"Stop," Warren said.

Julia paused. He pushed to his feet and approached her slowly. She didn't move, but a visible tremble rippled through her when he stopped in front of her.

He tilted his chin up, drawing her eyes to the top of the doorframe and the mistletoe dangling over her head. Her gaze darted back to his, colliding into him like a thunderbolt.

Her slender throat worked with a swallow. Her eyes were dark sapphires, the Caribbean sea, the sky before a storm. She drew back, her breasts rising and falling with the force of her breath. A crease formed between her eyebrows. Her lips parted.

The heat in his veins flared into a firestorm. Before he could think, he moved closer, sliding one hand to the back of her neck. The air thickened with tension.

"Warren?" Her voice shook.

He pulled her toward him and brought his mouth down on hers.

CHAPTER 3

The snow globe fell from Julia's hands and bounced once, unbroken, on the thick carpet.

This.

This right here was what she *wanted.* What she'd been wanting for a very long time. For him to take control, to take *her*, to surrender to the desires she'd kept concealed for too long. The stifled longings broke free...either a flock of butterflies rising into the sky or the opening of Pandora's box, she didn't know which.

All she knew right now was that his lips were on hers, and his hands were holding her in place. Disbelief and outright pleasure washed through her. She wanted to fall into him like she was diving through a cloud of everything warm and good. Because...*oh my God.*

Though their unusually intimate talk and his closeness had warmed and softened her, the touch of his lips fired her with heat, melting away the brittle emotions hardening her insides. She curled her fingers into his arms, stunned by the realization of a moment she had imagined more often than she ever wanted to admit.

Warren Stone was kissing her under the mistletoe. And she was letting him. More, she was kissing him back, surrendering to the spicy taste of him, her head spinning with the intoxicating combination of wine and the man she had secretly craved for so long.

He glided his mouth easily over hers, urging her lips apart, sliding his tongue against hers with an expertise that jolted her with desire. Lord in heaven, the man knew how to kiss, the pressure of his mouth firm yet gentle, his possessive grip on her neck keeping her in place.

Not that she wanted to move. The familiar scent of his shaving cream—orange and spice—filled her nose. He trailed his lips from her mouth to her cheek, his whiskers abrading her skin deliciously. Julia shivered. Long-dormant hunger flooded her veins. He brought his mouth back to hers, his big hands sliding up her midriff to her breasts. Her nipples stiffened against his palms, and a moan escaped her throat.

"Christ, you feel good." His voice was rough, his body lined with tension.

Dizziness swept through her. She couldn't think. All she could do was feel—his hands on her breasts, his lips against hers, his body...oh, his *body*.

How many times had she imagined what his broad shoulders and chest would feel like under her fingers? How many times had she admired how beautifully his tailored suits fit his muscular physique, and then pictured herself unknotting his tie and stripping off his jacket? How many times had she secretly fantasized...

She placed a trembling hand on his chest. *Good lord.* He worked out regularly and had been increasing his climbing and bouldering efforts, but she hadn't expected him to be so...*powerful*, a wall of hard, sculpted muscle coiled with leashed strength. His heart hammered against her palm, a fast-paced rhythm matching hers.

What would it feel like to ease her hand under his shirt, touch his taut skin and explore his astonishingly solid body? She pulled in a ragged breath, her senses swimming. He lifted his mouth from hers, his breath puffing hot against her lips, his brown eyes darkened with urgency.

"You're beautiful."

Pleasure soared through her. He frequently told her she looked great, he liked her outfit, whatever, but never before had he told her she was beautiful while gazing at her as if he wanted to consume her. And she wanted him to. Wanted him to swallow her up, rid her of all thought, electrify every part of her being.

He lowered her to the floor, his mouth locked back to hers. She went willingly, heedless of any resistance, a dandelion puff surrendering to the force of the wind.

His kiss was everything she'd imagined it to be and more—a caress, a claiming, a question. Soft nibbles at her lips alternating with the slow, probing quest of his tongue. His hands tightening in her hair, his scruff grazing her chin. Pulling back and advancing. Feather-light touches of his mouth on her cheeks, her forehead, then back to take her lips.

Thirteen—no, *thirty*—years folded and collapsed in time, distilling to this moment alone. She slid her hands to his back, gripped his shirt, arched up against him. Her breasts brushed the hard wall of his chest, stimulating her tight nipples. She squeezed her thighs together. God, already she was wet and starting to ache.

He broke the kiss and levered himself over her, one hand on the floor beside her head. His gaze probed hers as if he were already stripping her naked. She parted her legs, letting him fit his body against hers.

Oh. He was hard, an impressive bulge pressing against the front of his trousers. Emboldened, she ran her hand over his chest, rubbing her fingers across his hard abs, then down to his erection. A groan rumbled through him, but the instant she closed her hand around him, he grabbed her wrist.

Julia froze. "What's wrong?"

He cursed under his breath, his mouth tightening with self-restraint. "If you want me to stop, I—"

She almost laughed, caught in a wave of dizzy excitement. She couldn't believe how *light* she suddenly felt, as if all the frustrations of the past week had lifted from her heart and flown away like birds.

"Warren," she breathed. "What I *want* is for you to finish what you started."

His mouth curved with a smile, his brown gaze softening.

"What I want..." he pressed his hand to the side of her neck, lowering his mouth to hers again, "...is you."

He slid his hands over her breasts, his breath increasing. He stroked lower, across her midriff and between her legs. He cupped his hand over her, easing one long finger right into her cleft. Julia gasped. Lust exploded through her. She'd almost forgotten what a man's touch felt like on the most intimate parts of her body—and he was only touching her on the outside of her clothes.

She ran her trembling fingers over the length of his erection where it rested against his thigh. A shiver of trepidation rattled through her because...heavens, the man was *big*. The thick ridge of his cock pulsed heat clear through his trousers, sending a responding throb right to her core. His breath skimmed over her like a hot breeze. But instead of hauling her close again, he put his hand under her chin and lifted her face to look at him.

Her heart hammered at the gleam in his brown eyes—dark, lustful, possessive. Electric currents, burning stars, the center of a candle flame. She'd known him longer than she'd known anyone, harbored everything from a secret crush to outright desire for him. There was no one she trusted more.

She tugged his shoulders and pressed her lips to his again. He pushed his hands under the hem of her shirt, his fingers gliding over her bare skin. Shivers rained down her spine. *Up, up*...his hands closed over her breasts, plucking at her taut nipples.

Julia shifted, her breath coming faster, all rational thought spilling away. Warren lowered her back onto the floor, his weight pressing her into the carpet, his cock throbbing against her thigh. She wound her arms around his shoulders as he lowered his head to kiss her neck, her throat, trailing his lips back to her mouth.

"Wait." Julia eased away from him slightly to shed her T-shirt. A rush of purely female satisfaction filled her when he groaned at the sight of her lingerie-clad breasts.

"If you only knew how often I've imagined you naked," he muttered, undoing the bra clasp with an expert flick of his fingers. Her breasts popped out, nipples sticking straight up.

"Ah fuck..." He bent to capture one of her nipples in his mouth.

Sparks flamed in her blood. Julia gasped, arching upward and tightening her fingers into his shirt. A hint of disbelief rose in her at the realization that *Warren* was flicking his tongue over her nipple and sucking the tight little bud, but everything else about him—his presence, his scent, his body—was achingly, unbearably familiar.

He pulled away from her only long enough to grip her yoga pants and strip them off her legs, revealing the black lace panties hugging her hips. His breath hitched.

"La Perla, huh?" He ran his gaze across her body, his eyes crinkling at the corners. "I knew you could cross that one off your list several times over. But you could make cheap lingerie look incredible. You make *everything* incredible."

Stunned, Julia watched as he lowered his head to press kisses over her midriff, her belly button, down to her mons covered in sheer lace. Heat sizzled through her every time his lips made contact with her skin. He stroked his hands up and down her thighs in a mesmerizing rhythm, lulling her into a haze of sensual need.

She twisted her hand into his thick hair, brushing it back from his forehead. Her breath caught when he hooked his fingers into her panties and tugged them off. Then she was naked, and he was still fully clothed in his tailored suit and tie, and God in heaven, had any man ever looked at her with such smoldering lust, such hot possession, as if he'd unlocked and freed a thousand desires?

He stroked her bare legs, dipping his fingers toward her pussy. An intense feeling of vulnerability washed over her. She tensed, bringing her legs together. He stopped her, gently pressing his hands against her inner thighs.

"Don't hide, Jules." His voice husky, he traced little circles on her skin. "Not from me."

Her heart fluttered like the beat of a hummingbird's wings. And then he lowered his head to kiss her again, and all doubt slipped away like water over smooth, polished rocks. She moaned into his mouth. Their tongues met, tangled, danced. She lifted her knees to hug his hips, bringing his erection right up against her pussy.

"Oh, God, Warren." Julia gasped, squeezing her eyes shut as that hot ridge of flesh pressed against her pulsing clit. She writhed against him, already feeling her arousal mounting. "I could come just from...*oh*..."

"Do it," he ordered, bringing one hand up to twist her nipples. "Work yourself on me. Show me how much you want it."

Sweat broke out on her skin. She gripped the front of his shirt and rubbed her spread pussy against his cock. He was so fucking *hard*, his erection throbbing heat straight into her blood. The material of his trousers abraded her sensitive folds, simulating her arousal higher and higher.

"Warren..." She squirmed harder in an increasingly desperate drive for that final explosive release.

He shifted, changing their positions enough that her clit rubbed against just the right spot. She fisted her hands in his shirt and wrapped her legs around him, squirming frantically on his cock until pleasure burst through her like a thousand shooting stars. She shrieked, her body trembling and arching as Warren's deep voice rained into her ear and the sensations slowly ebbed.

"Holy shit." Panting and sweating, she fell back against the floor and stared at him in a daze. "I don't think I've ever done that before."

A smile curved his mouth. He rose to his knees. A damp spot spread over the front of his trousers, evidence of her orgasm. A hot flush rose to her cheeks.

He unbuckled his belt and stripped it off. Julia swallowed to ease her dry throat, mesmerized by the deftness of his hands as he unbuttoned his pants and worked the zipper. She stared in awe when he pushed the trousers over his hips, revealing navy boxer briefs that did nothing to conceal the massive length and breadth of his cock.

"God, Warren," she whispered.

He moved forward, straddling her hips. "Take them off."

Trembling, she hooked her fingers into the waistband and tugged the boxer briefs down. His erection bobbed upward like a living creature, directly in her line of sight. Long and straight with a smooth, veined shaft and thick, glossy knob, his cock looked as if it had been made for pleasure. *Her* pleasure.

Lust and more than a little trepidation flared through her. She swallowed again, her heart hammering. She gestured to his shirt and tie.

"Take it off," she said, unable to prevent her pleading tone. "I want to see you naked."

He pulled at the knot of his tie and pulled it off, letting it fall to the floor with the pile of other clothes. His gaze never leaving hers, he unbuttoned his shirt and removed it, revealing a sculpted expanse of chest and shoulders that would have put a Greek statue to shame. And though Julia had a vivid imagination, she'd never pictured Warren looking like *this*.

His muscular shoulders sloped to thick, solid pecs and a washboard abdomen whose ridges she wanted to lick one by one. With his cock sticking straight out like an invitation, he was suddenly less the Warren she'd always known and more a crazy hot stranger with a body that could take her places she'd never been before.

"You're...you're really built." She lifted a tentative hand to touch his chest. "Like *built*. I had no idea."

"Side-effect of nearing retirement." Warren put his hands on either side of her head. "More time to work out."

Though surely a physique like his required an Olympic-sized workout, Julia didn't bother questioning him further. Instead she ran her fingers over his chest and traced all the grooves of his muscles as if mapping the landscape of his body.

Warren didn't move, letting her have her fill of exploring him before she finally stroked down to his jutting cock. She closed her fist around his shaft and squeezed, emboldened by his sharp intake of breath. She was an experienced-enough woman, but God knew she'd never had a man as powerfully virile as Warren Stone was turning out to be. The realization both excited and unnerved her.

Warren tangled his hand into her hair and levered his body over hers. In one movement, he brought them together, their legs and arms twining and flexing. The full contact of his naked body against hers flooded Julia with fresh desire and pleasure. He kissed her deeply, his tongue sweeping into her mouth as he edged his hands between her thighs. He dipped his forefinger into her cleft, circling her clit with his thumb.

"Wet and hot," he murmured, biting gently down on her collarbone. "Exactly the way I'd imagined my ice queen under all that frost."

She arched her hips into his touch. She couldn't tell him that no other man had ever made her *melt* so effortlessly. He worked his finger into her, groaning when she clenched around him.

She pressed her lips to his shoulder, scraped her fingernails down his back. Urgency flared, prickling over her skin like a shower of sparks. His muscles tightened, and his cock jerked against her thigh. He lifted his head with a sudden curse.

"Condom," he muttered. "I—"

"It's okay." Julia tightened her hands on his arms. "I'm past that now, and I haven't been with a man in over a year, and I know you're clean too. I want to feel you inside me without a condom, so please do it."

He lowered himself back over her. His gaze collided with hers. Time froze.

Julia's heart pounded, her breath emerging in rapid gasps. Disbelief descended over her, and she half-expected the fog would lift to reveal that this was all a mulled-wine-induced dream, but oh my god…that was definitely Warren spreading her open with his fingers before easing his thick cock inside her. She fumbled for something to grasp and closed her hand around the leg of the coffee table. Her blood lit with sensation, every part of her body stretching and pulsing with desire.

He braced his hands on either side of her head, his jaw tight with self-restraint.

"God, Warren." Julia drew in a breath. Sweat dripped between her breasts. "Do it. *Fuck me.*"

With a low grunt, he sank into her, his cock filling her with such exquisite pressure that the fog of lust intensified, driving her toward bliss. She moaned and wrapped her legs around his hips. He pulled back and pushed forward, easing into a hard, swift rhythm that stimulated her every nerve. She fell into the friction and thrust of their bodies, the scent of Warren filling her head, the rough abrasion of the carpet. She gripped his back, his arms, opened her mouth for his bruising kisses, and wondered at the power of his body, the flex and pull of his strong muscles.

Time slipped away. Bliss rolled and swept through her again, causing her to bite down on his shoulder to quiet her instinctive scream of pleasure. She sensed his own ascent, his shout guttural and hot against her neck as her body took the full force of his powerful release. He rolled to her side, the only sound the heavy cadence of their breath.

Julia still felt him inside her, as if he'd imprinted himself on her body the way he already had on every intangible part of her.

The words rose up from the depths of her being, the center of her soul, the soft, gentle area around her heart she so rarely let anyone see.

"I…"

The sound of her own voice, the simple *I*, broke through the fog of lust. She swallowed. A sudden alarm dispelled her lingering pleasure. She pushed the words down deep, horrified that she'd almost confessed.

She sat up slowly, trying to ignore the temptation to surrender to the warm strength of Warren beside her. She wanted to curl into him, rest her hand against his chest, slide her leg between his.

As she reached for her discarded shirt, she caught sight of the framed photo of Warren, Rebecca, and their children that she'd left on the coffee table.

Her heart seized. Tendrils of cold snaked through her, turning her blood to ice.

CHAPTER 4

"Well, that was fun."

Injecting a cool note into her voice, Julia turned away from Warren and picked up her crumpled panties.

He didn't respond. She fumbled to find her bra, calling upon every reserve of strength she possessed to collect her composure.

"I have an early meeting tomorrow." She got to her feet, still not looking at him, and slipped into her lingerie. "I need to go."

She felt his gaze as if it were a touch. He pushed to his elbows, his eyes hooded. Unselfconscious in his nakedness, his skin still damp with sweat and muscles taut, he was totally unfamiliar to her—a man who'd fucked her raw and made her come hard enough to see stars. Not Warren Stone, her sister's husband, the widower who'd become her best friend.

The man to whom she could never confess her love.

She smothered a stab of guilt, blocking an image of Rebecca with her elegant, lovely features, her sleek blonde hair, always cut in a fashionable bob, her model-like figure.

As a child, Julia had worshipped her older sister, and at first she'd resented Warren when he'd captured all of Rebecca's attention and then swept her off into marriage. Later, Julia had learned they'd wed partly due to Rebecca's unexpected pregnancy, but the circumstances appeared to have no effect on their rock-solid devotion and love.

Julia hadn't envied their marriage—in her eyes, they'd been tied down with children, Warren working all hours of the day, Rebecca stuck at home—but they'd been committed to both each other and their life together. That part Julia *had* envied. She'd told Warren as much on the night when she'd so shamelessly thrown herself at him.

A hot flush rose to her cheeks. She bent to pick up her shirt. Warren turned away from her and pulled on his boxer briefs. Her focus snapped involuntarily to the flex and stretch of his back muscles, the straight vertebrae of his spine and slopes of his shoulder blades. A sharp longing rose in her to slide her fingers over his back, trace the structure of his bones, learn every part of his body the way she'd learned every inch of his character.

She backed away, afraid she would act on the urge the way she'd almost confessed.

He turned and advanced, his expression set with determination.

"Julia, we need to talk about this," he said.

"*This* was a mistake."

"The hell it was. You're wrong if you think this hasn't been *waiting* to happen."

She held up a hand, trying to ignore her racing heart. "Spare me the post-coital discussion, please. I'm accustomed to men rolling over and going to sleep."

Warren frowned. "Don't you turn Ice Queen on me."

"I'm not turning anything," she snapped. "This is who I am."

"You're a lot more than that."

She couldn't respond. Warren was Rebecca's husband. He'd always been hers. Her presence had filled their lives for thirteen years through the children and the foundation. So much of the work she and Warren did together was in honor of Rebecca. To keep her alive.

How could Julia have allowed them to cross the invisible line they'd always kept so firmly drawn? How could she have let herself almost confess the deepest secret of her heart?

"I admit it's been quite a while since I've gotten laid," she remarked crisply. "Thanks for scratching my itch. We should do this again in another thirteen years."

"All right." He crossed his arms over his bare chest, his features steeling. "If that's what you want, I can play the game. We're doing this again tomorrow. You'll get on your knees and wrap your pretty lips around my dick. Maybe I'll let you swallow, or maybe I'll fuck you again and come on your tits."

God. A hot shudder rippled through her. She turned away, not wanting him to read on her face that his crude words inflamed her all over again.

"I'll check my agenda and let you know if that works for me." She jerked her shirt over her head.

Before she could grab her pants from the floor, Warren clamped his hand around her wrist. He yanked her against the solid wall of his chest, trapping her with the strength of his grip.

"Oh, it will work for you, honey." His voice was dangerously low, his dark eyes burning through her. "Because you're mine now. You want me to scratch your itch? Sure. But that means you do whatever the fuck I say whenever the fuck I say it. If you think you can shut me out with your ice, you're wrong. I have a goddamned inferno."

Her heart pounded so hard she could hear it inside her head. She'd never seen him so controlling, so determined. Part of her longed to lock herself right up against his body and let him *do* things to her. She wanted to get on her hands and knees for him, to feel him driving into her from behind, her ass slamming against his flat stomach. She wanted to ride him, pushing his cock inside her as deep as it could possibly go. She wanted them both to come, over and over, until they were exhausted and spent.

Then she wanted him to take her in his arms and fucking *cuddle* her until she fell into a deep, dreamless sleep.

He put his hand between her legs, edging his fingers underneath her panties to where she was still wet and aching from his cock. He circled her swollen clit. A tremble rocked her. She struggled not to writhe against the pressure of his fingers, to beg him to make her come again.

Just as she was about to surrender to the urge, he let her go.

Julia scrambled to put on her pants and shoes, her face hot. She'd lost this battle and it was her own damned fault. Trembling, she hurried to the door.

"We're not done here, Jules," Warren said. "No fucking way."

The steely certainty in his voice lanced into her like an arrow. No one knew better than her that Warren Stone was a man who got what he wanted.

But he'd never had to battle *her* hard-edged resolve, the brick walls she'd constructed to keep people out.

She hurried outside, slamming the door behind her. As she drove home, she tried not to think about the fact that Warren was the only man in the world who could demolish those walls with nothing more than a kiss.

"Here's the final line-up for Deck the Halls." Marco handed Julia a sheet of paper. "I'll meet you over at the theater tomorrow night for rehearsal number one, unless you need me to escort you so you don't cut and run."

"Don't get your hopes up." Julia scanned the schedule.

"I put Poodle-O-Doodles in the first act because apparently the dogs have a naptime at…"

Marco's voice drifted from her attention, as had pretty much everything else today. Except for her memories of Warren.

A shiver rippled down her spine. Her body still ached deliciously from their encounter last night. She hadn't been able to keep it—to keep *him*—far from her thoughts. She certainly hadn't been able to stop reliving his touch, the scrape of his stubble on her skin, the thrust of his shaft inside her, over and over—

"...and then the Wee Tinsel Dancers will come out for their tap dance with the Gingerbread Man," Marco said.

"Fine." She waved for him to take the paper away. "Looks great."

"Did you just say *looks great?*"

Julia sighed. "It will *suffice for now*, Marco. You may leave. Really, I insist."

He smirked and left her office. Julia suspected he would bring her a kale salad for lunch, the little toad.

She rose from her desk and went to the private studio adjoining her office. Unlike her business space, her studio contained a drafting table, mood boards covered with photos, textiles, and graphics; shelves of fabric rolls and samples; mannequins, and a sewing table cluttered with measuring tape and scissors.

She sat at the drafting table, which was covered with sketches for her proposed Appear line. She studied a drawing of a tailored shirt, trying not to hear Vincent Peck telling her it was outdated and old.

She'd been in the fashion industry long enough to know how trends worked. And her recent experiences with Polly and Kate had taught her that younger women didn't always care for high-end fashion, but they did need flattering, well-made clothing that was easy to mix and match. With the right patterns and fabrics, some whimsical, fun touches, *Appear* could be a unique line for young, working women.

Though the Evermore deal had hit her right where it hurt the most, she had to find a way out. A way *up*. She had to believe in herself, to *not believe* Vincent Peck's criticism that her designs were uninspired. That she didn't have the credibility to create an authentic line for young women because...well. Her young days were behind her.

Fuck him. It wasn't as if Peck was any spring chicken, so what did he know?

She set her drawings aside. She'd get back to them later when she had time to think of new concepts.

She left her office and strode to Enzo's desk. His head jerked up at the sound of her heels clicking across the floor.

"The Zuzu photo shoot proofs?" She held out her hand.

He shuffled through papers on his desk and produced the folder. Julia took it with a nod, eyeing the surface of his desk. It was covered with stacks of paper, a musical Christmas tree, two dying plants, hand sanitizer, and a number of little trinkets—troll dolls, a dinosaur paper clip holder, wind-up robots, and a tabletop air hockey game.

"This is unaccept..." Julia stopped. "What is that?"

"What?" Enzo whirled around, as if ready to defend himself.

"*That.*" Julia stabbed her finger at the multicolored cube half-hidden behind the printer. "Is that a Rubik's Cube?"

"Oh, this. Yes." Relieved, he held up the cube.

Julia snapped her fingers and opened her palm. Enzo dropped the cube into her hand and backed his swivel chair away. She studied the mixed-up cube. They'd been popular when she was a kid, but she hadn't seen or attempted to solve one in years.

And why would she have? It was a ridiculous waste of time, trying to get the colors on a cube to align.

"Uh, will there be anything else?" Enzo asked.

"May I borrow this?" Julia closed her fingers around the cube.

"Yeah, sure." Enzo looked mildly baffled. "You can have it, if you want."

Julia nodded her thanks and stepped away. "Clean your desk. I want it spotless by the end of the day."

"Yes, ma'am." Enzo grabbed the wastepaper basket and got to work.

Julia returned to her office. She closed the door and sat behind her desk, studying the silly little Rubik's Cube.

Really, how hard could it be? If she twisted the right side, she'd have a row of white along the edge, and then she just had to bring the other two edge pieces to the same side…except then that screwed up the yellow row she had created on the other side, which meant she had a mess in the middle section of the… Well, hold on. She needed a different approach, maybe instead of focusing on the rows she needed to get the center square first.

She worked a bit more, concentrating on the white center square before evaluating the other squares to see if she could optimize the rows and…

"Julia?"

She looked up. Marco peered around her office door, his coat and briefcase in hand.

"Okay if I go?" he asked.

"I suppose." She tossed the cube onto her desk. "Why are you leaving early?"

"I'm not." He pointed to the clock. "It's seven p.m."

"Oh." She blinked. There must have been a wrinkle in time because there was no way she'd been working on a Rubik's Cube for over an hour straight.

She waved Marco away. "I'm just going to finish up a few things here."

"Sure." He glanced at the cube, his eyebrows raised. "See you tomorrow."

"Yes, you will."

When her office door closed, Julia gave a huff of irritation. She opened the bottom drawer of her desk to throw the cube inside, then changed her mind and put it in her handbag instead. That way, she wouldn't forget to return it to Enzo tomorrow.

She closed up the office and walked along Ocean Avenue, assessing the evening holiday decorations with a critical eye. The charm of downtown Indigo Bay lay in the rows of high-end shops and restaurants clustered beside art galleries, boutiques, and coffee-houses. Historic cottages spoke of the architects and artists who had once lived here, and ivy-covered stone buildings with arched entryways led to hidden courtyards. Multicolored lights wound around the iron lamps lining the streets, wreathes and stars decorated posts, colorful Christmas trees and reindeer adorned the flower beds.

Julia loved the beauty and history of Indigo Bay. She loved the way Sugar Rush presided over the town like a benevolent king, sustaining so much of the economy and residents. She loved that the Rebecca Stone Foundation was the town's unofficial charity and that it did so much good.

But, god in heaven, did she wish the town didn't expect the holidays to be something out of a hyperactive, animated Christmas movie.

She went into Asante, an upscale bar and restaurant, and hitched herself onto a stool at the bar. A quick drink might take her mind off the fact that her list of action items was still a mile long, which meant she'd have to put in some hours this weekend.

She had no intention of cutting into her time with her family, especially since Hailey would be back in Indigo Bay for the Stone family tree-trimming party. The tension in Julia's shoulders relaxed a bit. She hadn't seen her niece in several months and had planned some outings for them when Hailey returned. Julia couldn't wait to spend time with her niece. Hailey was a bright spot in the holidays, the Cindy Lou Who of Julia's Grinchy Christmas.

"What can I get for you, darling?" The bartender placed a cocktail napkin in front of her.

"Scotch. Neat."

He lifted an eyebrow.

"Did you expect me to ask for a glass of white wine?" she asked dryly.

"No, but I've got a Christmas peppermint martini, if you're feeling festive."

"Bah humbug."

He grinned. "*Unfestive* scotch coming right up."

"Aunt Julia."

She turned to find Tyler waving at her from a booth where he was seated with Luke and Evan. Pleased, she took the glass from the bartender and walked over to her nephews. Tyler moved over to make room for her.

"What're you doing here?" he asked. "Waiting for a hot date?"

"Hardly." She spoke with derision, hoping he didn't notice the flush creeping up her cheeks. She usually deflected Tyler's teasing remarks about her love life with a roll of her eyes, but this time his mention of a *hot date* brought up an image of…his father.

Julia took a gulp of scotch. She'd had sex with the boys' *father*. And while she'd been totally into it at the time, now in the clear light of day it seemed all the more wrong. What in the world would the boys say if they knew she'd been writhing around on the floor of the great room while Warren—

No need to go there.

She squirmed a little and cleared her throat. "Just getting a drink. What are you boys up to?"

"We're talking about Dad." Luke reached for his beer. "The whole retirement thing that came out of nowhere."

"I believe he didn't tell you sooner because he knew you'd try to talk him out of it," Julia said.

"Right. Like we won't now?" Evan asked.

Julia gave them both a repressive frown. "You have no right to try and stop your father from retiring. He's earned the right to retire early and do something else with his life."

"What's he going to do?" Luke argued. "Play poker? Build model airplanes? Without Sugar Rush, he'll be lost."

"Unlike you, Lucas Stone, your father's entire identity has not been wrapped up in Sugar Rush," Julia reminded him. "I strongly suggest you all listen to him and work to restructure the company instead of attempting to convince him not to retire."

"I'm telling you, man." Tyler tilted his head back to take a swallow of beer, then eyed Luke pointedly. "It's a chick."

Luke made a scoffing noise. Evan shrugged. Julia's shoulders tensed. She regarded each of her nephews in turn.

"What are you talking about?" she asked evenly.

Evan sighed. "Ty thinks Dad is seeing someone."

Julia's heart stuttered. "You mean a woman?"

"No, a duck," Tyler replied dryly. "Of course a woman."

"He *has* been dating more recently," Evan admitted. "And he's been going off with his climbing buddies too. With the retirement thing coming out of nowhere, there's gotta be something else he's not telling us."

"Exactly." Tyler nodded in satisfaction.

"So you think Dad's playing the field?" Luke asked. "*That's* why he wants to retire?"

"Maybe." Evan took a few chips from the bowl in the center of the table. "He was vague about his post-retirement plans, right? And a few times over the past month, Hannah and I have asked him to go with us somewhere on the weekends—to dinner, down to Catalina, trip to San Francisco. He turned us down every time."

"So?" Luke asked. "He's never been into going out."

"So maybe that's changing. And maybe he doesn't want to tell us yet."

"Why would he not want to tell us?" Luke argued. "We know he's seen a few women over the years."

"A few women." Tyler rolled his eyes. "What about *one* super-hot woman? Who's also into climbing and hiking and stuff?"

Luke's forehead creased. "You think he's getting serious about one woman?"

"It's possible," Tyler said. "He seemed pretty into that lady Gia a while back. And he's going on a ski vacation after Christmas, right? He never said he was going alone."

"Boys." Julia's voice came out sharper than she'd intended, honed on the granite rock that had settled into the pit of her belly. "Speculating about your father's love life is both rude and disrespectful."

The three of them all blinked in faint surprise.

"Uh, why?" Tyler asked.

"It just is," Julia snapped. "He wouldn't speculate about *your* love lives."

"Yeah, he probably would," Evan remarked.

Julia took a swallow of scotch, appreciating the burn as it spread through her chest. Her insides knotted like a ragged hemline. Warren wouldn't have had sex with her if he was serious about another woman. He had far too much integrity for that. And despite the lustful combustion of their fuck, he also possessed more than enough self-control to have stopped things before they'd gotten out of hand. If he'd wanted to.

Julia wasn't at all certain she could say the same about herself. And now more than ever, she hated the mere *idea* of Warren with another woman, which made her nephews' speculation all the more vexing.

"I'm telling you to stop it." She slid out of the booth. "Your father's love life is none of your business. So instead of gossiping, I'd suggest you check your emails and see where I've volunteered you for the Deck the Halls finale."

"Can I dress up as an elf again this year?" Tyler pulled his phone out of his pocket and swiped the screen. "Please say yes. I could use the costume when Kate and I get busy…uh, delivering toys to the children's hospital."

Evan grinned. Julia compressed her lips and reached for her handbag.

"You're selling roasted chestnuts," she informed Tyler. "There is no costume."

He gave a drawn-out groan.

"What am I doing?" Evan asked.

"You're setting up seating, and Luke, you and Adam are supervising backstage. There will be more, but those are your jobs for now."

"Come on, Aunt Julia." Tyler's pleading gaze locked on her. "Can't I help at Santa's Sleigh or something cool like that?"

"No." Julia rose, her spine straightening. "You all have your assignments. And stop gossiping about your father's love life or I'll give you a whole new definition of the term *roasted chestnuts*."

She strode away just as the boys burst into laughter.

CHAPTER 5

Curses blistered through Warren's brain. He ran faster, his breath burning his lungs. Sweat dripped down his back. He charged up the hill toward his house, ignoring the pain in his muscles. He ran the steps up to the redwood deck and came to a slow halt and checking the time on his watch. Thirteen seconds faster than yesterday's run. He pulled the fifty-pound backpack off and dragged in a few breaths.

The dizziness hit him like a brick. He grabbed the deck railing. The world spun for a few seconds before grinding to a stop. He straightened slowly, smothering the unease spreading through his chest.

He'd never had vertigo before, not even on the smaller-scale climbs he'd done over the past year in preparation for the Matterhorn. But three months ago he'd started having dizzy spells and a strange pressure in his ears that wasn't related to an infection or even a common cold. He leaned his forearms on the railing and closed his eyes.

He'd always been into physical fitness, but over the past year he'd taken it to a whole new level in preparation for the climb. Four times a week, he met the others at the gym for strength training, and every day he did some form of cardio and endurance work. They'd also been stepping up their local climbs, hiking to higher elevations with heavier packs.

He went into the kitchen and downed a glass of water. In the morning, he ran the hills and valleys of his estate, knowing he needed more training than the younger guys to keep up. He was in better condition now than he'd been his whole life, but he was the oldest guy of the group. Aside from occasional digs, the other guys respected both him and his seniority, which only fueled his determination to lead the grueling climb. And not let a little dizziness get in his way.

He headed upstairs to shower, the hot water and start of his daily routine shifting his mind back to his retirement. A little over a week until Christmas. Then he'd leave for the climb, which he'd purposely planned to give his sons complete authority over Sugar Rush. If he wasn't available, they'd have to restructure and start working without him.

Whether or not they wanted to.

He dressed and checked his phone, trying not to be irritated by Julia's lack of response to his calls and texts. She'd been ignoring him way too much lately. Maybe that was what had pushed him over the edge.

He got into his car and drove to the Sugar Rush campus. He didn't often feel badly about his actions. He tried to live and act with integrity, to be a good role model for his children, to treat women well. In fact, the last time he'd felt such sharp regret and guilt had been years ago…with Julia.

Except this time it was magnified tenfold. He'd been unable to stop touching her, his desire reaching a fevered breaking point. It had felt like years of pent-up lust had suddenly exploded. He could have fucked her for hours, not wanting to leave the soft tight grip of her body. In the hours since their encounter, he hadn't been able to stop thinking about her sweet, warm taste, the sound of her moans, the vibrations rippling through her.

But despite the explosive heat, her multiple orgasms, her unmistakable response, she still thought it had been a *mistake*. Like their kiss from thirty years ago, but cranked up a thousand degrees.

He hated the idea that she would connect the two events in her head, as if what had happened then had any impact on what had happened now.

Unless it had.

He shook his head. An image of Rebecca emerged in his mind, followed by the usual ache of sorrow. She'd never seemed to twist questions and mistakes around, trying to look at them from all angles and come up with answers. Not for the first time, he wished he had her certainty.

He straightened his lollipop-pattered tie and strode toward the main office of the Sugar Rush campus—a sprawling complex of buildings nestled in the hills overlooking the ocean. He nodded greetings at several employees as they crossed the curving, flagstone pathways and manicured gardens between the buildings. He was immensely proud to be a member of the Stone family, to have been born into the legacy of Sugar Rush, but he was ready to leave the company to others and their visions of the future.

He took the stairs to the seventh floor. Luke's new executive assistant, Anne, wasn't at her desk, but the office door was half-open. Warren knocked and entered. Luke was at the seating area, the company's end-of-the-year reports spread on the table.

Luke motioned him over. "Hey, Dad. Have a seat."

Warren sat beside his son, and they spent an hour reviewing the reports and discussing points to bring up at the next board meeting. When they were finished, Luke stacked the files and glanced at him.

"Have you rethought retirement yet?"

Warren's insides twisted. He needed to get Luke on his side

about this. If his eldest son supported him, the other boys would follow his lead, and the transition would be smooth.

"No," he said. "I don't plan to, either."

Luke's forehead creased with a scowl. Warren tried not to smile. Even now, he still saw the boy in his sons—as rough-and-tumble and rebellious as they were smart, kind, and energetic. As the eldest, Luke had always been the protector, especially of Evan. It hadn't been a surprise that he'd felt the same way about the family company.

Warren's soft spot for Luke lay in the fact that the boy was his first-born, the heir to the throne. Luke was both the reason Warren had become a parent, and he was the son who'd taught him how to be a father. He'd made mistakes with Luke that he'd been able to correct for his other children. And since he'd been so young when Rebecca got pregnant, in some ways he and Luke had grown up together. Warren had become an adult because of Luke.

It hadn't been the same for Rebecca. She'd already been an adult, easing into motherhood and marriage as if she'd simply stepped into her life's role. Warren hadn't found the transition nearly as easy, but he'd worked hard to do right by his family. He only needed to look at his children to know he'd succeeded.

"You knew I'd retire eventually," he told Luke.

"Not so soon." Luke rubbed his jaw, still frowning. "And not when we're expanding and launching new projects. Alpine Chocolates, the Corporate Social Responsibility Division, the Cocoa Bean Team...plus all the new packing technologies, the work Spencer is doing with flavenols and product blending... Sugar Rush is right at the edge of becoming a global leader in sustainability and innovation. How can you leave right now?"

"Son, I'm not abandoning Sugar Rush," Warren said, "Or you. The company will always face new challenges and technologies. As it should. And you and your brothers will continue to steer the ship on the right course with your strong leadership. I have nothing but faith and trust in you. *That's* how I can leave right now."

He rose to his feet. "I've asked Mary to leave room on the meeting agenda so I can make the announcement. You should have a preliminary list of potential successors on hand. Don't give the board a chance to think too much about their own choices. You be first."

Luke didn't respond, but the creases on his forehead deepened. Again Warren ignored a pang of regret as he started toward the office door. All of his children had to find their own way at some point, just like he had.

He pulled open the door and stopped in his tracks. His heart crashed against his ribs. Dressed in a pale blue linen sheath that skimmed her figure like water, Julia stood in front of the executive assistant's desk in all her imperious glory, her hands on her hips and her eyebrows arched. With her Grace Kelly features and her sleek blonde hair glowing like honey, she was a vision of flawless, elegant beauty.

But Warren's mind flashed back to the disheveled, eager woman she'd been last night. The woman who'd writhed underneath him, dug her manicured fingernails into his back, convulsed around his cock as if she could have milked him dry. He'd wanted to turn her over, spank her pretty ass, drive into her from behind.

Hell. He wanted to do that to her *right now*. Mess up her hair. Tear off her dress. Rip off her stockings. Make her moan and beg and—

His cock twitched. He took a breath, willing himself to calm down. He was at work. He needed to get his shit together. Focus.

"It's quite simple," Julia was telling Anne, her tone arctic. "Luke needs to review the Sugar Rush charity schedule *before* we send it out to all employees. Would you distribute the board meeting agenda without his approval?"

Anne, who was powerfully capable and efficient, opened her

mouth to speak, then snapped it shut when Julia leaned closer. Though Warren was used to intervening in Julia's ice storms without undermining her authority, he was having trouble smothering his instantaneous lust.

"Of course you wouldn't," Julia continued frostily, her blue eyes narrowing on Anne like lasers. "Because that's *Executive Assistantship For Dummies*, isn't it? As is the fact that we announce the Sugar Rush holiday party after we've finalized the arrangements. So I strongly suggest you surgically excise your head from your—"

"Julia." Warren moved swiftly forward.

She startled at the sound of his voice, but recovered quickly and shot him a glare dripping with icicles. Anne stood, her expression flashing with relief over his interruption.

"Sir, I didn't realize you were in Luke's office," she said. "I'm sorry I didn't offer to see if you need anything."

"What he *needs* is for the executive assistants in this company to stop acting like deer caught in the headlights," Julia said crisply. "Luke seems to think you're a competent adult, but I have my doubts."

"She'll take care of it," Warren said, his tone hardening. "Anne came with excellent credentials and recommendations." He glanced at the younger woman. "But you need to review the company procedures. In detail."

"Of course, sir."

"You never know when there might be a pop quiz." Julia swiveled on her stiletto heel and strode away.

"She's like that with everyone," Warren assured Anne. "You'll get used to her."

"Like I'll get used to a snake bite?" Anne sank back onto her chair with a groan.

Warren almost smiled in sympathy. All the Sugar Rush employees were accustomed to Julia's wicked-queen ways because they knew she was usually right, but everyone was still scared of her—the newer hires most of all.

"Luke has only good things to say about you," he told Anne. "And that's far more important than the company party."

She nodded in gratitude. Warren made a mental note to send her a gift box of Sugar Rush chocolates, then headed after Julia. She walked like she expected people to bow at her passing, her spine straight and her hair shifting like spun gold. No one would dare to imagine Julia Bennett with messy hair and kiss-stained lips, writhing and gasping beneath him...

A mixture of possessiveness and irritation filled his chest. He stepped beside her, matching his longer stride to hers.

"God, I miss Kate." Julia didn't glance at him or break her pace. "Of course, I'm delighted that she's able to use all her talents in her new position and improve Sugar Rush's social responsibility, *et cetera*. But as Luke's assistant, that girl never missed a beat. Except in her choice of clothing, so we can all thank the good lord I corrected that misfortune."

She paused at the top of the stairs and turned to face him, her expression cool and remote. "Kate is still handling the sign-ups for the soup kitchen. Did you get her email?"

"Yes. Now step into my office."

Julia blinked at his hard tone, her gaze shifting to his closed office door. "I beg your pardon?"

Warren opened the door. "In. Now."

Her features tightened with resistance just as the elevator doors opened and several employees emerged, their voices rising in chatter. Julia crossed the hallway in front of them, her shoulders rigid. He caught a whiff of Chanel No. 5 as she passed him.

He entered the office behind her and closed the door, flicking the lock shut.

"You are not to take out personal crap on *my* employees," he said. "That's not how I run this company."

Julia's lips compressed. "Odd that you've never before questioned my treatment of *your* employees. And it wasn't personal. She needed to know she'd screwed up."

"Announcing the holiday party early is not screwing up," Warren replied evenly. "You're pissed off because you've had a shitty week, you have too much on your plate, an old bucket list has thrown you off your game, and you don't know what to do with the fact that we fucked the other night."

Two spots of color appeared on her cheeks. "I seem to recall that what I *did* with that fact was tell you it wasn't going to happen again. After which you informed me in excellent caveman style that I was wrong. You seem to forget I'm never wrong."

About this, you are.

He bit back the words. He hadn't become the president of Sugar Rush by throwing his weight around. He knew how to bide his time, work his way into getting what he wanted. And damned if he didn't want *her* more with every passing second.

"Well?" Julia put her hands on her hips and glared at him. "Are we done here?"

Under her make-up, purplish smudges shadowed her eyes. Brackets of tension lined her mouth. His jaw tightened.

"You had a migraine yesterday," he said.

"What the fuck do you care?" Julia snapped.

Warren's hands flexed. He was used to her quick-fire cursing, all the more effective when delivered by a woman who looked like royalty, but he didn't like being the recipient of her wrath.

"I'm putting Mia Donovan in charge of the Sugar Rush holiday party," he said.

"You're *firing* me?" Julia stared at him, her eyes widening. "Are you serious?"

"Yes." He steeled himself against her shock and the knowledge that he was hurting her. "You've planned it for the past ten years, and it's time to hand it over to someone else."

"You don't get to decide that."

"Yes, I do. Sugar Rush is my company. This is also the event where I'll be announcing my retirement. You're not going to plan it."

"Because I have too much on my plate?" Julia stopped in front of the windows, her arms crossed and her fiery gaze fixed on him. "Thanks for your concern, Daddy, but I assure you I can handle everything I take on."

"That's why you're such a success. It's also why your headaches are getting worse."

"You are not my fucking doctor."

"Stop swearing."

She barked out a laugh. "You need to rethink this retirement thing, Warren. It's making you soft."

Given the state of his dick, he was anything but *soft*.

"If you won't delegate your projects, I will," he said.

"Because you can't stop being the boss, even if you think otherwise." Julia paced angrily to the desk, her eyes flaring with blue ice. "Why *are* you retiring, Warren? Everyone knows you're the power behind the throne, much as you've let the boys take all the glory. Three months—hell, one month from now when you have nothing to do and no one to order around, you're going to wonder why you made such a bad decision."

Warren's jaw clenched. He was sick of getting pushback from all sides. "I've been in business my entire life. I know what I'm doing."

"So do I, dammit," Julia retorted. "I don't need you looking out for me."

"I will *always* look out for you."

She came to a halt, her whole body stilling. By contrast, Warren's heartbeat kicked up, sudden heat flooding his veins. Their gazes met across the room, a crackling electric current firing through the air.

Julia took a breath, her breasts heaving beneath her jacket.

"Goddamn you, Warren Stone," she whispered.

"I told you to stop swearing." He advanced, his own breath increasing, his hands fisting and unfisting at his sides.

Rebellion tightened her features. "And if I don't?"

"You sure you want to find out?"

He closed the distance between them, his lust flaring like a match to dry leaves.

What the fuck was going on with them?

The question flared like a comet through his mind and died just as fast—because he didn't care about the answer. His mind was consumed with the thought of tasting her red lips again, sweet like cherries, spicy like peppers. Her mouth could deliver an insult as sharp and searing as a blade, but he knew—had always known, even if he'd smothered the knowledge—that the sounds issuing from Julia Bennett's mouth could also be smooth, hot murmurs of lust that rushed straight to his blood. Weakening him of all thought, all control, inciting him with the urge to—

He grabbed her shoulders, hauling her soft, slender body against him. He'd always loved the *contrast* of Julia, the sharp-tongued, acidic queen and the relentlessly devoted aunt. The rigorous boss who shot orders like arrows, and the loyal friend who bought Hailey's favorite peanut butter, sent care packages to Gavin Knight when he was deployed in Iraq, spent hours on end with Evan at the hospital.

He stared down at her fine features, pale skin, and wide blue eyes that he'd seen almost every day of his life for the past thirteen years—and suddenly now it felt as if he were looking at her for the first time. Had he never noticed that tiny birthmark right beneath her left eye? Or the silver flecks in her irises, like falling snow? Or the perfect curve in her upper lip, tempting him to put his tongue there and—

Oh, he'd noticed all right. He'd just tried to pretend he hadn't.

"What the hell am I going to do with you, Julia?" he muttered.

"Fire me, apparently." Her tone was bitter, her eyes blue fire.

Her gaze flickered involuntarily to his mouth, her lips parting.

He slipped his hand beneath her chin, lifting her face to his. His heart jackhammered. Her breath brushed against his mouth, the familiar scent of her—Chanel No. 5, lavender soap, pure Julia—suddenly exotic and tantalizing.

"I'm going to let you go," he said slowly, "and take two steps back. I want you to reach under your skirt and take your underwear off…if you're wearing any."

Her breath caught, her eyes widening with shock. "Are you fu…"

"No. I am not *fucking kidding you.*"

He released her and stepped back. His dick pushed against his fly. His blood boiled with lust. Julia stared at him, her hair tousled and her breath still fast. She curled her hands on the edge of his desk. Tension stretched between them, thick and hot, crackling with a challenge.

"Your move," Warren said.

She breathed out a curse. He saw the instant her defiance snapped in two. She lowered her head and bent to the hem of her skirt. Instead of reaching under it like he'd instructed, she grasped the hem and tugged it up her legs to reveal her long, stocking-clad legs.

Warren's mouth twitched with a smile. Of course his Julia wouldn't just obey without trying to subvert his authority. She wouldn't succeed, but he loved watching her try.

She wiggled her skirt all the way up to her hips, showing him that her silk stockings were attached to black garters over lacy black panties. His breathing increased, his pulse pounding. She met his gaze briefly, eyes darkened with lust, before she unsnapped the garters and peeled her panties off.

"Put them on my desk," he said.

She did. Her hand trembled.

"Come here," Warren ordered.

She approached and stopped in front of him. He rested his

hands on either side of her neck just below her jaw. Her lips parted. He kissed her.

Cherries and spice exploded through him, firing heat into his blood. His dick stiffened further, pressing against her soft belly. Julia moaned into his mouth, her body lacing with erotic tension. His mind emptied of thought, all of his senses centering on the feel and taste of her. She parted her lips, let him inside, and drew her tongue across his with an eagerness she couldn't hide.

Ah, fuck, yeah. His Julia was straight fire underneath her ice-queen façade. Burning heat and lust. If he touched her pussy, he'd find her already wet and ready for him. He'd sink into her with no resistance at all, slow at first to make her beg for more, then faster until he was slamming into her and driving them both to orgasm.

"Did I win that move?" she breathed.

"We both did."

She slid one hand to the back of his neck, her curves shaping to the hard planes of his chest as if she'd been made to fit against him. He deepened the kiss, swept his tongue through her mouth, bit down gently on her lower lip. She pulled at his tie, a sudden frenzy lighting her eyes. When she yanked at his shirt front, the buttons popped off and clattered to the floor. He crushed his mouth down on hers again. He slid his hands down to cup her ass, dipping his fingers between her smooth thighs. Her damp heat turned his blood nuclear. He tore at her stockings, ripping the silk.

Julia pulled her head away from him. "Those are hand-crafted French silk stockings from—"

"I'll buy you a hundred more." He backed her toward the desk, the smoldering heat in his blood rising into a firestorm. "But first you have to spread your pretty legs and take my cock in as deep as you can."

A visible shudder rippled through her. "God, Warren."

Her ass hit the desk. She curled her fingers into the lapels of his suit jacket. He grabbed her hips and lifted her onto the desk, pushing between her thighs. Her skirt rode up to her waist. She parted her legs. He ran his finger over her pussy to her clit. His pulse throbbed.

"Hungry girl," he murmured.

"Jesus." She closed her eyes, a hot flush rising to her cheeks. "What are you doing to me?"

"What I should have done years ago." He edged his finger down and circled her tight little hole. Julia moaned, her muscles tensing and her thighs trembling around his hips. He pushed into her slit, his breath escaping as her pussy closed tight around his finger.

"You want my cock here?" He worked his finger back and forth.

"Yes." She rubbed the front of his trousers, cupping his hard dick. "I haven't been able to stop thinking about the other night, about what it felt like to have you inside me..."

"Turn around."

She lifted startled eyes to his. "I don't..."

"Turn *around*."

She hesitated. Just like he suspected she would. She was used to giving orders, not taking them. And he was used to being obeyed. Their gazes met, a brief hot battle of wills. She broke first, her eyes lowering and her flush deepening.

She eased off the desk and turned. Satisfaction flooded him. He grasped her skirt and pulled it up over her hips, his heart hammering at the sight of her perfect ass upturned and naked. He put his hand on her lower back, pressing her onto the desk.

Julia made a low noise in the back of her throat, closing her eyes as she rested her cheek on the desk's surface. He unfastened her garter belt and tossed it to the floor. Then he stepped back and admired the sight of her—this gorgeous, regal woman bent submissively over a desk with her naked ass jutting upward in invitation. Her shapely, long legs balanced on her strapped stilettos, and her manicured fingers clenched and unclenched on the edge of the desk.

She was *perfect*. So fucking perfect that he couldn't fathom how he'd managed to restrain himself from touching her all these years.

He unbuckled his belt and pulled it off, then yanked his trousers and boxer briefs down. His cock jutted outward, so hard it ached. He grabbed the shaft and stroked a few times, his gaze locked on her tempting cleft. He moved forward, pressing his knee between her thighs to spread them wider.

"Open," he ordered.

She squeezed her eyes shut, her lips parted and her chest heaving with the force of her breath. She was still fully clothed from the waist up, and though he burned to see her naked again, he needed to be inside her *right now*. He ran his hands over her ass, her skin soft and velvety under his palms. He drew his finger slowly down the cleft between her cheeks, pausing at the tight little ring of her anus. A gentle probe with his finger caused her to gasp, her body stiffening.

"Warren."

A hard shiver rocked through her. He moved his hands to her pussy, running his finger over her folds, circling her swollen clit. She gasped, wiggling her hips like she wanted more. She was the most responsive woman he'd ever been with, reacting with hot little moans and writhings to his every touch. He took her wrists and pulled her arms back, settling her hands on her rear.

"Hold yourself open for me," he said.

A deep flush swept over her skin. She put her trembling hands on the lower part of her ass and spread herself nice and wide. He eased the head of his cock over her slippery folds, intense pleasure ricocheting through him as he positioned himself at her slit. With a groan, he drove forward, sinking so deep into her tight heat that her body jerked forward. Julia cried out, her back arching as if she were offering herself to him.

"Oh my god, Warren, *yes*," she gasped. "Harder...ah, I feel you so deep..."

Her voice melted into incoherent moans. Warren moved her hands away so he could grip her ass himself, increasing the pace of his drive. Fuck, but she was perfect, taking every heavy thrust with a cry of pleasure, her body clenching around his shaft, her legs spread wide. Tension coiled through his body. Sweat dripped down his back. His blood was on fire, the explosion building with intense pressure.

Deeper, deeper, his pelvis hitting her bouncing ass, her body jostling back and forth. Some dim part of his mind thought he might be hurting her, but when she twisted to look at him again, nothing but urgency and desperation shone in her expression.

"Warren." Her voice was strained taut as wire.

He slowed the pace of his thrusts and found her quivering clit.

"Poor baby," he murmured. "Do you want to come?"

"No, I want to dance the tango." Julia arched her back, thrusting herself toward him. "What the hell do you think?"

He smiled. He flicked his fingers over her clit and rubbed.

"I'm so close," she gasped. "Harder...just like that...oh *yes*."

She cried out, her body convulsing and vibrating with the force of her orgasm. Warren stroked her until she'd crested the wave and was sliding down the other side. He plunged into her again, back and forth, his own urgency building and building...

"*Fuck*."

With a growl, he pulled out of her and fisted his cock, stroking twice before shooting all over her trembling ass. Pleasure ripped through him, the explosion painting her skin with a spray of his seed. *Marking* her.

He dragged in a breath and rested his palm on her lower back. Trembles coursed through her in unending waves, and her whole body heaved with the force of her breath. He lowered himself over her, pressing his face into her neck. She lifted a hand and speared it through his hair, her fingers gripping the strands for an instant before she slid her palm over his jaw.

He pushed to his feet, tugging up his boxers and trousers. He went into his private bathroom and dampened a cloth with hot water to clean her up. When he returned to the office, Julia was seated in a chair, pulling off her torn stockings. Though she wasn't in full Ice Queen mode yet, it was creeping up on her, like frost collecting on the edges of a windowpane.

He handed her the cloth and returned to the bathroom, giving her a chance to get herself together. When he returned, she was fully dressed—the only evidence of their encounter her wrinkled clothes and flushed cheeks.

"This can't happen again," she said.

He frowned. "Why not?"

"Why not?" She shook her head in astonishment. "Because there's a reason we haven't done this before. We both knew it would be a terrible idea, a mistake that could ruin everything."

Irritation ripped through him. "Who the fuck ever said it would be a terrible idea? Or a mistake?"

"We didn't have to *say* it." Julia's eyes flashed with responding annoyance. "We both knew. Why else would we have kept things platonic for so long? Because our relationship is about your children and keeping this family strong and solid. It's about Sugar Rush, Rebecca's memory, and the Stone reputation. What would people think if they found out Warren Stone had hooked up with his late wife's *sister*?"

"I don't care what they'd think," he said. "I don't owe anyone explanations about anything. And yeah, we could spent a shitload of energy feeling guilty about Rebecca, but the fact is that she's been gone for almost fourteen years and nothing you and I do together is a betrayal of her. Just the opposite. Everything you've done for the Rebecca Stone Foundation, for her children, has honored her. And I've got news for you, Jules."

He approached, determined to make her see the truth. She

stepped away and brought a hand up between them. Wariness shone in her eyes.

"Our relationship has always been about a hell of a lot more than just the kids and Sugar Rush." Warren took hold of her upper arms, digging his fingers into her soft skin. "It's been about *us*. As friends, partners, confidantes. Why not lovers too?"

Her throat worked with a swallow. "What...what would the boys and Hailey think if they knew..."

"I don't care what they'd think," he repeated. "We've done everything we could possibly do for them. I don't need their approval to be with you."

Julia's teeth came down on her lower lip. "You do, you know. Because what if they don't like me stepping into the space where their mother once was? What would you do then?"

He expelled a frustrated breath. "I'd tell them to mind their own business."

"And that would be good enough?" She shook her head again. "Not to mention, the majority of your employees knew and loved Rebecca. Hell, we've all but deified her with the Rebecca Stone Foundation and all the good works we've done in her name. Don't you think people will...*react* if they find out we've suddenly started an affair?"

"There is nothing *sudden* about this," Warren retorted. "If anyone *reacts*, they're more than likely to say, 'Well, it's about fucking time.'"

"And if they don't?"

"I'll take that risk."

"Maybe you will." She strode to the door, her spine stiff. "But I won't."

"Julia, get back here," he snapped.

"Sorry, boss." She threw him a cold glance over her shoulder. "Game over."

No. This game was just beginning.

CHAPTER 6

Julia's inner Grinch was snarling.

"Deck the halls with boughs of holly...fa la la la la...pfft tee be...pfft..."

The hip-hop rap beat of the Christmas carol thumped through the theater auditorium. The barbershop quartet, decked out in blindingly bright red vests and green bow-ties, began snapping and beat-boxing onstage.

Two more full hours, minimum, before she was freed from the tethers of another Deck the Halls rehearsal.

She glanced at her phone. Warren hadn't texted her since their encounter that morning, not that she'd know what to say to him in her turmoil of confusion.

What in the hell was going on with them?

Hot, raw sex was what was going on.

Despite her assertion that it couldn't happen again, she'd been lost the instant lust had exploded between them like a supernova. Consumed by his kiss, craving his touch, desperate to have him inside her again.

Even now, her heart sped up at the memory, her—

"They're pretty good," Marco said from his seat beside her. "Great rhythm."

Julia forced her mind back to the present.

"Thank you, gentlemen!" she called, cutting off the singers mid-beat. "Please remember to exit stage left."

...and keep going.

The men grinned and bowed before sauntering offstage. Julia checked the schedule as a choral group came out with a rendition of "Let it Snow," followed by two local elementary school teachers performing some sort of Star Wars snowman skit that she did not remotely understand.

"Exit stage left." She flipped the pages on her clipboard. "Wee Tinsel Dancers, you're next."

The spotlight danced back and forth across the empty stage.

"Wee Tinsel Dancers," Julia repeated sharply.

Nothing.

With a groan, she hauled herself out of the third-row auditorium seat and made her way backstage—where chaos reigned. Poodles yapped from their crates, teenaged magicians practiced their rope acts, a ventriloquist inexplicably gave his reindeer puppet a southern accent, and a dozen five-year-old girls simultaneously cried, whined, or sat pouting with their arms crossed.

Julia approached one of the Wee Tinsel teachers. "Sarah, is there a problem?"

Sarah, a young woman with flawless skin and a willowy body, sighed and put her hand on her forehead. "They don't want to do it."

"What?"

"They don't want to do it," Sarah repeated. "They were apparently told they would get candy canes, and they won't do it if they don't."

Julia turned to the little girls with a forced smile that felt as if it would give her a thousand wrinkles.

"Girls," she said in her most gentle, Mrs. Claus voice. "This is the rehearsal for your big night. You want to be stars, don't you?"

"I want to be a monkey!" announced a pig-tailed cherub. She jumped on the chair and pretended to climb the curtains.

"Get down, please," Julia said. "You know that performers need to rehearse for their performances, don't you? Isn't that why you're taking classes with Miss Sarah?"

"I need to pee," said a curly-haired angel.

"I want a candy cane," demanded a blonde munchkin, glowering at Julia. "You said there would be candy canes."

"On performance night, everyone will get a candy cane," Julia promised. "Now if you'll all please line up to—"

"Look!" yelled a cinnamon-haired sprite. "I'm a fire truck."

She ran around screeching at the top of her lungs.

Julia gritted her teeth. And people wondered why she didn't particularly enjoy small children.

"Where's the Gingerbread Man?" she asked Sarah. "Isn't he supposed to join them in the dance?"

"He had to work late, but he's on his way."

"All right." Julia stepped away from the noisy girls. "Let's move on with the next act. Let me know when he arrives."

She hoped to God the girls didn't throw a fit on the night of the actual performance. She checked the schedule and approached four middle-aged women standing together and talking in low voices.

"Jingle Belles?" Julia checked her roster for their names. "Are you ready?"

"Yes." Sharon, a plump woman with badly cut mousy brown hair, turned from the circle. "Did you get my email about our costumes? I'm afraid we can't wear the Santa suits like we'd planned."

"We were getting them custom-made, but there was a mix-up with the order," Beverly added.

Julia eyed the clothes the women were wearing—a boxy suit,

polyester pants and a sweater sequined with a Christmas tree design, an overlarge green shirt. Not to mention their lack of makeup, jewelry, and nail polish.

"So this is what you plan to wear?" She failed to keep the distaste out of her voice. Seeing women badly dressed, badly *put together*, was the visual equivalent of nails on a chalkboard.

"That's what I was asking," Sharon explained. "We can't afford to get matching suits or anything, so we can either wear individual festive clothes or just black pants and green shirts."

Julia attempted to suppress her instinctive urge to *fix them*. She did not have time to style anyone right now, much less four women for Deck the Halls.

"I have another sweater like this, but with a reindeer." Connie gestured to the sequined tree on her sweater. "One of you can borrow it."

"Or if everyone has something in plaid, we could coordinate with red scarves," Sharon suggested.

"What about Christmas-themed pajamas?" Beverly asked. "I saw snowman flannels on sale at Target the other—"

"We're short on time here, ladies," Julia interrupted. "Take your places onstage. Let's get this over with."

She strode down the steps of the stage. After resuming her seat beside Marco, she started checking her emails on her phone.

"O Come All Ye Faithful..."

A shiver rippled over Julia's skin. She looked up. The Jingle Belles stood in the spotlight, their voices rising in perfect acapella harmony. She'd known they were good, but onstage in the glow of the lights, they were...really good. Good enough to cause prickles to rise on her arms, and maybe even a bit of emotion to tighten her chest.

"...joyful and triumphant..."

A sudden memory came forth of her father singing this exact song at the piano of their little house in Palo Alto, his booming voice echoing through the room. She and Rebecca decorating the tree. Their mother making hot chocolate. Julia singing along, feeling the music opening inside her like light.

"Julia?"

She blinked at the sound of Marco's voice. The song had ended, the Jingle Belles' voices fading into the air. They stood looking at her, as if unsure what to do next.

"Exit stage…" Julia cleared her throat. "Thank you, ladies. If you can all stop by my studio at…" she consulted her phone calendar and decided she could fit them in before the family tree-trimming party, "…nine on Saturday morning, I'll see what clothes I can find for you. All right?"

The women all looked surprised. Julia felt Marco glance at her.

"You're serious?" Sharon asked.

"Of course I'm serious," Julia replied crisply. "Why wouldn't I be?"

"Well, you're a little…er…" Beverly started.

Connie nudged her with an elbow.

"…busy," Beverly finished.

Julia narrowed her eyes, suspecting the other woman had been about to use a different *B* word.

"Yes, I am *busy*," she replied. "But I'm willing to make time for you, unless you don't want my help?"

"No, no, we appreciate it," Sharon said hastily. "Thank you so much. Nine Saturday morning. We'll be there."

They had better be, if she was going to such lengths.

"Very well." Julia turned back to the schedule. "Exit stage left."

You think he's getting serious about one woman?

Luke's voice echoed through Julia's head. Throughout the entire rehearsal, everything *Warren* had simmered in a hot under-current beneath her thoughts.

She plucked the golden waffle from the waffle iron and dropped it onto a plate. After lathering it with butter and syrup, she sat on the sofa and dug her fork into the gooey goodness.

The waffle tasted like sandpaper—a result of her mood rather than the actual food. With a groan, she pushed the plate aside and leaned back on the sofa. The start of a migraine clawed at her head, pressure building behind her eyes.

Even though she couldn't—wouldn't—believe Warren capable of cheating, she had to resist the urge to text him about the boys' conversation.

What would she even say? *Did you fuck me while you're seeing another woman?* Aside from the fact that the answer had to be a resounding *No*, the question would make her sound like a raging jealous harpy—which, under the right circumstances, she probably could be. But she certainly didn't want to be that way about Warren.

He hadn't made his usual one p.m. call today. Hadn't texted her either. Apparently he was holding to his word that he'd *play the game*.

And damned her for rolling the dice first.

A hollowness broke open inside her. She always told Warren everything.

Whenever she was working through a difficult problem or situation, he was the one she went to. He'd take her to dinner, listen to her vent, talk her through possible solutions. By the time they were sharing a dessert, she was clear-headed, stronger, ready to tackle the issue from a different angle.

But this time, with two crazy-hot fucks burning between them like a bonfire, and all their arguing about her workload and the festival, and him firing her from the Sugar Rush holiday party...with so much upheaval, how could she possibly go to him for answers?

Longing stabbed through her. Much as she'd loved the sensation of him inside her, the touch of his lips, the way he made her feel both dirty and cherished at the same time...she needed *him*. She needed the Warren she'd known and relied on for thirteen years.

Yes, she'd always had feelings for him that were better kept concealed, but she'd been willing to make the sacrifice for the sake of their deep, loyal friendship. To keep Warren Stone as the one person in the world she could turn to with a problem.

And now? Who was she supposed to turn to when *he* was the problem?

She closed her eyes and leaned her head against the back of the sofa. Her mind flashed with images of herself bent over his big desk, her skirt hiked up and her panties pulled down. Balancing on her stiletto heels. Never before had ice-queen stylist Julia Bennett behaved with such wanton disregard.

Never before had she *liked* being told what to do. But with Warren she sure did. She liked obeying his commands, that deep firm voice twisting through her blood.

She was wet just thinking about it. Imagining Warren staring at her naked ass, his hands pushing her thighs wider and opening her for his penetration. And penetrate her he had, thrusting into her balls-deep, the delicious friction of his cock sending her urgency skyrocketing. She'd only caught glimpses of him over her shoulder and had to imagine what he'd looked like—his thick shaft sticking rigidly out of his open trousers, his tie loosened and his features a mask of lust as he drove them both toward bliss.

A half groan, half sigh escaped her. She wiggled, pressing her thighs together to ease the ache in her clit. She could still feel him, smell him.

If he walked into the house right now, she'd yank off her panties and spread her legs for him without even thinking twice. Because *oh my fucking god*, how she craved his cock inside her, his mouth crashing against hers, his deep voice murmuring orders into her ear.

She lifted a hand to her breast, twisting her hard nipple underneath her linen sheath dress. Heat shot straight down to her pussy. She could pull up her skirt just far enough to ease her hand between her thighs. It wouldn't take long at all, just a little tickle on her clit and she'd come with an image of Warren shooting all over her bare ass—

She pushed to her feet and went into her bedroom, stripping off her suit, leaving her bra and panties in a trail behind her. She retrieved her vibrator from the nightstand, and ten seconds later, she was working it against her pussy—no lube needed, since just the memory of Warren had made her wet and ready.

She closed her eyes, arching her body up to meet the rhythmic pulsations. She rubbed the vibrator over her clit and pressed it against her opening. Usually the toy was powerful enough to spark a quick, hard orgasm that left her reasonably satisfied, but this time her body was slow to react. Which was strange since she'd have come in a heartbeat if Warren had slipped his hand into her panties and fingered her damp pussy…

Julia groaned, pressing the round knob harder against her clit. Images flashed behind her closed eyelids—Warren naked, his cock projecting outward, his eyes smoldering. He fisted his cock and pushed between her legs, murmuring dirty phrases in his deep voice as he slid slowly into her and started to thrust… hard…harder…jostling her against the bed, filling her over and over…

"Ah!"

An orgasm wrenched through her. She gasped, stroking the vibrator over her folds as the sensations peaked and began to ebb. She fell against the pillows to catch her breath. Only when her body calmed down did she realize her cheeks were damp. She covered her face with her hands and choked back a sob.

Oh fuck *no*.

She would not do this.

She sat up and yanked on her silk bathrobe, determination

steeling her spine. She would not mope around regretting the past or worrying about the future. She'd take her recent setbacks and work her ass off to turn things back around in her favor because Julia Bennett got shit done. *Perfectly.*

She'd go back to drawing board on the Appear designs and find another way to launch the clothing line. She'd organize Deck the Halls so well it would be the best festival event the town had ever seen. She'd finalize all the family plans so her nephews and niece would have a memorable holiday they'd still be talking about years from now. She take her *Before Fifty* list and...well, she'd throw it away because it was silly, but that would give her closure from the past.

Her phone rang with "I Want Candy."

Julia pressed a hand to her heart, her nerves flaring to life as she reached for her phone and answered the call.

"Hi." His deep voice stroked her like a cat's paw. "How'd the rehearsal go?"

"It went."

"You okay?"

Her throat tightened. "I don't know."

"Jules, taking risks is *good*. Change is good."

"So is stability."

"We've been stable for years. That won't change."

"It already has."

Before he could respond, she ended the call and turned off her phone.

What happened to the words *I love you* when you kept them trapped inside for so long? Lacking air and light, did they wilt and fall apart like old flowers? Or was it like nurturing little seeds, keeping them safe and warm so that one day they might flourish in the sunlight? Or would they fossilize inside you forever, hardening like clay?

And what would happen if she ever dared to set those words free?

CHAPTER 7

Stupid Rubik's Cube.

Julia dropped the torture device back into her handbag with a scowl. She had a *million* other better things to do.

She picked up the *Before Fifty* list from her desk and scanned the items. *Learn to say the alphabet backward.*

How hard could that be?

ZYXWV...TU...no, UT.

ZYXWVUT. Why she'd thought at nineteen years old that knowing this would be in any way useful, she had no idea. But at least it was easier than the Rubik's Cube.

ZYXWVUTSRQ...If she memorized three letters at a time, she'd have it down in less than ten minutes. Not that this knowledge would be useful *now* either, but—

Julia shook her head and pushed the list away. She was an adult, for heaven's sake, not a teenager.

She opened her Montblanc planner to her bullet-point list of action items. The list that *mattered.*

Taking her mind off the alphabet, she set to work and crossed several items off her agenda—*staff holiday bonuses, schedules to volunteers, candy canes for Santa, Wee Tinsel to march in Fa La La Parade.*

With those completed, she went to her studio to retackle her Appear clothing line. She reworked some of her concepts, adding new embellishments and changing the fabrics and patterns. Though she wasn't struck with great inspiration, she ended her day with a sense of accomplishment. Not only had she gotten a fresh start and made a dent in her list, she'd also gotten her assistants to do their work without crying into their skinny lattes.

As she packed up to leave, her phone rang with a call from Minnie of the Holiday Festival committee. Julia sighed the sigh of a martyr and picked it up.

"Hello, Minnie."

"Good news, Julie."

"Julia."

"Julie, we just received word that we've been given a craploa... er, I mean a great deal of money for the Deck the Halls finale. Isn't that wonderful?"

Julia opened her mouth and closed it again, struggling to find her voice.

"Where did this donation come from?" she managed to ask.

"Oh, an anonymous donor," Minnie said cheerfully. "Now you should have plenty for everything, including the fireworks."

Julia's shoulders tensed. "I'll...I'll have to look into this."

"You'll figure it out, dear," Minnie said. "Make a new list in that fancy book of yours."

Julia hung up the phone and glowered at her "fancy book." Warren Stone. Sugar Rush superhero saves Deck the Halls.

Damn him.

She walked to her BMW and drove to Warren's house, glad to see four of her nephews' cars in the driveway. Cowardly though it might be, she needed the big, burly presence of her nephews as a buffer against their father. Their smoldering, muscular father who sent her into flames with one...

Stop it!

ZYXWVUTSRQ...ZYXWVUTSRQPO...

"Hello, boys." She crossed the great room, where Adam and Carson were watching TV, and entered the kitchen. Hailey sat at the kitchen counter working on her tablet, and a rush of pleasure filled Julia at the sight of her niece.

"Hi, Peanut."

"Aunt Julia!" Hailey leapt off the stool and hurried over to throw her arms around Julia. "Carson said he didn't know if you'd be here because of the Holiday Festival stuff."

"Nothing could keep me from seeing you." Julia embraced her niece tightly, then stepped back to drink in the sight of her. With her shiny, shoulder-length brown hair and fine, elegant features, Hailey had an understated beauty enhanced by her quiet, reserved personality. At twenty-four, she'd recently graduated from Stanford with a degree in botany and was working at the Golden Gate Park Conservancy while considering graduate school options. In Julia's eyes, Hailey was one of the few people in the world who could do no wrong.

"How's your job going?" she asked.

"Great. I get to hang out with plants and flowers, and they're really good listeners."

Julia smiled, even as sorrow twined through her. Hailey had been eleven when she'd been injured in the same car accident that had killed Rebecca. The subsequent weeks in the hospital combined with the trauma and grief of her mother's death had unsurprisingly changed Hailey from a bright, outgoing girl to one who was far more introverted and cautious. Though with a great deal of work and therapy, she'd made a full physical recovery, the psychological effects lingered and she still preferred solitude over socialization.

Not that that was a bad thing. Warren and the boys had always been overprotective of her, but after the accident they'd circled around her like guardian lions to keep anything harmful at bay. She'd branched out on her own when she went to Stanford, but the shelter of home and family had always been close by, and her "brotherhood of lions" guard remained firmly in place.

And while Julia wanted her niece's emotional and physical safety more than anything, she also wanted Hailey to enjoy her youth and freedom. To not *miss out* on anything.

"Any new friends?" she asked casually.

She didn't want to be the aunt pestering her niece about her social life, but frankly, with her six hulking, hovering brothers stalking her Facebook page and scrutinizing the few boyfriends she'd had, Hailey didn't have a lot—if any—secrets. But Julia still preferred getting the intel directly from Hailey rather than secondhand.

"Don't ask," Hailey muttered, hitching herself back onto the stool.

Julia frowned. "What happened?"

"Dickhead boyfriend ditched her for a friend." Tyler ambled into the kitchen, grabbed Hailey with one arm, and gave her a noogie. "Good riddance to bad garbage, is what I say."

Outrage flickered in Julia on her niece's behalf. "I should say so."

"Oof. Quit it." Hailey scowled at Tyler and shoved him away. "That is not what happened. Pete and I had been friends throughout our senior year. Then he asked me out, and things got weird so we broke up. Now we're neither friends nor dating."

"You want us to go have a *talk* with the guy?" Carson came into the kitchen and opened the fridge. "Say the word."

"No, but thanks for the offer." Hailey rolled her eyes, but her voice was filled with affection.

Being at home for the holidays, especially with her large, protective brothers, would heal her niece's hurt. Hailey had a strong bond with all the boys, especially Adam. When she'd been in the hospital, he'd brought her a seed starter kit complete with a growing tray and heat lamp. Everyone else had been a bit baffled by the gift—especially considering neither Adam nor Hailey had ever expressed the slightest interest in gardening. But he'd told her, "When these are ready to plant, you'll be out of the hospital."

He'd been right. Caring for the seeds and watching them grow had given Hailey a renewed hope and a goal. When she'd finally returned home, she and Adam had planted the flourishing seedlings in the garden. And Hailey's love for plants had taken root.

"I meant to tell you I have tickets to the San Jose Ballet perfor-mance of the *Nutcracker* tomorrow night," Julia told her niece. "Would you like to go?"

"Didn't you know?" Hailey frowned. "I have to head back to the city tomorrow. I'm in charge of the plants over the holidays, and I can't leave them alone for too long. I'm sorry."

Julia smothered a stab of disappointment. "That's all right. I have other plans. For a break from all things Christmas, I booked us a spa day on Wednesday. Massages, herbal wraps, the works."

"I won't be back until the Sugar Rush holiday party." Hailey's forehead creased. "I'm so sorry, Aunt Julia. I thought Dad told you."

Dad hadn't told her much of anything lately. Except to bend over his desk and spread her legs for him.

"I'll go with you," Tyler offered. "I like herbal wraps, especially with turkey and extra mayo."

Julia shook her head at her nephew. "How does Kate put up with you?"

"She loves me just the way I am." Tyler arched an eyebrow. "Speaking of which, what's going on with Dad?"

Julia sighed. Gossip in the Stone family spread like a bad rash. Warren's alleged "dating" would be no different.

"We don't know for sure," Carson said. "He's being kind of James Bond secretive about it, but we think he's getting—"

"Carson," Julia said repressively.

"...into the dating scene," he finished, giving her an engaging grin. "Maybe even serious with one woman."

"Not Gia, I hope." Hailey's mouth twisted, and she turned back to her tablet. "She seemed like she'd be more into Dad's status and money than him as a person. And there are plenty of other women better for him. What about you, Aunt Julia?"

For an instant, Julia misinterpreted her niece's remark as a query about whether or not she, Julia, was "better for" Warren than Gia. She swallowed the automatic *"Of course I am"* that rose to her throat.

"What about me?" she asked.

"Are you seeing anyone?"

Julia didn't respond. She slanted her gaze past Tyler to where Warren was crossing the great room to the kitchen. Her heart forgot that she was angry with him because it did a little hopscotch. Which was ridiculous because she saw Warren practically every day.

But did she notice *every day* how mouth-watering he looked in worn jeans that hugged his long legs, and that navy T-shirt stretching over his broad chest and impressive biceps...wow, how had she never noticed those biceps before? Good heavens, the sleeves of his shirt were too tight around his muscles. He must be hitting the gym extra hard these days.

She unwillingly recalled the boys' speculation about their father also apparently hitting the dating scene extra hard.

Warren was watching her, his brown eyes shuttered. Unease rose to her chest. When had he ever been shuttered from her?

The looks they exchanged had always contained a hundred unspoken words that only they understood. In meetings for the Rebecca Stone Foundation, at family gatherings, charity dinners, Sugar Rush events—all she had to do was look at Warren to have a conversation with him.

Yes, we should definitely do that. Nope, that idea sucks. Warren, is it

time to go yet because these heels are killing me, and you look bored to
death...Jules, you need to wear that dress more often because I want to
rip it right off you and—

Well, maybe he hadn't said *that* with one look at her.

Or had he?

"I can't stay for dinner." Luke entered the kitchen, his voice breaking into her thoughts. "I gotta go help Polly at Wild Child. But we're going out to get the tree tomorrow, right? Carson said it was a one p.m. call, meeting here to carpool up to the mountains. Polly and I will bring lunch for everyone, if Dad can provide the drinks."

"Turns out I have plans tomorrow," Warren said. "I'll have to meet you at the site."

Tyler and Luke exchanged glances—one of the *knowing guy looks* that Julia had learned to decipher over the years. Jealousy stabbed through her.

She crossed her arms and leveled a dark scowl at Warren.

"Did I tell you the Deck the Halls show had a sudden infusion of cash from an anonymous donor?" she asked crisply.

"Great," Tyler said. "Maybe now I can get an elf costume."

"Bit of a coincidence," Julia continued. "All things considered."

"Sounds like the show needed some help."

"As long as it wasn't payment for services rendered."

His expression hardened. "Jules, we need to go over a few things in my office."

Their gazes clashed in challenge. Julia swept past Luke and strode down the corridor to Warren's office.

They entered the office, and he closed the door behind them. As soon as the lock clicked, Julia whirled to face him.

"Really? You really threw a bunch of money at Deck the Halls right after we..." She swallowed hard.

"...fucked?" Warren finished.

Jesus. That one word in his deep, gravelly voice jolted her like the thrust of his cock.

"I would hardly call it a coincidence," she said.

"So you think it's *payment for services rendered?*" Warren's expression darkened. "You know me better than that."

Yes, she did. And knowing him was the exact same as loving him.

"How about I did it because you're making yourself sick doing too many things and refusing my help?" Warren said.

"I told you I can handle it." Julia paced to the windows. "How could you do that without consulting me?"

"Because you wouldn't have taken the money if I had. You've never taken my help, not even when you *need* it."

"That's not the point!" She fisted her hands at her sides. "The point is that you shoved your way into a situation that is not yours to control. It's mine. I took on the responsibility of the show, and I don't need you swooping in to rescue me just because things got a little rough."

"I didn't do it to rescue you," Warren retorted. "I gave the money to the city council for the festival. I did it for the town."

"Oh, please. You told Minnie it was for Deck the Halls, didn't you? Because in addition to firing me from the Sugar Rush party, you needed to find another way to take responsibilities away from me."

"I did not do this to take anything away from you." Warren's mouth tightened with frustration. "I did it to give something back to you."

"What?" Julia spread her arms out. "What did you need to give back to me, Warren?"

"Christmas, dammit. *Time.* Your enjoyment of the holidays spent with your family."

"Oh, God bless us every one, Tiny Tim."

He narrowed his eyes at her. "I'm not tiny."

An unwelcome laugh bubbled into her throat.

"Well, I know *that*," she muttered.

"Jules." Warren approached her, his gaze on her face. "Use the money for the show. Give the festival committee the fireworks finale and whatever else they want. Everyone will love it, and you won't need to drown yourself in mulled wine to get through it. Please."

The *please* broke through her anger. And the truth that having a much bigger budget would ease her stress considerably.

"Well, I can't tell the committee to give the money back," she grumbled. "Now that they know about it, they're ready to turn the show into a TV special. I hope you're happy."

"If it eases your workload, I am." He strode to his desk and riffled through the papers spread over the surface.

Julia took a breath, trying to reconcile her emotions. She'd always relied on Warren for many things—support, advice, friendship—but she never wanted to be financially beholden to him or his company. It felt wrong, like she'd be taking money that rightfully belonged to his children.

And, much as she didn't want to admit it, relying on Warren financially would negate all that she'd done on her own up to this point. Unlike her sister, Julia had been independent almost her entire adulthood. She'd worked her way up, started her own business, built her own company. Sugar Rush, Warren, the boys, and Hailey had all given her a home and a family, but her career remained hers alone.

"If you do something like this again, please tell me first."

"Only if you promise to take what I offer."

"It'll have to depend on the offer."

He glanced at her. Electricity sizzled between them. She averted her gaze, heat rising to her face.

"So where are you going tomorrow?" she asked.

"Out with a friend."

"That's more important than getting the Christmas tree?"

"Right now, yes." He appeared unfazed by her sharp tone.

She willed herself not to feel jealous at the idea of him with a *friend.* A week ago, she wouldn't have given his plans a second thought. But why was he being vague?

"Who's the friend?" she asked casually.

"Amelie. We met in Switzerland. She's visiting for the next week."

Julia had had enough experiences in life to know not to make assumptions or take anything at face value. "Amelie" could be the VP at another company Warren was negotiating with. She could be his new financial advisor or a Sugar Rush supplier or—well, she could also be a woman he was seeing. He'd spent a lot of time in Switzerland over the past year, and it wouldn't be any great surprise if he'd hooked up with a Swiss Miss who'd decided to visit him in California.

He was checking his phone, his head bent, his thick hair falling across his forehead. Her fingers itched with the urge to smooth it back, to tunnel her hand through the dark strands. The muscles of his arms shifted in the light, and his shirt stretched so beautifully over his broad chest that she wanted to slide her hands underneath it and touch his warm, strong muscles.

A tremble rippled across her skin. He lifted his head, their gazes meeting with a hot spark.

"The boys think you're seeing someone." Julia curled her fingers into her palms, her remark coming out almost involuntarily. "That that's why you're retiring, because you're getting serious about a woman, and she might even be joining you on your ski trip. Is it *Amelie?*"

"Julia." Warren set his phone on the desk and regarded her with faint amusement. "Amelie is just a friend. But if the boys want to think I'm hooking up with someone else, great. At least they're not plotting to put me in an old folks' home."

"Knowing you, you'd get some geriatric action there anyway," Julia remarked dryly.

"I intend to polish my cane regularly no matter where I am." He winked at her.

She couldn't help smiling, the tension in her bones easing a bit. Their relationship was strong enough to withstand even a big mistake. Even Warren's need for control.

Though she had liked it when he'd controlled *her*. A lot.

A shiver rippled down her spine.

He crossed to the door and stopped in front of her. Julia's heartbeat accelerated, her nerves lighting up at his mere proximity and the thought that he was about to touch her. He leaned closer, his breath brushing her ear. Her blood heated.

"And the only woman I want to *get serious* about right now," he murmured, "is you."

He straightened and walked out.

Julia watched him go, her knees weakening.

What if she set all her feelings for him free? What would happen to them?

She pushed the question aside, not daring to go to a place she'd tried not to imagine over the years. Rebecca had been the only wife Warren would ever have, the paragon against which he measured all other women. Julia never wanted to step into that role—first because it had belonged to her sister, and second because she didn't want to come up short in comparison.

And most of all because she was scared to death at the thought of losing what she and Warren had spent thirteen years building.

CHAPTER 8

"ZYXWVUTSRQPONMLKJIHGFEDCBA."

Hah. *Take that, Rubik's Cube.*

Julia strode to her office desk, grabbed a blue pen, and put a checkmark beside #27: *Learn to say the alphabet backwards.*

Of course, this was an utterly useless skill—if one could even call it a skill—but she couldn't deny there was a strong satisfaction in checking even one more item off her *Before Fifty* list. And finding another way to keep constant thoughts of Warren at bay.

She started to fold the list when her gaze caught #43: *Memorize all the verses of "It Came Upon A Midnight Clear."*

Had that once been her favorite Christmas carol?

Had she once *had* a favorite Christmas carol?

She turned to her computer and typed the song title into a web browser. After playing a few vocal recordings, she found an acoustic version with a video play of the lyrics.

Well, this was silly. She hadn't sung in years. She *used* to enjoy singing, way back when she was with Sam. He'd play the guitar and she would sing old classics—"The Sound of Silence," "Blowin' in the Wind," "Hallelujah."

The strains of his guitar drifting on the smoky air from the campfire, the press of his thigh against hers. Lying together in the back of his van, fingers entwined, feet dangling through the open door as they looked at the stars.

The pain of his abandonment had exceeded the bliss of those moments, but she was still grateful for having known, deep in her heart, what it felt like to be happy and in love. Even if it had been thirty years ago.

She studied the Christmas lyrics again and restarted the music. *"It came..."* She cleared her throat. Started, stopped, started again. *"It came upon a midnight clear, that glorious song of old."*

Her voice was rusty, her pitch off, but something lit inside her, the same glow she'd felt when she'd listened to the Jingle Belles and their perfect harmony. Like her heart was lifting.

"From angels bending near the earth to touch their harps of gold..."

And what poetic lyrics—*peaceful wings unfurled, cloven skies, ever-circling years...*

"To hear the angels sing."

"Ahem."

Julia jerked her head up, her voice stopping in her throat. Marco stood at the door, staring at her. Heat flooded her face. She fumbled to close the website.

"I was just—"

"Damn, lady," he interrupted with a cluck of his tongue. "I had no idea you were hiding an inner Mariah Carey."

"Don't be ridiculous," Julia snapped. "What do you want?"

"Jingle Belles all the way," Marco said. "They're in the dressing room."

"I'll head over there now. Send in Enzo, Isabella, and Anisa."

Her assistants were working on a Saturday to style several personal clients for a swanky Christmas ball that night, but those high-society clients wouldn't arrive until later in the afternoon. Which meant Julia intended to put her assistants to work on the Jingle Belles.

She rose from her desk and slipped into her suede YSL blazer before walking to the large, airy room where she styled her clients. Her assistants hurried out of their offices to join her when they heard the sharp click of her heels. The four Jingle Belles clustered in the middle of the room, looking as if they weren't sure whether this had been a good idea or not.

"Hello, ladies," Julia said. "May we offer you a cappuccino or vitamin water?"

"No, we're fine," Sharon said. "We don't want to take up too much of your time."

"Nonsense. We've discussed your...issue already, and my assistants have chosen several options. Let's get your measurements and see what we can do."

She skimmed her gaze over Sharon's untucked, overlong shirt, Beverly's floral print blouse and belted jeans, Connie's cable-knit reindeer sweater.

Time to wave her Christmas fairy wand. Vigorously.

She nodded at her assistants. Enzo hauled out clothing racks filled with designer suits, skirts, blouses, and dresses. Anisa and Isabella took the women's measurements. Julia examined the cuts, styles, and fabrics of the clothes while studying the women's figures and determining how the lines of the clothes might suit them.

A flurry of fitting and assessments followed—cap-sleeve dresses, sateen mini-skirts, off-the-shoulder jumpsuits. As Julia worked with the four women, she unwittingly learned more about them. Beverly was a retired teacher with two college-aged children (Nick, an education major, and Donna, a physics major); Sharon was in her twenty-first year as Indigo Bay Library's head librarian and had a beloved husband who snored terribly; and Connie volunteered for a nonprofit nature conservancy. Gail had a two-year-old grandson who was the next Einstein, and her daughter was due any minute now with another baby. The Jingle

Belles had been singing together for six years and got together regularly for lunch and movie-going.

Though Julia had never been one of the girls, she found herself rather enjoying their chatter about their lives. Not that she could relate to grandchildren or husbands, but she appreciated their references to the '80s and their somewhat bemused approach to technology.

However, they were difficult to fit. Aside from Gail, who was strikingly toned, nothing flattered the other women's rounded figures. Sleeveless dresses displayed too much of their upper arms, and none of them were comfortable in anything too tight or low-cut.

"This is why I *hate* shopping for clothes." Sharon groaned, trying to force the button closed on a suit jacket. "Nothing ever fits."

"Or things are made for twenty-year-olds," Gail agreed. "I'm sorry, but a fifty-five-year-old woman in a graphic tee and mesh leggings is not a good look."

"Preach it, sister," Isabella remarked.

"Everything is either too young, too tight, or too frumpy," Connie said.

"I still say we should wear pajamas," Beverly mused, picking at the metallic fabric of a skirt meant for a woman thirty years younger.

Julia tried not to groan. "Pajamas should only be worn at night in bed, if that. I'd suggest a nice chemise or babydoll instead."

The women looked at her as if she were speaking a foreign language.

Julia snapped her fingers at Enzo. "Bring out the gowns."

Anisa's eyes widened. Enzo hurried to wheel out a rack of high-end gowns that likely cost more than Sharon's family sedan. Julia had the women try on several of the gowns—split-sleeved, ruched, asymmetric, V-necked. Even if the fit could be tailored, the color didn't work, or it didn't coordinate well with the style of one of the other women's gowns.

By the time they were finished, the women looked harried and tired, and Julia's frustration had started an ache in the middle of her forehead.

However, she never—*never*—failed a styling challenge.

"Anisa, Isabella," she ordered sharply. "Take all their measurements again and input them into a spreadsheet. Enzo, bring me some fabric samples. Jersey and cotton blends with good structure. Nothing shiny."

"What are we doing now?" Beverly took off her glasses and rubbed her eyes.

"Jingle Belles." Julia took out her pencil and sketchpad. "I'm going to design your dresses myself."

❧

"It's crooked."

"It is not."

"Tilt it to the left."

"It'll be lopsided."

"Turn it ninety degrees clockwise. There's a big hole right in the front."

"It's *crooked*."

"Would you stop being such a douche?"

Julia set a box of tree ornaments on the coffee table as the boys continued their bickering and their girlfriends rummaged through the ornaments. The usual good-natured arguing had gone on all afternoon as they tramped through the Christmas tree farm to pick out a tree. Normally she'd have enjoyed being out on the mountainside with her family, the air fresh and crisp, but her hollow feeling from the previous night had remained.

Because normally Warren was there. Instead he'd texted them

all that he was running late and would see them back at the house.

When had he ever missed the tradition of cutting down and decorating the Christmas tree, even this late in the month? *Everyone* was here except for him. Apparently *Amelie* was more important.

Irritation clawed at her. If she and Warren hadn't gone suddenly stratospheric with their physical relationship, would she be so irked? Was it just the sex making her jealous and possessive? If so, what did that mean?

The questions and lack of answers made her head ache.

All afternoon she'd tried *not* to let her thoughts get away from her. She tried *not* to look at the spot on the floor where they'd first fucked. She tried *not* to feel his hands on her skin, his shaft pulsing inside her. She tried *not* to want it yet again.

And now that it was almost five, her bones felt as if they were about to crack with all the self-control and resistance she'd been mustering up.

"Dinner call."

Warren's deep voice boomed through the entryway. Schooling her expression into one of composure, Julia straightened from picking through a box of decorations. The boys all perked up at the smell of hot sub sandwiches and hurried to grab the paper bags from their father. Warren stomped into the great room, shedding his jacket. His thick hair was disheveled, his face ruddy from exertion, his eyes bright.

"Sorry I missed the afternoon," he said. "But the tree looks great."

A flurry of activity ensued as everyone dove into the food he'd brought.

"Julia, where's the pickle?" Tyler rummaged through a box of ornaments.

"At home. I'm not putting it on until Christmas Eve because I know you'll try to find it before you're supposed to."

"What's the pickle?" Kate asked.

"Old German tradition," Spencer explained. "Julia hides the pickle ornament and whoever finds it first on Christmas morning gets an extra present."

"Oh, Julia, I forgot to tell you that I had to change your slot for the soup kitchen." Kate stood on a stepstool to hang an ornament near the top of the tree. "Did you get the donations for the giving tree?"

"Yes. I'll bring them by tomorrow afternoon."

"What about the family dinner over at the foundation?" Carson asked.

"The invitations have been sent out." Julia picked up crumpled wrappers to throw into the trash.

"Can you give us a list of where we need to be and when?" Tyler asked. "I get confused with all that's going on."

"You're making cinnamon rolls for Christmas morning, aren't you?" Spencer asked.

Crap. Cinnamon rolls. She'd forgotten to add that to her list.

The Stones were very generous with their community giving throughout the holiday season, but Christmas Day was always spent with their family at Warren's house. The brothers had developed a number of inviolable Christmas Day traditions over the years, including cinnamon rolls, board games, backyard and TV football, family photos with silly Christmas props, charades, the *Charlie Brown Christmas* special, a baked ham dinner with all the trimmings, and a massive amount of boisterous ribbing.

"I'll make the cinnamon rolls," she assured Spencer.

"You're the best."

"We also have to get the props together for the photos," Adam said.

"Julia is upping the game for the pickle," Tyler said. "I told her no gift certificate for a wax job like last year. Maybe we should get another tree for the family room, make it more of a challenge to find the pickle."

"Can I invite a couple of friends over for the game on Christmas Day?" Adam asked.

"Boys." Warren's voice cut through the chatter like a steel blade.

Silence fell. Everyone looked at him.

"Your aunt Julia is not in charge of giving you whatever you want for the holidays," Warren said pointedly, his expression stern. "Nor is she in charge of planning your personal parties. If you want certain things done, then do them yourself."

Julia turned, her insides tightening. "I'm happy to do it, Warren."

"You don't have to."

"I don't mind." Her tone was clipped.

"Tyler will be in charge of the infamous pickle this year." Warren eyed his youngest son. "Since he's so eager to carry on the tradition."

"Does that mean I need to come up with a present?" he asked.

"Warren." Julia crossed the room, her leather boots clicking sharply. "I am *delighted* to plan family events and traditions. There is no need for you to *delegate*."

His mouth compressed. "The boys are adults, last time I checked. They are more than capable of doing their fair share."

"Or is it that you can't stand not giving orders?" Julia snapped, unable to stop herself. "Now you're going to fire me from planning the family holidays?"

"I'm not *firing* you from anything."

"You fired me from the Sugar Rush party." She planted her hands on her hips. "You remember that, don't you? The most important party of the last fifteen years when you're going to announce your retirement to the whole company? Maybe even a successor? And yet you decided I couldn't handle planning it."

"I never thought you couldn't handle it." Warren's eyes flashed. "I just didn't want you to *have to*."

"Like you don't want me to handle the fucking *pickle*?"

"If Tyler wants the fucking pickle, he can deal with it himself."

Julia opened her mouth to snap back at him, then stopped when she realized that the silence had thickened. Everyone was staring at her and Warren as if watching a spectacle—which she supposed they were. She and Warren occasionally disagreed over little things, but they never fought in front of others. Certainly not the boys, their significant others, and Hailey.

She closed her mouth and stepped back, her heart racing. Warren stalked toward his office.

As soon as the door slammed, Julia marched out to the terrace, welcoming the cool evening air on her hot skin.

She wished she could erase the past week, rewind to long before Warren had kissed her and she'd responded as if she were a dried-up plant drinking a stream of cool, fresh water. If she'd agreed to meet him at Lotus for dinner the other night, none of this mess would have happened. She'd have confessed all the disparaging things Vincent Peck had said about her designs, and Warren—after threatening to kick the Evermore president's ass—would have helped her figure out what to do next. He'd have given her advice about Deck the Halls, made suggestions that would ease her schedule.

A sudden loneliness hit her. No matter what happened, she and Warren could never go back to the way things had been *before*. No one could.

CHAPTER 9

"You fired her from planning the Sugar Rush party?"

Hailey stood with her hands on her hips, radiating indignity on her aunt's behalf. Warren hadn't expected to battle both Julia and his daughter on this issue, but last night's argument had placed Hailey firmly on Julia's side.

"I didn't *fire* her." Warren poured coffee into a travel mug and handed it to his daughter. "I *excused* her."

"Oh, please. Dad, she's been planning that party for ten years. She loves doing it. Why would you take it away from her?"

"Because she's doing way too much. It's not good for her." He didn't tell Hailey he was concerned about Julia's migraines—no one else knew she even had them. "And she has enough on her plate with Deck the Halls."

"Well, she didn't seem any too happy about being *excused*." Hailey lifted her backpack onto one shoulder. "I'm going to stop by her office on the way out and say goodbye."

Warren nodded, deflecting the usual stab of fear at the thought of his daughter driving back to San Francisco. He'd had to work hard over the years to let Hailey do…well, anything, and still he was plagued by worry that something could happen to her. He'd managed to work through his grief over Rebecca's death—though it would shadow the rest of his life—but if anything happened to his daughter...

"Hey, I hear you might be dating someone new," Hailey remarked as they walked to the front door. "Is that gossip or the truth?"

"A little of both." Hardly a lie. He wasn't *dating* Julia, but she wasn't *someone new* either.

"Well, I hope it works out." She moved closer to hug him. "It's nice to see you doing something else besides working on your models."

"When are you coming back?" He wrapped his arms around her. As usual, he didn't want to let go.

"The night before the party." She reached up to kiss his cheek. "I'll call you as soon as I arrive, I promise."

"Sure you don't want me to drive you?"

"Yes, Dad." She rolled her eyes and opened the door. "I love you."

"I love you, Hailey's Comet." Warren watched her leave, sending up a silent prayer to the universe to keep her safe.

He headed back upstairs to get ready for work, and was pulling into the Sugar Rush parking lot within the hour. Luke was in his office with a list of potential presidents for Warren to review.

"Looks good." Warren dropped the list back onto his son's desk.

Luke studied the paper and shook his head. "I can't see someone outside the family stepping in. But I can't see Carson or Evan doing it either. We work great where they are, but as president...I don't know."

Warren understood. The president-CEO relationship could be challenging to develop, though he and Luke had created a seamless partnership. Luke guided the company with a big-picture vision and strategy, while Warren focused on successful execution of day-to-day operations. They didn't always agree, but they both knew how to negotiate and compromise.

The added challenge for them had been getting past the father-son dynamic, but Luke had stepped up to such a degree after Rebecca's death that he'd proven himself early on. And Warren had been the one to guide the company through the rough waters of Luke's false paternity suit, which had given them new levels of trust in each other.

A knock came at the door. At Luke's invitation, Kate Darling, the vice-president of the Corporate Social Responsibility division, came into the office. Smart as a whip and organized beyond belief, Kate had been Luke's executive assistant up until recently, when Warren, Evan, and Luke had promoted her to VP.

Warren had seen a lot of young people both rise and fall at Sugar Rush, and he'd known from the start that Kate would be an incredible asset to the company if they tapped into her full potential. Rarely had he seen someone so gifted.

"Oh, hello, Mr. Stone." She smiled at him en route to Luke's desk with a heavy binder. "I didn't know you were here, but I'm glad you are. I can kill two birds with one stone...oh dear, that was an unintentional but terrible joke. Here's a draft of the report I'm working on linking Sugar Rush's social impact to business benefits and metrics. I'm focusing on three avenues of data collection and usage, internal and external communications, and alliances. I'm going to submit it for presentation at the business summit in Europe next year."

"Excellent, thank you." Luke leafed through the book, shooting Warren a *"she's a rock star"* glance. "I'll talk to Evan and HR about connecting you with the other businesses slated to be there. Do you have a minute?"

"I'm free until two."

"Let's stop by his office." Luke rounded his desk and started to the door, pausing to look at Warren. "Dad?"

Warren shook his head. He'd been purposely backing out of

meetings and decision-making. "Go ahead. I have other things to finish up."

Luke's mouth twisted, but he nodded and stepped aside for Kate to precede him. She glanced from him to Warren, appearing somewhat baffled before heading out the door.

Warren returned to his office, walking past the framed historical photos and advertisements of Sugar Rush's history. One week until December twenty-third and the Sugar Rush company party where he'd announce his retirement. No turning back now.

He'd been so focused on the Matterhorn climb and the mechanics of retiring that he hadn't thought *past* those two things. He had vague plans to do other things he'd never done before—scuba in the Great Barrier Reef, take a cross-country road trip, fix the garage door that had been rattling for months. Try the dating scene again.

He hadn't seen himself with one woman, though. Not until now. And now he had to convince Julia that all of their years had been leading up to this—a life meant to be lived together.

He had no intention of returning to Sugar Rush—and that thought opened a hollowness inside his chest. He wanted to retire. Had been wanting to for well over a year. But he hadn't yet gotten past the worry underscoring his decision, the one Julia had sensed from the beginning—*would he regret it?*

After he'd walked away, after the climb was over, would he wish he could still come to work every day? To the company that was part of his blood, the people who were his family, the culture that he'd lived his entire life?

The questions filtered through his mind, unwanted and unspoken. If his answers were all *yes*, then tough shit for him. He'd made his decision. Told his sons. Nothing—not even regret —could make him change his mind now.

He finished up paperwork and checked his email on the computer. He opened a message from Hans, the head of Alpine Climbs.

Warren, still don't have your medical info for your file. Please send
ASAP.

He ignored a flicker of unease and checked his calendar. He had a doctor's visit tomorrow for a full physical. He hit the reply button and wrote:

Will have it to you by the end of the week.

He sent the email and checked his phone. Julia still hadn't responded to his texts or voicemail, which didn't surprise him. She was becoming an expert at giving him the cold shoulder.

Even though nothing about her was *cold*. Just the opposite. She was fire, spice, the sun. He'd never forgotten his first taste of her. And he'd spent over thirty years hating himself for *not forgetting*.

Old, raw guilt rose in him. He'd never betrayed his wife, his children, his sense of honor. At least, he didn't think he had. But was remembering a form of betrayal? He had no way to rid himself of the memory. And God knew he'd had to restrain himself from Julia for the past thirteen years, as if not touching her was a penance.

But now? Touching her, kissing her, making love to her—it was all so damned *right*, so perfect, that it was an absolution. What reason was there for guilt anymore? Life was too short. Time passed too quickly. If you didn't grab what was right in front of you, it was gone.

In mid-afternoon, he drove to her studios. Downtown Indigo Bay shimmered with holiday lights and decorations. Julia's touch was obvious in the massive Christmas tree that sat in front of the city hall, surrounded by a stage where Deck the Halls would take place. Santa's elaborate sleigh and North Pole Village adorned the square next to the stage.

His pride in her was endless. Even though he still believed

she'd taken on too much this year, she hadn't expected the bomb of the Evermore deal. But she was still coordinating Deck the Halls with the aplomb of an orchestra conductor—and, more than likely, a few dozen sharp commands.

He parked and went into her office, nodding a greeting at Enzo, who was staffing the front desk.

"Is she in?" he asked.

"Yes, but she sent out a notice that she's not to be disturbed. So enter at your own risk."

"I always do."

They exchanged commiserative looks before Warren headed down the carpeted corridor to Julia's office. His knock on the door went unanswered, so he opened it and stepped inside. She wasn't at her desk, but her coat and bag sat in their usual places, and her cell phone rested beside her computer—which partly explained why she hadn't responded to his texts. He crossed to the closed door of her private studio and knocked.

"Julia?"

No response. He tried the knob and pushed the door open.

She sat on a stool at the drafting table, the sleeves of her white shirt rolled up, her high heeled red shoes kicked off, a pencil tucked behind her ear. She looked up at the sound of the door opening, the crease of concentration on her forehead turning to a frown.

"What are you doing here?" she asked.

"Melting you."

"Not possible."

"I disagree."

She threw him a glower. "You can go *pickle* yourself, Warren Stone."

"Well, I am kind of a big dill."

"I'm not smiling."

"You are on the inside."

He stopped by her desk, eyeing the black-and-white and

colored drawings spread out in front of her. The pages were filled with intricate images of models wearing an array of clothing—gowns, skirts, dresses, pants, and shirts. Though Warren had known Julia was an excellent artist, he was struck by the sheer amount of detail she'd conveyed, from the texture of fabrics to the anatomy of the models.

"What are these?" he asked.

She waved a dismissive hand. "Enzo should have told you I don't want to be disturbed."

"He did. Unfortunately, I like disturbing you."

An appealing flush rose to her cheeks, indicating she liked being disturbed by him.

"I'm designing dresses for a few Deck the Halls performers," she said.

"Really?"

"If I didn't step in, they might have shown up onstage wearing Christmas flannel pajamas," Julia said. "I couldn't let that happen. My reputation is tied to the show, after all."

Warren picked up a sketch of a mini-dress. "Is this one of the designs?"

"No, that's for my Appear line." Julia sketched the hem on a drawing of a red gown, shooting a derisive glance at the mini-dress. "I have to rework those concepts too, maybe change the lines and patterns. Hopefully I can secure an investor next time."

"Nice." He studied the drawing. "I'd love to see you in this little dress."

She scoffed. "Those are for women in their twenties. Not fif— I mean, forties."

"What's wrong with being in your fifties? Longevity is power."

"Not in fashion." Julia shaded the edge of the red dress. "Fashion is all about the young."

"So there's a lot of competition for young women consumers, right?"

"Loads of it." She slanted him a glance. "Why?"

"From a business angle, why try and break into such a highly competitive market?"

"Because it's the biggest market." She set her drawing aside. "Some people would probably say it's the *only* market."

"Is it your market?"

"I style a lot of women in their twenties. Of course, many of my clients are also older women who have no idea where to start creating a personal style. Or where to find flattering clothes."

"Which is why they need you to help them."

"Exactly."

Warren had the same feeling he sometimes had at Sugar Rush when they were developing a new product—the sense that something was missing but he didn't know what. Spencer often had the same instinct, though he worked through it with science. Warren examined everything else—market research, competition, advertising, focus groups.

What was Julia missing?

"I need to get going." She put her colored markers away. "We're getting the Deck the Halls stage decorated this afternoon, and I need to supervise."

She got to her feet, bending to put on her shoes. Warren let his gaze wander to the slight gap in the neckline of her shirt, which exposed a pale V of skin and a hint of cleavage. That alone heated his blood. He'd always been *aware* of Julia as a woman, but now that he knew exactly how she felt and tasted, he'd never be able to get enough of her.

"Hey." He rested his hands on the table and leaned closer to her. "Sorry about last night. I'll take you to dinner to make it up to you."

She hesitated, then straightened and shook her head.

Irritation bit at him. "Julia, we are the *same*."

"No, we're not."

"Yes. And we can be even better than we are."

Her mouth tightened. She started to pass him. He closed his

hand around her arm, bringing her closer, her shoulder against his chest. The scent of her perfume, of *her*, washed over him like a hot summer breeze.

"She's not here anymore," he whispered.

Julia closed her eyes. Something inside her seemed to give way, like the turning of a lock.

It wasn't enough, he knew that. The past—Rebecca—was too much a part of them to be settled with easy platitudes. But it was the truth. And Julia had become a part of him too, as essential to his and his children's lives as sunlight to a garden.

He brushed his lips over her temple, settled his hand on the back of her warm neck.

"You can't hide from me," he said. "You can try to ignore me, freeze me out, pretend like you don't want me...but you won't succeed. I *know* you."

"You don't know everything about me."

"I know more than I did last week. I've always known you're sharp and controlling, and now I know that in private, you want to give up that control. And I want to take it."

Her slender throat worked with a swallow. "Don't you dare think you can—"

"You're not pushing me away." He tightened his grip. "And I won't seduce you here either. Because the next time we make love, we're doing it in your bed or mine. I'm going to strip you nice and slow so I can enjoy every part of your gorgeous body. I'm going to kiss you all over, watch the way your eyes darken and your skin gets that pink blush that makes you look like a sunrise. Then I'll slide my hands over every part of you—your breasts, your thighs, your hips, your ass. I'll feel you start to tremble and get all tense and hot. Then I'll spread your legs and touch your pussy. You'll already be wet and ready because you'll want it as much as I do. You'll arch your hips and say *Warren, please* in that throaty voice that sets my blood on fire."

"God." The word escaped her on a low breath. "I can't battle you. You're too strong for me."

"No." He slid his arm around her waist, preventing her escape. "We're perfectly matched. That's why we've been so good together all these years."

He brought his other hand around to her throat, turning her face toward him. Heat burned the air. Her eyes flickered with a thousand fires, her breath caressing his lips. A memory emerged of the first time they were this close, when his thoughts had been a tangled mess and he hadn't known what to expect.

Now he knew. Longevity was power.

He'd seen the best and worst of people. He'd been with other women, traveled the world, walked through dark tunnels of pain in search of light. He'd been strong when he hadn't wanted to be. He'd hated being helpless in the face of circumstances he couldn't change. He'd wondered if there was a god and he'd prayed to the stars. He'd loved fiercely, felt joy so big his heart couldn't contain it all, and clawed his way up through the black hole of grief.

Now he knew the touch of Julia's lips was a gift. *She* was a gift.

He touched his mouth to hers. The pulse in her throat beat against his palm. She slid her hand over his chest, up to his shoulder. Her body fit against his, her soft breasts pressing against him, her other arm twining around his waist.

He deepened the kiss, sweeping his tongue into her mouth. His nerves flared with heat, pressure tightening his groin. She tasted like everything good—honey, spices, the sweet flavor of cherries that belonged only to her.

"I wanted to forget that night," he murmured against her lips. "But I didn't."

"Neither did I." She eased away from him, her eyes dimming with guilt. "But I can never live up to my sister. And what if you and I take that step and it messes everything up?"

"It won't. We're stronger than that."

She plucked at a button on his shirt, not looking up but clearly listening.

"I want you because I know you so well," he continued. "You're an incredibly strong woman who's overcome a lot. A selfless, amazing friend who goes out of her way to help others, even if she'd never admit it, and who will always be there for my children."

"The kids don't even really need me anymore."

"Yes, they do. So do I."

He lowered his mouth to hers again. She sank against him, her hand spreading over his chest.

A buzzing noise sounded in his ears. He tightened his grip on Julia. For a heart-stopping instant, he braced himself instinctively for an attack of dizziness.

"...have to take that." Her voice filtered past the sudden fear, her hand sliding reluctantly away from him.

He took a breath and let her go. She walked to her desk and pressed the buzzing intercom.

"Minnie the Pitbull is trying to reach you," Marco announced through the speaker. "Line one."

Regret laced Julia's expression as she glanced at Warren. "I should take that."

He nodded and stepped back toward the door. "I'm not letting you get away, Jules."

Before she could respond, he left the office. He pushed away his lingering unease as he got into his car and drove home. Julia's earlier words echoed through him.

This was a mistake.

No, it wasn't. He wouldn't let her keep thinking that, much less *believe* it. Yeah, they'd both made mistakes years ago, but they'd made up for them countless times over. They'd spent their lives doing the right thing, helping and supporting their family, working hard for their careers. They'd done good deeds for the community, for their friends and employees. No fucking way was any part of their relationship, especially a blazing new facet of it, a *mistake*.

He needed to make Julia see that. They'd gone through too much together. He wouldn't tolerate her self-condemnation or regrets. He wouldn't let her distance herself from him.

He wouldn't let her run away again.

CHAPTER 11

Twenty-nine years ago

"Becca, you don't get to decide how I live my life!" Julia snapped.

His muscles tensing, Warren edged in front of his wife as if to protect her from her younger sister's wrath.

Julia was on fire—her blue eyes blazing, her long blonde hair a tangled mess around her shoulders, her pale skin flushed with anger. In a red cotton tank dress that left her tanned shoulders bare, her arms lined with silver and string bracelets, she vibrated with righteous anger, like the rattling of a shiny bell.

By contrast, Rebecca was as composed as a marble sculpture in her navy pleated skirt and silk blouse, her hair pulled into a smooth chignon at the base of her neck. She crossed her arms and leveled a cool look on her younger sister.

"I'm not *deciding* anything," she said. "I'm telling you it's about time you *grow up* and figure out what you want to do with the rest of your life."

"Just because *you* did?" Julia spread her arms out. "That's what you really want, isn't it? You're embarrassed by my divorce because you always wanted me to be like you, to get married to someone like him..." She waved an irritated hand toward Warren, "...and live in suburban torture."

Rebecca's lips tightened. "What I want *for* you is that you stop roaming around the country like a hobo and do something with your life. Go back to school. Get a good job. Meet a man who isn't going to lure you into a quickie wedding and then dump you just to get back into favor with his rich family."

"Rebecca." Warren rested his hand on his wife's back, hating the undiluted distress on Julia's face, the angry tears shining in her eyes that she still refused to let fall. "There's no need for that."

"Clearly there is a need if she can't figure this out herself," Rebecca replied tartly.

"I *can* figure it out," Julia cried. "Look, I came here because I need a place to stay just over the holidays until I make plans to go to Mexico. I *thought* you'd be happy to help me out, but apparently I was wrong."

"Of course we'll help you," Warren said.

"But you have to get your act together," Rebecca added. "And you can't go to Mexico, for heaven's sake. What on earth would you do there?"

"Whatever I want." Julia tossed her head with a sneer.

Rebecca sighed. She crossed to take Julia's shoulders, her expression softening as she gazed at her younger sister. "Julia, I hate that you married Sam because he ended up hurting you. I hate that you find it necessary to roam the country like a gypsy when you have so many other gifts to offer. You're so smart, you're a fantastic artist, you're incredibly creative, you sing like an angel...but you're wasting your talents. You're wasting your *life*."

"I am *not*." Julia yanked away from her and stalked to the other side of the kitchen, her fists clenching. "Just because I'm not living my life the way you are doesn't mean it's a waste. And you telling me that makes you no better than Sam's stupid parents!"

His wife's anger rose again in the set of her shoulders. Warren put his hand on her arm, again stepping between her and Julia.

"This argument is getting us nowhere," he said. "Julia, you can take the guest bedroom on the second floor. Get a good night's sleep and tomorrow we can—"

"Oh, shut up." Julia whirled to pin him with an angry glower. "You don't need to act like my father, just like *she* doesn't need to act like my mother. I'm twenty-one years old, which means I can do whatever I want."

Rebecca shook her head. "Not if you're staying in this house with our children."

Julia made a noise of frustration. The back door banged open, and seven-year-old Luke ran through the living room past the elaborately decorated Christmas tree. He entered the kitchen, trailed at a slower pace by Evan. Both boys were covered in dirt and grass-stains from whatever epic game they'd invented in the backyard.

"Can we have gingerbread cookies?" Luke shouted, grabbing a stepstool to clamber up to the kitchen cabinets.

"Hands washed first." Warren grabbed hold of his son and carted him over to the sink, moving to make room for Evan.

As always, his heart clenched painfully at the sight of the younger boy, who'd already seen more hospital rooms and faced more health problems than any six-year-old boy should have to. But Evan was a force, battling his heart condition like a prize-fighter and always trying his damnedest to keep up with his older and younger brothers.

His focus shifted to his sons as he helped them clean up and procure several cookies.

"Want one, Aunt Julia?" Evan extended a cookie to Julia, who was standing by the windows, hugging her arms tightly around herself.

She managed to smile at the boy, reaching out to ruffle his dark hair. "No, thanks, kiddo."

He shrugged off the oddness of anyone turning down a cookie before he and Luke ran back toward the door. Rebecca stepped into the doorway, her arms outstretched to block their exit.

"What's the password?" she asked.

"I love you, Mom," Luke yelled, throwing his arms around her in a hug. Evan did the same, and Rebecca latched both boys into a tight embrace before stepping aside to let them pass. They ran outside amidst shouts of *"Ahoy, matey!"*

A heavy silence fell over the kitchen. Julia looked at her sister —such a blatant plea in her eyes that something inside Warren wrenched painfully. He caught his wife's eye and indicated that he wanted to speak to her in the adjoining room.

"We'll be back in a minute," he told Julia, who huffed in annoyance.

When he and Rebecca were in the dining room, he closed the door and gave his wife a pointed stare. "Sweetie, *you* are all she has left."

Pain flashed in her eyes. "I know. But I've tolerated her running around for the past three years, and look what happened. What if she keeps doing this and ends up in an even worse situation? She can't go to random festivals and sleep in cars or camp out with people she doesn't know. What if someone hurts her far worse than Sam did? I'd lose my mind, Warren. I just want her to be safe."

She pressed her hands to her cheeks, her eyes glistening with tears. Warren gathered her into his arms, inhaling the sweet, familiar scent of her. His heart softened, an old sense of awe rising in him at the reminder that she was his. Even now, he didn't know what he'd done to deserve Rebecca in all her good-ness, her certainty of her place in the world, her natural ease with motherhood.

No wonder she was so frustrated with Julia, the wild child

who wanted to explore forests, sleep under the stars, stow away on ships just to see where they'd take her.

Rebecca slipped her arms around his waist and hugged him tightly. "We also have to think about the children, Warren. If Julia hooks up with a bad crowd…"

"No. We won't allow that." He pressed his lips against her forehead. "She's still upset about Sam. She'll see reason once she's calmed down."

"I will not!" Julia shouted from the kitchen.

Warren and Rebecca exchanged wry, exasperated looks.

Yes, she will, he mouthed to his wife. She smiled, standing on her tiptoes to kiss him before they returned to the kitchen.

Julia was pacing like a caged tiger, her bracelets rattling and her hair flying around her shoulders with every sharp turn. She stopped to glare at her sister.

"I'm not you," she snapped. "I will never be like you."

"I am aware of that fact," Rebecca replied, her spine stiffening in response to Julia's irritation. "However, if you intend to stay in this household, you will abide by our rules."

"Like washing my hands before eating a cookie?" Julia retorted. "I'm not seven, in case you forgot. I know how to be an adult."

"And yet your actions speak otherwise," Rebecca said.

"Oh, forget it. I don't need this shit." Julia whirled on her heel, grabbing a patchwork cloth bag from the table before stalking to the door. "So sorry to trouble you with my request."

Rebecca sighed, dismay etching her features. "Julia, don't go. Look, we want to help you but you need to meet us halfway."

"What I need is to get away from my fucking perfect older sister who will *never* like me exactly the way I am." Julia yanked open the door, her tears finally spilling over. "So to hell with you. I'll find somewhere else to go."

"Julia!" Alarmed, Rebecca hurried to the door, but Julia escaped first. She slammed the door behind her and ran toward her rusty yellow VW Beetle. In seconds, she was backing out of the driveway, tires squealing.

"Warren. Oh God, why did I say that?" Rebecca pressed her hands to her eyes. "No one gets me as riled up as she does."

Warren pulled on his jacket and grabbed his car keys from the counter. He stopped beside Rebecca, tugging her quickly against him. "I'll find her."

"Bring her back safely," she called as he headed out the door.

"I will."

He'd never before broken a promise to his wife. He got into his car and headed in the direction Julia had gone. Night had fallen. For the past seven years, they'd been living on the outskirts of San Francisco while Warren worked at the Stone Confectioners' factory. His father had given him an entry-level corporate position, slated to begin the following year, so in a few months he and Rebecca would move their family south to Indigo Bay.

Warren drove, his gaze sweeping the streets and parking lots for Julia's car. Christmas lights shone in shop windows, a weary attempt at cheer. Two hours passed without success. His concern intensified. He didn't have the same antipathy toward Julia's life-style that Rebecca did—in fact, he kind of envied it—but he sure as hell didn't want anything bad to happen to her.

He stopped once at a pay phone to call Rebecca and tell her he was still looking before he started his search again. For all he knew, Julia had left town already.

He passed restaurants, coffee-houses, bars. Nothing. He stopped at several gas stations to ask if they'd seen her car, but no one had. He circled the outskirts of town, stopping at a red light near the onramp to the freeway. He peered through the dark at the bars clustered along the streets.

Jackpot. The yellow Beetle sat under a lamp in the parking lot of a rundown bar. Warren pulled over, parked, and hurried inside.

Smoke hung in the dusky interior, along with the smells of beer and liquor. Blue-collar workers sat at the bar and the round tables, a sagging Christmas tree sat in the corner, and "Silent Night" came from a jukebox.

There she was.

Relief flooded him. Julia sat in a dimly lit corner of the room, the table in front of her scattered with both empty and half-full glasses. An instant later Warren noticed the man standing beside her, leaning too close to chat her up. Her expression was tight, and her eyes burned.

Warren stalked to the table, his fists clenching. "Leave her alone, man."

The guy straightened with a frown. "Who the fuck are you?"

"Her husband."

Julia's eyes widened. The guy stared at him, eyes narrowed in suspicion. Warren held up his left hand and pointed to his wedding ring.

"How come she don't got one?" the guy snapped, jerking his head toward Julia.

"She just walked out on me," Warren explained. "I'm trying to get her back."

The man's expression cleared. He gave a short laugh and shook his head. "Well, good luck with that, man. She's a feisty one."

He saluted Warren with his beer bottle and sauntered away. Warren pulled out a chair next to Julia and sat. A wary glint flickered in her gaze. Her skin was flushed, her eyes glassy and pupils dilated. The strap of her dress had fallen down her arm, exposing the top part of her breast. He reached out to put it back in place, trying not to notice the soft warmth of her skin.

"Thanks," she finally said, reaching for a half-full glass on the table. "I mean, he was getting aggressive. I didn't like it."

"You shouldn't be here alone."

Her mouth tightened. "You sound like my sister."

"Your sister made some good points."

"So did I."

He acknowledged that with a nod, gesturing to the clutter of glasses on the table. "How much have you had?"

"Not enough to forget." She laughed, then swallowed the liquor and wiped her mouth with the back of her hand. "You want one?"

Warren shook his head. Julia rolled her eyes.

"'Course not. Because you're perfect too, aren't you? Perfect fucking Warren Stone and his perfect fucking wife."

"I'm not perfect."

"Yeah, well, you *look* perfect," she muttered. "You and Rebecca. Like...what's his name? The movie actor and his wife. The super-hot guy who was in the movie about the cops."

"I don't know." He pushed a glass out of her reach. "Come on. I'll take you home."

"I don't have a home." Her forehead creased. She studied the glasses and chose one that still had liquor at the bottom. "I wish I did. I wanted to. I thought Sam and I would have a home one day, you know? Like you and Becca. I mean, I didn't want to *be* like you because you have really boring lives, but I wanted...I thought we could get a little beach house or something, a place to go after we travelled. A place where we could be happy."

Her blue eyes filled with fresh tears. Warren's insides twisted.

He hadn't liked Sam when they'd first met a couple of years ago, his defenses locking against the other man's disingenuous vibe and lack of direct responses. *What do you do? Oh, you know. A little of this, a little of that. Where are you going next? Wherever we want, man. Any plans for the future? Sure, after I consult my fortune teller.*

He'd told Julia as much, but she'd been starry-eyed with love for the guy. Next thing Warren knew, they'd gotten married in Vegas and were starting a cross-country road trip that would conclude with a visit to his family.

That hadn't ended well. Or maybe it had, because at least Julia had escaped the fucker before getting in deeper than she already was.

"…like Laura Ingalls Wilder," she was saying.

"Sorry, what?"

"I wanted to be like Laura from *Little House on the Prairie*. It was my favorite book. I thought it would be so amazing to travel in a wagon, run barefoot on the prairie, wade in the creek…I just wanted to be free. I thought I could be with Sam. So much for that dream."

She tilted her head back and drained the glass.

He took the glass from her. "Enough, Julia. You always have a home with me and Rebecca."

"Right, where she treats me like a five-year-old."

"She only wants you to stay safe."

"What about you?" She blinked at him, her eyes shiny and unfocused.

A warning signal flashed in Warren's brain. "I want you to stay safe, too. Which means you can't come to places like this and drink too much."

"I don't usually drink so much." She peered at the glasses. "I'm just so bummed out, you know? I loved Sam. Like really *loved* him. I know Becca doesn't believe that because we weren't like *you*, but love doesn't have to have just one definition."

"No, it doesn't."

"But he obviously didn't feel the same way about me." She sniffed and wiped her eyes with a crumpled napkin. "Because he picked money and a law firm over me. What kind of man does that?"

"Not a good one." Warren pushed his chair back and stood. He didn't want her staying here, but he couldn't bring her home drunk. Rebecca would be upset, and there'd be yet another rift between the sisters.

"Come with me." He pulled his wallet from his pocket and

dropped a few twenties on the table. "You need to sober up before we go home."

"I was pregnant."

He went cold. "What?"

"When we got married." Tears rolled down her cheeks. "I didn't know before, but I found out a month later."

Warren's hands fisted. "Did *he* know?"

Julia nodded, her breath hitching on another sob. "I thought for sure he'd tell his family to go to hell when he found out I was pregnant, but he didn't. He didn't tell his parents anything. Then after the divorce was final, I wanted to get my shit together before going to Becca because I wanted to prove to her I could handle being pregnant by myself. But I...I miscarried a week after the divorce was final. I never told anyone. Please don't tell Becca. I don't want her to think I did something to cause it."

She put her head in her hands and sobbed. Anger—no, a red-hot burn of rage toward Sam Craven—filled Warren's chest. He put his hand on her head, stroked her hair.

"Rebecca would never think that of you," he said gently.

"She might." Julia lifted her head and swiped her arm over her face. "Don't tell her."

"I won't," he promised. "Come on. Let's get out of here."

She regarded him through reddened eyes. "You're so nice, Warren. You know that? You're, like, a *nice man.* You'd never choose a law firm over my sister."

"No, I wouldn't." He slipped his hand under her arm and helped her to her feet. "I promise, it'll all work out."

She sniffled again, but grabbed her bag and walked with him to the parking lot, gripping his arm to keep her pace steady. He steered her away from her car and toward his sedan.

"We'll get your car later." He opened the passenger side door. "Get in."

"Where are you taking me?"

He had no idea. He closed the door, went around to the

driver's seat, and started the car. He'd drive around for a while, maybe find a 24-hour diner where he could get her some coffee.

"Can we get ice-cream?" Julia asked.

"Ice-cream and alcohol are not a good mix."

"I'm hungry."

Warren drove, scanning the streets before finding a take-out pizza joint. He ordered a large coffee and an order of breadsticks, bringing it back to the car.

"Oh, wow. That smells amazing." She took the bag from him and inhaled. "You are *so* nice."

He started the car again, hoping she'd be sober enough after eating that he could take her home.

"Can you pull over so I can eat?" Julia asked. "I don't want to get carsick."

Warren drove into the empty parking lot of a park and came to a stop. Julia opened the door and got out with the bag of food, taking a deep breath of cool night air. He picked up the coffee and followed her out.

"I feel better already." She hitched herself onto the hood of the car and opened the bag. She ate a breadstick and moaned with pleasure. "So good."

Warren checked his watch. Past one. On the way home, he'd find another pay phone to call Rebecca. He leaned against the fender beside Julia, studying her as she worked her way through the breadsticks. She wasn't beautiful like Rebecca, but she had a tousled, gypsy-girl appeal, a wildness that his lovely wife lacked. Julia's hair was thick and tangled, her skin browned from the sun, her legs long and bare.

"Want one?" She extended the bag to him.

He shook his head. "Drink the coffee, too."

"Yes, sir." She took the lid off the Styrofoam cup and sipped, eyeing him over the rim. "You like to order people around, huh?"

Unease prickled his chest. He'd known Julia for seven years, and though they didn't see each other regularly, he'd never gotten a flirty vibe from her. He'd sure as hell never felt anything inappropriate toward her.

"I *strongly suggest*," he corrected.

"Too bad you weren't around when Sam and I were at the chapel." She crumpled up the bag, her mouth twisting. "You could have strongly suggested I said *no* instead of *yes*."

"Would you have listened to me?"

"Maybe."

"I doubt that."

"Frankly, so do I." She tilted her head back, squinting up at the stars. She pulled her legs into a cross-legged position, wavering off-balance for a second. "Oh, shit."

She clutched Warren's arm. He let her steady herself on him. Julia gave a breathless laugh, curling her fingers into his shirtsleeve. Her breasts pressed against his forearm, the strap of her dress slipping down again. Warren cursed under his breath and grabbed her shoulders.

"Careful," he warned.

"I don't like being careful." She pushed closer, blinking up at him, her blue eyes luminous in the stark light of the parking lot. "I like being care*free*."

She tugged him so they were face-to-face—her seated on the car hood, him standing. Warning signals flashed in his brain again.

"Come on." He took his keys from his pocket. "We're going home."

"Becca will be mad at me for getting drunk."

"As well she should be. If you want to stay with us, you need to be responsible."

She wrinkled her nose. "What a horrible word. Responsible. You sound like Becca."

He tugged his arm away from her. "Let's go."

"Not yet."

He turned the instant she fisted the front of his shirt and

pulled him closer. Her mouth crashed down on his, open, hot, and wet. She moaned, gripping his arms, her fingernails digging into his skin. In the instant of shock before his rationality broke through, he tasted butter on her lips, lemons, something sweet like cherries.

"Julia!" Warren yanked his head away, his chest filling with an unnerving combination of irritation and heat. "Stop it."

"I don't want to." She scooted to the edge of the car hood, twisting her fists into the front of his shirt. Her breathing increased as she hooked her legs around his waist. "Kiss me back."

"No."

He grabbed her wrists, untangling her grip from his shirt. She tugged again, rising up to press another open kiss to his mouth. Christ, the girl kissed like she was made for the act—all eagerness and soft, wild heat. She drew his hand to her breast, and again before he could think straight, he felt her hard little nipple against his palm, the heaving of her chest, the warmth of her skin burning through the thin material of her dress. She murmured his name, crushing her body against his.

Goddammit. He ripped away from her so fast she almost lost her balance again. She gave a growl of frustration and slid off the hood, wavering as she took a step toward him.

"Steady." Warren darted forward, sliding his hand under her arm before she fell.

She lowered her head, her long hair sweeping down to conceal her face. Trembles ran visibly through her body, and he realized she was crying.

He groaned inwardly. "Julia, let's go home. It's been a really long night."

"I don't want to go," she wailed, dropping her head against his chest. "I'm sick to death of her being the perfect one and me being the screw-up. I have a life too, and just because it's not like hers doesn't mean it's worthless."

"She never said it was." Warren patted her arm gently. "Now get in the car."

"And go back to your house so you can be with her?" Julia sniffled. "I'm so jealous that you guys have this, like, perfect marriage and I couldn't even get mine to last more than three months. Why can't you just give me a taste of what you and Becca have? No one needs to know."

"Julia, I am married to your sister. I'm...oh, for fuck's sake."

She'd pulled away from him and was starting to lower the straps of her dress to expose her breasts.

"Julia, stop it." Warren held up his hands, his spine stiff enough to break.

"Is that an order or a strong suggestion?" she asked mockingly, twisting one strap between her fingers, lowering it just enough to—

"Everything okay here, folks?" An authoritative voice boomed through the night air, a bright light suddenly shining in their direction.

Shit.

Julia froze. Warren turned to find a police car parked nearby, two officers standing outside the open doors. He moved between Julia and the officers, blocking her from their view, his hands still up.

"Everything's fine, officers," he said. "My friend here just had too much to drink and is walking it off."

"Looks like she's doing a little more than walking," the second officer observed, peering past Warren's shoulder.

"She'll be fine," he said, sensing Julia's distress like a sudden storm. "If you need my ID, it's in my wallet. Okay if I reach for it?"

The officers exchanged glances.

"Never mind, but you'd both better move along," the first one said. "We'll wait for you to go."

Warren nodded, turning to grab Julia's hand. She was trem-

bling, her eyes dark and her skin burning red with embarrassment. He guided her around to the passenger seat and got her
buckled in. Giving the officers another nod of thanks, he climbed
into the driver's seat and left the parking lot.

Julia huddled against the car door, wiping tears from her
cheeks.

"You okay?" He couldn't help reaching out to touch her hand,
hoping to offer some measure of comfort.

"I'm so sorry." Her voice was very small.

"It's over. Everything will be different in the morning."

And it was. Because Julia was gone.

CHAPTER 10

Julia is a Latinate feminine form of the Roman family Julius. Julius is derived from the founder Julus, son of Aeneas and Creusa in Roman mythology. The name may also derive from the name of the Roman god Jupiter.

Interesting. Not mind-blowing, but interesting.

But considering Julia-derived-from-Julus had one week left before the Deck the Halls final performance and needed to finish the Jingle Belles' dresses, she really didn't have time to sit at the Wild Child bakery searching name websites on her laptop.

Although it *was* nice to be able to check another item off her *Before Fifty* list.

Julia put a blue checkmark beside #39—*Learn the etymology of my name*—and slipped the paper back into her handbag.

Conversation, music, and the scent of coffee drifted in the air around her. She sometimes came to Wild Child to work, both to get away from the office and because she enjoyed the comforting, bohemian atmosphere Polly had created with rustic tables, flowering plants, and local artwork.

She turned back to her laptop. Instead of opening her email, she found herself looking up "Rubik's Cube solutions" and "vodka gummy bears" and "1000 piece puzzles." Then, clearly because she was possessed, she placed overnight express orders for several items.

Tomorrow's news headlines would surely read: *Fashion stylist Julia Bennett Loses Her Last Thread of Sanity.*

"Here you go." Polly Lockhart, Luke's wife and owner of the Wild Child Bakery, set a black coffee in front of her.

"Thank you." Julia closed her laptop and picked up the coffee.

Polly pulled out a chair, which meant she was in a chatty mood.

"So whatcha doing?" She rested her chin on her hand and studied the designs on the sketchpad open on the table.

"Working on some new designs." Julia attempted to close the cover on the pad, but Polly got to it first.

"Can I see?" she asked. "Hey, Mia, come and look at Julia's new designs."

Julia sighed as pretty blonde Mia sauntered over with a coffee drink topped with a pile of whipped cream so high it was lopsided. While Julia liked Mia, the sight of her was a sharp reminder that Warren had *fired* her from planning the Sugar Rush party and turned the job over to the other woman.

"Oh, I'd love to see them." Mia sat beside Polly, eagerly scooting her chair closer. "Fashion is so much fun."

Julia forced her mind away from Warren—again—and watched the two younger women study her designs. A few years ago, after Luke had been slammed with a damaging false paternity suit, Julia had eyed her nephews' girlfriends—any woman who approached them, in fact—with deep suspicion and dislike.

So far, however, her wariness had proven unfounded. Luke's wife Polly, whom Julia had wrathfully accused of gold-digging (not without reason), had not only earned her respect for having one hell of a backbone, but also her trust and affection. Polly's sister Hannah had healed Evan's heart in ways that went beyond the physical. Kate Darling, Tyler's significant other, was even more efficient than Julia herself, not to mention highly intelligent and an excellent partner for the youngest Stone brother. Her nephews had chosen well.

"These are nice," Mia remarked, though her tone was oddly subdued.

Julia frowned. "Just nice? They're for young career women like you. You should love them."

Mia closed the book and smiled. "Oh, sure. I love them."

"She hates them," Julia told Polly.

"Totally."

"I don't hate them," Mia protested. "They're just a little too...I don't know. They remind me of stuff my mother used to wear."

Julia bared her teeth in a forced smile. "Do you mean they're *old*?"

"No!" A horrified look flashed across Mia's face. "I didn't say that. Did I ever tell you I want to be like you when I'm...er, a few years from now? I was only talking about the clothes. Oh my God, you're going to put a curse on me now, aren't you?"

Hah. Mia was so sweet that even a curse from Julia would probably come to a screeching halt in front of her and burst into a bouquet of flowers.

"No," Julia said. "I appreciate your honesty."

Polly blinked. "Wow. Have you been infused with the Christmas spirit?"

"I could use some Christmas spirits, if that's what you mean."

"Hey, come with us to the Tipsy Angel tomorrow night." Mia turned and waved over Kate, who was working on her laptop at another table. "Kate, come here."

"What's going on?" Kate came over with her laptop and latte.

"We're going to the Tipsy Angel tomorrow, and Julia's coming with us."

"Really?" Kate arched one eyebrow.

"I am not," Julia said. "What is the Tipsy Angel anyway?"

"It's legit the hottest club in town." Mia pulled out her phone and scrolled. "The Blooming Onions are there tomorrow. Come with us and get your groove on."

"My groove doesn't need to be got on, but thank you for the offer." Julia rose to her feet and zipped up her satchel. Much as she liked the younger women's company, the thought of sitting in a crowded, smoky, noisy club while they fired off words like *legit* and *hunty* was…less than appealing.

"I have a great deal of work still to do for Deck the Halls," she said by way of an explanation. "I hope you all got my email with your volunteer duties?"

"How could we miss an email with the subject line *Open this or be cursed*?" Polly asked.

"I'm glad it worked."

Julia reached for her coat, catching the eye of a nice-looking man at least ten years younger than her seated by the window. He was staring at her with unabashed interest, which was not at all unpleasant. He lifted his coffee to her in a salute and winked.

She almost smiled. *Almost.*

She turned to pick up her handbag. All three younger women were watching her with raised eyebrows and knowing expressions.

"What?" she asked.

"He's cute," Polly offered. "You should totally have a Wild Child hook-up. I'll get you a plate of muffins, and you can go over and say hi. Maybe he'll show you his baguette."

"Or you can ask him if he wants to *bake* you happy," Mia said.

"Or tell him you like his buns," Kate suggested.

They all giggled.

Julia huffed and buttoned up her coat. "As if I have time for that sort of nonsense."

"I'm guessing Mr. Stone wouldn't like it either," Kate said.

Julia and Polly exchanged looks. Aside from the fact that Kate still had trouble calling Warren *"Warren,"* she never just randomly brought him into a conversation.

"Why would Warren not like it?" Julia asked, her tone clipped.

Kate shrugged and swiped her tablet. "I thought you two had something going on, that's all."

"I beg your pardon?" Julia swallowed, her heart thumping against her ribs. "Why would you think that?"

"Just a suspicion." Kate took a sip of her latte, her expression totally uncalculating. "I've seen the way you two look at each other. Right, Polly?"

"Uh, sure." Polly gave Julia a *'Yeah, I didn't get that at all'* glance.

Julia's stomach tensed. Had she really been that transparent? She'd always kept tight control over her suppressed feelings for Warren. That was part of the reason she'd honed her cold reserve —the better with which to conceal her emotions.

But Kate had just said, "The way *you two* look at each other."

Did that mean Warren had also been unable to hide his feelings for her? Exactly *how* had he been looking at her? Had anyone else noticed? And would he pass her a note in English class and ask her to sit with him at the cool kids' table in the cafeteria?

For God's sake. She was a fif—*forty-nine-year-old* woman who did not need to speculate about a ridiculous crush on a man she'd known most of her life. Even if that man had shot her clear up into the stars.

"Don't be silly." She picked up her coffee and placed a plastic cover over the top. "Warren and I have better things to do than sit around making goo-goo eyes at each other."

"Well, if you're going to make goo-goo eyes at any man, he's certainly worthy," Kate remarked.

"He is *super*-hot, right?" Mia agreed.

Julia gave an exasperated sigh. She really didn't have time to sit around listening to younger women wax rhapsodic about Warren's "hotness." Even if it was the truth.

"I'll see you all at Deck the Halls on Christmas Eve," she said.

"If you're not at your stations at your allotted times, I'll unleash my flying monkeys."

"And how will that be different from any other day?" Polly asked sweetly.

"They'll be wearing Santa hats and sleigh bells."

❧

Julia crossed her arms and tapped her fingernails against the sleeves of her Dolce & Gabbana suit jacket. The Jingle Belles stood in a row in front of her, each woman clad in a deep red, matte dress that Julia had designed in record time. She'd then mobilized every person on her staff to help get the dresses made. Though the color was the same, each dress had a different cut and length depending on the woman's figure—empire waist, sweetheart neckline, tea-length, A-line, and a sheath for Gail, whose work as a personal trainer accounted for her toned figure.

"Turn," Julia ordered.

The women, having become accustomed to obeying in the course of numerous hasty fittings, rotated in slow circles. Julia ran a critical eye over their hips and rear ends, assessing the fall of the skirts, the straightness of the hems, and the narrowing at the waist. She moved closer to ensure that the seams didn't pucker, the necklines lay flat, the fabric didn't sag or bulge anywhere, and that the slit on Gail's skirt was perpendicular to the floor.

Finally, she stepped back and gave a short nod.

Behind her, Enzo and Anisa breathed out audible sighs of relief.

"I can't believe it." Sharon stared at herself in the mirror on the opposite wall. "I mean, I really can't believe it."

"You're a miracle worker." Connie ran her hands over her skirt. "I've never worn a dress like this."

"I've never been able to *find* a dress like this," Beverly said. "It's like it was made for me."

"It *was* made for you," Julia reminded her.

"Thank you so much," Sharon said. "But...er, this all must have been terribly expensive."

"I told you there's no charge." Julia eyed the other woman's hair. "However, styling is not only about the clothes. We need to work on the rest of you as well."

Sharon touched her hair, faint worry appearing in her eyes. "What are you going to do?"

"Don't even ask," Enzo advised. "Julia is at her best when she does whatever she wants.""Which is, like, always," Anisa muttered.

Julia slanted the younger woman a mild glare before turning back to the Belles. "Let's get to work on your hair and makeup. Then my assistants will be ready to recreate the looks for your Deck the Halls performance."

The women changed back into their regular clothes—the sight of which still made Julia's nostrils flare with their boxy, unflattering cuts. Enzo and Anisa got the women situated at dressing tables, and a flock of hairstylists and make-up artists entered.

"You know, there are plenty of places where you can find nice, ready-to-wear clothes that suit your body type." Julia stepped back to let the hairstylists do their work.

"I've tried." Connie shrugged. "So many clothes for women our age are just frumpy."

"I'm not that far removed from your age," Julia said, not that she enjoyed disclosing that fact. "And I would never wear *frumpy* clothes. I don't even like saying that word."

"Well, look at you," Sharon muttered. "With your figure, frumpy isn't an option. Unfortunately, for the rest of us..."

"It's not that hard to find clothes that fit well," Julia said.

The women laughed, almost startling her.

"In the real world, it is," Connie said. "The regular retail world, not the world of designer stuff and special alterations that none of us can afford."

"If you're over fifty, forget it," Sharon said. "Welcome to baggy shirts and pleated pants with elastic waistbands. Next stop, orthopedic shoes and girdles."

The other women chuckled in agreement.

"Not to mention, get used to black and brown," Beverly added.

Julia, who was standing behind Sharon, looked in the mirror above the other woman's head. Compared to all four women, she looked *perfect*—well-dressed, her hair a shining honey-colored waterfall to her shoulders, her features artfully enhanced with subtle cosmetics. She worked hard to look like this, and she made no apologies for her belief that the right clothes, hairstyle, and make-up could increase a woman's inner power. She saw it all the time in the wealthy women she styled—the socialites, politician's wives, corporate CEO's daughters, heiresses.

So who did "regular" women like Sharon and Connie go to for help bringing their interiors to the surface, like Julia had done with Polly and Kate?

Old. Tired. Passé.

Longevity is power.

Her thoughts continued working as the women were transformed with flattering haircuts and highlights, and their features accented with perfect color tones. They stared at themselves in the mirrors as if they couldn't believe the reflections matched who they were. It was an expression Julia often saw on her clients, and one which she always enjoyed the most.

"We'll schedule appointments on the day of the performance so everything will be fresh," she assured them. "You can leave the dresses here, and we'll bring them to the dress rehearsal."

She waved away their profuse thanks, telling Isabella to get them samples of all the beauty products. She checked her tablet, adding appointments into the schedule and double-checking the Deck the Halls line-up.

"We're going to stop by that soup and salad place on Thistle Street for lunch," Sharon said as she got up from the dressing table. "Would you like to join us?"

She should really put the Jingle Belles in a spotlight position, either right before intermission or, even better, as the grand finale before the fireworks.

"Julia?"

She glanced up at Sharon. "Yes?"

"Would you like to join us for lunch?"

Julia blinked. "You were asking me?"

"Yes." Sharon's forehead furrowed, and a sudden embarrassment flashed in her expression. "I mean, I'm sure you're really busy and all, but you've been so generous that we'd at least like to take you to lunch."

"Oh. I'm sorry, I...I would like that, but I have a business call in twenty minutes."

"Too bad. Well, maybe another time."

"Another time." Julia watched the other women disappear behind the changing screens. A few seconds later, they started chattering and admiring their new looks all over again.

Julia returned to her office, oddly disappointed that she couldn't join them for lunch. Not that she had anything in common with four women from regular walks of life. They'd sit at a table and talk about their husbands and children, their book clubs, the best place to buy groceries...

No, that wasn't her kind of conversation at all. Then again, neither was the millennial talk she often heard from her assistants about the latest tech gadget and viral social media video.

She straightened her shoulders and went into her studio, where the youthful designs for her Appear line were scattered on the surface. Julia studied them, her mind shifting back to the idea of flipping her target demographic to focus on older women.

Women in their fifties, sixties, seventies who had seen and done a great deal in life. Maybe, like the Jingle Belles, some of them had lost a spouse or had children in college. Maybe they were still working or looking for a new job. Maybe they were librarians, grandmothers, personal trainers, business owners, professionals, teachers. Maybe they were seeking a change or entering a new phase of their lives.

She picked up a design of a flirty, ruffled miniskirt meant for a woman in her early twenties with an unrealistically perfect set of legs.

Her designs had always been about empowering women. Making them feel good, confident, strong.

Warren had pointed out the truth—young women had so many choices in fashion. Too many choices, in fact.

But older women? If the Jingle Belles were right, they faced racks of clothes that were either old-fashioned or too expensive. Drab, boxy, *outdated*.

And yet clearly those women were as active as ever with their work, families, clubs, community groups, volunteering…

They needed clothes that showed the world they wouldn't be written off just because they were mature. Classic styles with modern touches. Vibrant colors, fabrics, textures…

Julia texted Marco and told him to cancel her scheduled call. She turned her sketchpad to a fresh page. A feeling rose that she couldn't name, an instinct telling her when an idea was *good*.

She picked up a sharp pencil and set to work, envisioning classic looks whose conservative edge was softened by a sense of adventure and brightness. Fitted blazers, blouses in soft, vivid reds and greens. Silk, jacquard, linen, cashmere. Skirts of a flattering length, shirts with sleeves that showed hints of skin without being overly revealing. Pants made of a high-quality jersey fabric and tailored to fit, therefore eliminating the need for horrible "slimming" underclothes. Nothing baggy, high-waisted, or too long. Nothing *frumpy*.

By the time she was finished for the day, she'd filled her sketchbook and started to work out fabrics for prototypes. She uploaded her preliminary designs to her online portfolio and contacted a select few colleagues for their opinions.

A clothing line for older women. What could she call it? Terms for women over fifty were so unappealing. Matron. Spinster. Dowager. Or just...*old woman*.

She left her studios and drove downtown, where the lighting and stage technicians were doing a run-through on the Deck the Halls stage. Ocean Avenue was a nonstop bustle of shoppers and families trying to get in a last-minute visit with Santa.

"Aunt Julia."

She turned, her world brightening as she saw Hailey coming toward her—a vision of Christmas cheer in a red coat and plaid scarf. She put down her clipboard and hurried to meet her niece.

"I thought you weren't coming back until the weekend."

"I was able to leave early." Hailey hugged her tightly. "Dad said you'd probably be here, so I wanted to see if you needed any help."

"Not until the final show." Julia eyed her niece, noticing the faint worry in the girl's brown eyes that were so much like her father's. "Hey, let's go get a coffee or hot cocoa. My treat."

"Don't you need to work?"

"They'll be fine without me." She waved a dismissive hand toward the stage. "In fact, they'll probably enjoy being without me for an hour or so."

A few minutes later, they were sitting at a window table at Wild Child, with two cappuccinos and a plate of Declairs. After chit-chat about Hailey's work and her thoughts about graduate school, Julia sensed her niece shifting toward confidentiality.

Though it had taken some time for Hailey to trust her enough to confide in her, over the years Julia had learned to recognize the signs of Hailey's need to talk about something specific. Julia had never wanted or tried to take her sister's place as Hailey's mother, but she had become the girl's main confidante in a family full of boys. It was a role she both cherished and did not take lightly.

"Is everything all right?" she asked. "Is that break-up still bothering you?"

Hailey shook her head, lifting her cup to her lips. "Have you noticed anything going on with Dad?"

A humorless laugh bubbled in Julia's throat. Had she *not* noticed Warren in recent days? He'd infiltrated every area of her thoughts.

"Like what?" she asked casually.

"Well, when I went down for breakfast this morning, he was sitting at the kitchen table, kind of...I don't know. Slumped. I asked him what was wrong, and he got up really fast, like he didn't want me to see him like that. Then he said nothing was wrong, he was going out for a run and would be back later."

Unease pricked at Julia. "He might be a little discombobulated about retirement. He's been acting like it's no big deal, but of course it is. Maybe he didn't want you to see him upset."

"Maybe." Hailey didn't look convinced. "Adam told me Dad is doing a lot more climbing and bouldering, but do you think that's good for him?"

"He wouldn't do it if it wasn't," Julia said. "Your father has never been reckless."

"Here you go." Polly swooped over to deposit a plate of Declairs on the table. "Hailey, are you coming with us to the parade? We're leaving around four."

"Sure, I'll meet you over at Luke's."

Polly turned to Julia. "What about you, sunshine?"

"Hah. I would rain on the silly parade."

Polly cracked a grin and headed over to another table. Hailey ate a Declair and shook her head, as if ridding herself of worrisome thoughts.

"Well, I just wanted to ask," she said. "I know I don't live all that far away, but I kind of hate leaving Dad alone, you know?"

"Dearest, all of your brothers are at his beck and call, much as they would like to believe otherwise. He just needs to snap his fingers and they'll come running."

"I know, but I still worry about him." Hailey shrugged, studying the design on the mosaic tabletop. "Evan thinks all of Dad's modeling has been a way of isolating himself. I want him to retire, but not if he's going to spend all his time holed up in his workshop."

"I'm sure he has all sorts of grandiose plans," Julia said. "And he would be dismayed to know that you were worrying about him."

"I'll try not to." Hailey smiled and reached for her coat. "I'm so glad he has you, Aunt Julia. Not just to keep an eye on him, but as a friend."

After they'd said goodbye, Julia watched her niece leave the café. Hailey still had a guarded way of moving through the world, as if she had an invisible shield in front of her.

I'm so glad he has you.

It had been an offhanded statement, but one that settled in Julia's heart like a bird in a nest. Maybe that meant the idea of her and Warren as an actual couple wouldn't be a difficult transition in Hailey's mind.

Julia slid into her coat and stood. Hope and fear warred inside her. She'd lived long enough to know that fear seemed stronger. Sharp claws and gnashing teeth.

But hope, green leaves and star-sprinkled skies, was deceptively gentle. And it always stood an excellent chance of winning the battle.

"Y ou're in better shape and better health than most men half your age." The doctor removed his stethoscope and made a note on Warren's chart. "Great heart, blood pressure, lungs. We'll have your bloodwork by tomorrow. All the training you're doing has clearly served you well."

"What about the dizziness?" Warren asked.

Dr. Anderson studied his chart, a frown creasing his forehead. "Could be nutrition related or just because you've taken your training to a whole other level. Possibly a vitamin deficiency. I'll know more when I get your blood results. If everything is normal, I'll refer you to an ENT. Otherwise keep doing what you're doing, and send me a selfie when you're at the top of the Matterhorn."

Warren thanked him, dressed, and left the office—glad about the good report but still uneasy about his sudden attacks of vertigo. The Matterhorn route required climbing vertical rock faces, some with drops that led hundreds of feet to the glaciers below. Narrow ridge lines, constant exposure, an unstable, difficult descent.

A climber had to be as sharp and focused as he or she had ever been in life. Warren had been working to his limits for a year in preparation for the challenge. Mentally, emotionally, physically—he was ready.

He couldn't let a little dizziness dent his confidence. Dr. Anderson was right. Probably dehydration or a nutrition issue. He'd pay more attention to what he was eating and drinking.

He got into his car and used his tablet to send an email to Hans at Alpine Climbs, attaching a copy of the completed health form listing no medications or pre-existing conditions. Hans's reply came a few seconds later:

Thanks. We'll know before Xmas if we are green-lighted.

Reminding himself that the uncertainty of climbing was one of its appeals, Warren drove home and parked in the garage.

He went into his office, his gaze falling on his model workshop, which he hadn't used in months. The long table was still covered with parts of an RAF fighter plane he hadn't finished.

He hadn't had much of an urge to work on the models lately, not with his focus on the Matterhorn and retirement. He didn't miss it much either. He liked putting models together, but he liked being out in the world more.

He liked the challenge of Julia more.

He passed the workshop and stopped at the built-in shelves loaded with books. He scrutinized the titles—everything from history books to novels.

On the bottom shelf sat a row of paperbacks. He pulled one out—a worn yellow-edged children's book. *Little House on the Prairie.* He flipped the pages and took a folded sheet of paper out from between them.

After sitting in a leather chair, he unfolded the paper. His heart hammered. How many years ago had he last read this letter? Twenty-eight?

Dear Warren,

*I hope this reaches you. I'm writing from London, a little flat in
Battersea. I've been here about three weeks and am looking for a job or
maybe to enroll in art classes.*

*I want to apologize for what I said and did. Kissing you was a terrible
thing to do. I don't usually act that way, though I hope you know that.
You were so nice. There were things you did that you didn't have to do,
and things you could have done that you didn't.*

*Not to be weird, but I've been thinking about you a lot. The kind of man
you are, like one who wouldn't ditch me because you were too cowardly
to stand up to your father. Especially if you knew I was pregnant.
Maybe it's a good thing Sam bailed out on me because I don't think we
would've had a very good marriage if he could do that.*

*Anyway, I guess I just wanted to say I'm sorry. And to thank you too
because you've always reminded me that men who are kind of perfect
are really out there. Maybe one day I'll find one.*

Sincerely,
Julia Bennett

Kind of perfect.

Even now, the phrase twisted through him like a corkscrew.
She'd thought he'd been *nice*.

That night had been the first break, the start of the domino
effect that apparently still hadn't ended.

How was it that a few hours could still discolor a person's life
thirty years later? When were people allowed to stop feeling
guilty and to admit that making mistakes was part of being
human? Was there one person in the history of time who hadn't
felt or thought something *wrong*?

Julia's quest for perfection meant that she couldn't forgive herself. But if she knew *he* hadn't been "kind of perfect"—far from it—she might find a way to allow herself a mistake.

He folded the letter and put it in the interior pocket of his suit jacket before heading back to his car. He drove to Julia's studios, only to be informed by Marco that she'd gone home early. Which, unbeknownst to anyone else, likely meant that she was trying to stave off a migraine.

His insides clenched as he headed to her house. She'd never had very bad migraines until the onset of menopause, when they'd started getting increasingly severe. Despite his insistence that she see several different specialists, none had come up with a medication that worked.

He pulled into her driveway and approached the front door. He knocked instead of ringing the bell. The loud noise of the bell exacerbated her headaches.

No response. The faint sound of music came from inside. She'd never listen to music if she had a headache. Warren knocked again and turned the knob. The door opened.

He stepped inside, breathing in the scent of baking—cinnamon and sugar. Music filled the air—the dynamic, thumping beat of Cher's "If I Could Turn Back Time" accompanied by the singer's rich voice...

Wait a second. That wasn't Cher. That was—

Warren stopped in the kitchen doorway. A cake sat on the counter alongside a bowl of white frosting. And clad in yoga pants, a T-shirt, and a flour-covered apron, her hair pulled into a messy ponytail, Julia danced around the kitchen, holding a spatula like a microphone and belting out the lyrics about regrets and lost love as if she were singing to a stadium full of people.

And holy shit...she could *sing*.

Warren couldn't take his eyes off her. She wiggled her hips, flipped her hair, strutted in circles, and sang with everything she possessed. Her voice was strong, rich, rising and falling in time with the melody like a ship rolling over a sea.

She grabbed a spatula and loaded it with white frosting, then slapped it onto a cake. Still singing, she whirled around. Her gaze collided with his. She stopped, her eyes widening with shock and her skin flushed.

"What…what are you doing here?" she asked breathlessly.

"You didn't hear me knock, so I came in. Sorry to interrupt."

She suddenly seemed like a different woman than the one he'd known for so many years. How the hell had he never known she could sing like…like *that*?

Fear lanced through him, sharp and unexpected. His hands flexed and unflexed. He had a vague memory of Rebecca telling him Julia could sing, but it hadn't registered much and he'd never heard her. If he hadn't even known Julia could sing like a dream, what else didn't he know about her? What was she hiding? What had she not told him?

As if reading his thoughts, Julia's flush deepened. She moved toward the music player to hit the stop button. Warren was across the room before she could reach it, grabbing her around the waist. She startled. The song changed to Modern English's "Melt with You."

Warren pulled her against him and spun her around, grabbing her right hand with his left. He guided her into a slow dance, losing himself in her blue eyes and the lingering echo of her voice. He led her on several turns around the kitchen and was rewarded by her spontaneous laugh. She came to a halt near the sink, the smile still curving her mouth.

"You're incredible, Jules." He cupped his hands on either side of her face. "Why didn't I know you could sing like that?"

"I haven't sung in years." She shook her head dismissively. "I just used to do it for fun."

He rubbed his thumb over her lips, suppressing the thought that she'd stopped singing because of him. That she'd *missed out*.

He lowered his hand to the side of her throat. Her pulse beat rapid and hot against his palm.

"And the cake?" He tilted his head to the cake resting beside them.

"On my *Before Fifty* list." She ran a hand down his chest. "Bake a carrot cake."

Tenderness flared beneath his awe and desire. "You're working on your list?"

"Not really. Well, sort of." Faint embarrassment shone in her eyes. "It's completely stupid, but I don't like the fact that I didn't finish what I started. So I'm…well, I guess I've been working on a few of them. With varying degrees of success."

Christ, he loved her. She didn't wallow in regrets or missed chances—she met them head-on and figured out a way to turn them to her advantage. Unable to resist the temptation, he lowered his mouth to hers. She sank into him, her breath heating his lips, her hands curling into the front of his shirt.

He grasped her wrists. She looked up, eyebrows lifting.

His heartbeat increased. He'd kept a secret for thirty years. Scared she'd hate him for it. But he wanted—needed—her to know the truth. If he was going to have any hope of convincing her they belonged together, he had to give her every part of himself.

He pulled the letter out of his pocket and handed it to her. A quizzical crease formed on her forehead. She unfolded the paper and read the first line.

"Oh my God." She lifted her eyes to his, her breath escaping on a rush. "You kept it."

"How could I not?"

"You never responded."

"No. I wanted to forget it ever happened."

A shadow of hurt appeared on her face, but she nodded and lowered her gaze back to the letter. A hundred emotions crossed her face as she read her thirty-year-old writing—regret, sorrow, bittersweet warmth.

"I'm glad I wrote this," she finally said. "I meant every word."

"Even though I wanted to forget…" He moved closer, his hand still on the side of her warm neck. "I told you I've never been able to."

"Neither have I," Julia admitted. "Even though I've always been ashamed of myself."

"Me too."

Her eyebrows drew together slightly. "What did you have to be ashamed about?"

"You don't remember?"

She shook her head.

"I'm not perfect, Jules. I've never been perfect. I'm not *kind of* perfect or anything even close. I make mistakes all the time. I regret things I've done and things I didn't do. And whatever you thought of me because of that night was wrong."

"What are you talking about?"

"I kissed you back." Warren forced the confession past his tight throat, deflecting a sharp, painful spear of guilt. "I was a married man with young children, and when my wife's sister kissed me, it was like…like fireworks. I felt that kiss down to my bones. And I should have pushed you away before your lips touched mine, but I didn't."

Confusion lit in her eyes. "I don't remember that."

"I do."

"So you…you've been punishing yourself all this time because of that?" Julia rested her hand on his chest, the warmth of her palm burning through the material of his shirt. "Warren, that was just a physical reaction. I threw myself at you, for heaven's sake. I started *stripping*. God. I don't even know what I was thinking. So even if you…if you *felt* something, it wasn't as if you took me up on my blatant offer. Heck, you spent hours searching for me because of Rebecca, because you told her you'd find me. You did nothing to betray your wife and family. *Nothing.*"

Warren swallowed past the tightness in his throat. He'd told himself that countless times over. Mostly he believed it. But a small part of him had always known he could have, should have, broken away from Julia faster than he had.

"Oh, Warren." She laughed suddenly, a hollow, sad sound. "I've known men who have cheated on their wives for years with different women. Men who are alcoholics, abusers, addicted to porn or gambling. I've known wives who've stayed married because of the children or because they had no idea what else they would do with themselves. I've known people who are desperately unhappy in their partnerships. Do you have any idea how *rare* your and Rebecca's marriage was? Everyone knew how much you loved each other, what great parents you were, how devoted you were to your family. Just because you didn't shove a drunk girl away from you in an instant doesn't dilute *any* of that. You're still the most honorable man there is."

"I've tried to be."

"You *are.*" She put her hand on his jaw, distress lighting her blue eyes. "It was all my fault. I hate that this has been gnawing at you for all these years."

"It's been gnawing at you, too," he reminded her. "You'd drawn an invisible line between us, one I always knew was there. It disappeared the instant I kissed you under the mistletoe, much as you've tried to pretend it didn't. Rebecca has been stopping you too."

Julia looked down, twisting a button on his shirt. "How do we let her go?"

"We don't." He brushed a lock of hair away from her forehead. "She'll always be part of us. We both loved her. She's the mother of my children. But Julia, she's gone. We're here. I'd like to think she'd want us both to have another shot at happiness."

She studied the button on his shirt as if assessing its construction. Her long eyelashes made shadows on her cheekbones, and that little crease of thought wrinkled her smooth forehead.

"For years, I've been focused on my children, the company, the foundation, the town." An ache pushed at him, but one of gratitude and hope rather than pain. "I'd never change any part of my past, but I've also spent a lot of time *not* doing things. I won't do that anymore. Life is for the living."

She leaned forward and rested her forehead against his chest. He settled his hand on the back of her neck. Pressed his lips to the top of her head.

How long had he loved her? He didn't know when his feelings for her had shifted from affection and gratitude to outright *love*. Long before they'd had sex, he knew that much. Falling in love with Julia had been like the easing from summer into autumn when the air turns crisp and cool, the leaves change slowly into brilliant colors of red and gold, and the sky becomes a cloud-swept blue circle arching overhead.

Warren had lived long and well enough to know that not only was it possible to have more than one love in life, it was the greatest gift a person could be given.

And loving Julia—being *in love* with her—was like everything good about autumn wrapped into one. Comfort, crispness, warmth, a chill. Hot cider, the bite of frost, a football challenge, the glow of jack-o-lanterns through the dark, salted caramel, wild geese soaring over the sky, the crunch of leaves, mist curling through the woods, wind carving whitecaps on the ocean.

Loving Julia was change. Intense beauty. A touch of melancholy. Leaving behind and starting new. The indescribable joy of knowing he had lived as well as he possibly could, but that it was far from over. With her, he could see the bloom of endless springs.

"I need to finish frosting the cake," she mumbled.

"I love you," he said.

She lifted her head, her eyes blue moons of surprise and disbelief. "Don't you try and distract me, Warren Stone."

A smile tugged at his mouth. He pulled her closer, settling their lower bodies together.

"I'm not," he assured her. "Do you know why Sugar Rush as a company has lasted for so long?"

She eyed him with suspicion, but didn't try to move away. "You're changing the subject."

"I'm making a point," he corrected. "When my great-great-grandfather started Stone Confectioners in the 1850s, he made a ton of mistakes. Wrong suppliers, unsuccessful recipes, poor advertising. But he kept going until he found one of his main customer bases in the Gold Rush miners. After he opened his first shop in San Francisco and realized he was making something of himself, he wrote a founding philosophy.

"He wanted the company to always focus on keeping customers happy, to never use low-quality chocolate and ingredients, to do good in the community, and to maintain integrity and respect in all relationships. And he was adamant about wanting to keep Stone Confectioners as a family-run company guided by those principles. If he were here today and saw the company, even with all our global growth and changes, I have no doubt he'd recognize that Sugar Rush is fundamentally the same company he started. More, that foundation is the reason we've been so successful. It's the bedrock on which we've built a thriving, vibrant city."

Julia was silent, clearly listening though her eyes were still narrow.

"And?" she finally said.

"It's like us," Warren explained. "I've loved you for a very long time, only now I finally have the guts to admit it. I love your fire and your ice. I love your loyalty, your dedication to this family, your perseverance, your drive. I love the way you call people on their bullshit. I love that you're an ice queen one minute and a marshmallow the next. I love the noises you make in the back of your throat when I kiss you. I love your fucking perfect body and your sharp, take-no-prisoners mind and the fact that you secretly love watching *Gossip Girl* marathons in your ratty old flannel pajamas. While eating waffles."

She opened her mouth to protest. He kept talking because no matter how hard she tried to deny it, he knew the truth of her secret passions.

"Do I wish I'd told you sooner?" he asked. "No. We have thirteen years of friendship and alliance behind us. We've been through rough times and come out of it together. We've been partners, allies, colleagues. Hell, we've been *co-parents*. And because we have an unshakable foundation, loving you is so damned easy. How can it not work when we have so much? I want to love you completely. I want us to…are you crying?"

"Of course not." Julia sniffed, her eyes pooling with tears. "I'm just…oh, damn you, Warren Stone."

She rested her forehead against his chest again and gave a choked laugh. "You're the only man in the world who could turn a lecture on Sugar Rush corporate history into a declaration of love."

"I'm pretty sure I made the declaration first." He wrapped his arms around her and pressed his lips to the top of her head. "Come on, Jules. Give us a chance. You've never been scared of anything or anyone in your life. Don't be afraid of *us*."

She didn't look up, keeping her forehead against his chest so he couldn't see her face. He stroked her back, absorbing the warm, soft feeling of her body pressed against his.

Finally, after the clock on the kitchen wall had ticked into eternity, Julia's voice emerged, small and muffled against his shirt front.

"Okay."

Warren's heart spun like a Ferris wheel and lit up like the Fourth of July. He wanted to haul her into his arms, to whirl her around in a circle and then back her up against the wall and kiss her senseless.

Instead he lowered his head and forced his voice to sound calmly inquisitive.

"Sorry?" he said. "I didn't catch that."

She pinched his ass. "I said *okay*."

"Okay...what?"

A laugh broke from her. She finally lifted her face from his chest and looked up at him. Tears streaked her cheeks, her skin was red and blotchy, and her eyes glowed. She was like a sunrise.

"I'll give us a chance, you beautiful, stubborn man. But how did you know about the TV and the flannels?"

He smiled and chucked her under the chin. "I know *you*."

"You're wrong about the waffles." She gave a little sniff. "No way do I sit around in flannels eating *waffles*, of all things."

"My mistake." He drew her closer, his thumb finding the pulse beating at the side of her neck. "But don't worry, I won't tell anyone."

He lowered his mouth to hers. She murmured a little noise against his lips and pressed closer, sliding one hand to his back. The fireworks spread to his blood, little sparks flaring into whirlwinds. He flicked his tongue out to press against the seam of her lips. She opened, let him in. The warm, sweet taste of her—sugar and cinnamon—flooded into him. He cupped the sides of her neck, tilting her head to just the right angle. Though she was much smaller than him, she fit against him perfectly, all of her slender curves surrendering to the planes of his chest.

He lowered his hands to the backs of her thighs and lifted her against him. With a murmur of pleasure, she wrapped her arms and legs around him, not taking her lips from his. He strode to the bedroom and lowered her to the bed.

He levered himself over her, drinking in the sight of her flushed face, the smear of frosting on her cheek, her tousled blonde hair. Possessiveness and gratitude washed over him. He saw everything in her—the extraordinary businesswoman, the gypsy girl, the fierce, beloved aunt, the devoted sister. Above all, the woman he loved.

She lifted her hand to his face, stroked the five o'clock shadow on his jaw. He rose to straddle her thighs. She was still wearing the flour-dusted apron, which gave her a domestic look he liked. He tugged on the apron straps and reached beneath her to unfasten the strings at her back. "Had no idea you owned an apron."

"I cook every now and then." She wiggled underneath him to shed the apron, the movement of her body jolting him with heat.

"You don't cook." He slipped his hands over her tight blue T-shirt to her breasts. Ah, her nipples were hard already, budding up against his palms.

"I cook some things." Her voice was starting to get breathless. "Just because I've never cooked for *you* doesn't mean I don't cook at all."

"Yeah?" He pinched her nipples through her shirt. "What do you cook, then?"

"Um…dinner. Sometimes. Oh…" She arched her back and pressed her breasts into his palms.

"Hmm." He pulled her T-shirt up and stroked the satin skin of her midriff up to her blue lace bra that was the exact same color as her shirt. His dick pushed against the front of his trousers.

"You'll need to cook for me one night, then." He flicked open the front clasp of her bra. "Maybe wearing nothing but your apron and stilettos."

Though Julia attempted a frown, intrigue and a spark of excitement lit in her eyes. Just the thought of her strutting around the kitchen with her tits barely covered by the apron and her delectable round ass peeking out from beneath the apron strings…damned if that wasn't enough to jerk his cock into full hardness.

He unbuckled his belt and dropped it to the floor, then

unzipped his trousers and took out his dick. Julia's hot gaze snapped to it, her lips parting. His blood went into a full boil. She rose to her elbows and licked her lips. He moved closer, nudging the head of his dick against her mouth. She opened and took him in.

Ah, fuck, yeah...

That was it, her hot gasp of breath, the soft yielding of her lips, the surrender of her body curving under his. Her warm, wet mouth enclosed his shaft like heaven. He gripped the sides of her head, forcing himself not to go too deep. She curled her fingers into his hips, working her lips and tongue over his cock with slow strokes that twisted pressure through his entire body.

She circled the base of his shaft with her hand and squeezed. He pushed forward, watching her perfect bow lips wrap around his cock. She made a muffled noise and slackened her throat muscles, encouraging him to thrust. He wanted to come in her mouth, to watch her swallow, see his seed coating her lips.

Instead he pressed the sides of her head in warning. She drew back to look up at him, her eyes glazed. He made a gesture with his hand. She hastened to shed the rest of her clothes, dropping them to the floor before scooting back on the bed.

He raked his gaze over the smooth, supple lines of her body, her tits topped with rosy nipples, the warm cleft between her legs. He stroked his hand over her breasts and belly, his jaw clenching when his fingers encountered her damp heat. She breathed his name, a tremble coursing through her.

"Warren, *please.*"

Her throaty plea fired his blood. He positioned himself between her legs, entering her with slow measured movements to ensure she'd feel every inch of his possession. Her breath rasped hot against his shoulder. The scent of her filled his head. His muscles tensed with restraint as he sank into her—hot, damp, welcoming.

"God, Warren...it's like you're doing it for the first time all over again...*oh*..."

He braced his hands on the bed, sinking as deep into her as he could go, his gaze locked on hers. Her pale cheeks were stained with pink, and her full mouth looked damp and well-kissed. Need glazed her blue eyes along with another emotion he could only define as pure and unadulterated trust.

She throbbed around him, her sweet body heaving with little gasps of need. Urgency coiled through him. He pulled back and surged forward, then repeated the movement with growing force until the rhythm of Julia's throaty cries matched the pace of their bodies. She trembled under him, gripping his biceps, her breasts rubbing against his chest.

Mine. The word fired through his brain with every plunge into her. *You're mine.*

Heat. She burned him. He clutched her hips, increasing the pace of his thrusts until she cried out and convulsed around him. He pushed into her, his muscles tensing as the coil wound tighter and tighter. He gave a rough shout. Julia's body continued to grip his cock as he spilled himself into her, pleasure searing away all thought.

He rolled off her, chest heaving, and pulled her to his side. She curled against him like a soft, warm bird, her breath feathering over his shoulder. He wanted to go to sleep every night and wake up every morning with this woman tucked against him exactly like this.

A dream he hadn't even known was there.

CHAPTER 12

I *love you.*
   Such a common phrase, almost overused. And yet when it was said *to you* by the one who'd owned your heart for years, suddenly it was the first time in all of history that a man had ever spoken those words to a woman.

I love you.

He loved her. As a friend, a partner, an ally, and now a lover. Warren had the same burning need for her as she did for him, felt the same sharp crackle of heat, desire, lust. He loved her because he knew her as well as she knew him, because they'd built a foundation—a *life*. Because they'd weathered storms both alone and together. She was his comfort, the person he turned to in both the dark and the light, his best friend, just as he was for her.

How could a romance between them possibly fail when everything about it was already such a success? They didn't have to go through any ridiculous "getting to know you" phase or try to learn more about each other. There was no awkwardness, no uncertainty, no *wondering*.

There was only knowledge, acceptance, and love.

As Julia lay alone in bed, drinking in the scents of coffee and bacon drifting from the kitchen, she almost didn't recognize the emotion spiraling through her. She'd felt happy before, of course, plenty of times. When the boys or Hailey had a personal achievement, when Evan's heart surgery was a success, when a Foundation event went well, when Tyler straightened up, when her business skyrocketed.

But this? This wasn't connected to anything tangible. Her heart didn't even know what to do with itself, fluttering rapidly in her chest like a hummingbird that had just discovered the sweetest, richest honeysuckle in the world.

This was a happiness that came from loving and being loved unconditionally. This was pure, like birdsong, a clear mountain stream, a new leaf.

This was *joy*.

She threw back the covers and grabbed her silk kimono, suddenly eager to see him even though they'd slept together all night. She hurried to splash water on her face and brush her teeth before going into the kitchen.

Her heart did an Olympic-sized hopscotch at the sight of him presiding over the pans sizzling on the kitchen stove. He wore trousers and a wrinkled dress shirt, open down the front to reveal his gorgeous chest. His thick hair, messy from her grip last night, fell over his forehead, and his profile was set with concentration as he studied the bacon to assess whether or not he should flip it over.

As if sensing her presence, he turned, his eyes warming.

"Morning, beautiful." He extended an arm.

She got all melty inside. What if she could walk into her kitchen every morning and have this man greet her? She crossed the room to tuck herself against his side, absorbing the strong, solid feel of him.

He kissed the top of her head. "Coffee's ready. Breakfast will be done in five minutes."

Julia slipped away from him to pour herself a cup of coffee.

She sipped the coffee and leaned against the counter, eyeing the high-end, professional double Belgian waffle iron plugged into the wall.

"Where did you get that?" she asked casually.

"Found it in the back of the cupboard." He gave an innocent shrug. "Must have been there when you bought the house."

"Must have."

"I decided to try it out."

He lifted a bowl filled with batter and ladled a portion onto the waffle maker. The delicious sizzle and aroma of hot baking elicited a rumble from Julia's belly. She attempted not to groan in anticipation of the golden brown nirvana about to emerge from the waffle iron.

She sat at the kitchen table and unfolded the newspaper as Warren filled plates with bacon and eggs. The waffle iron beeped. He lifted the lid, revealing a perfect, steaming waffle. Julia's mouth watered.

"Don't suppose you want any." Warren lifted the waffle with a spatula. "Seeing as how you don't eat waffles, of all things."

"I'll give it a try." Julia extended her plate. "I mean, I don't want you to have gone to all this trouble for nothing."

"Very charitable of you."

She gave a little huff. He winked at her.

He slipped half the waffle onto her plate and the second half onto his. Julia took the butter and syrup from the fridge and promptly slathered her waffle with both. She cut off a generous forkful and stuck it in her mouth. The fluffy, crispy, buttery-sweet flavor filled her senses.

"Oh my God." She groaned with pleasure. "This is incredible. What recipe did you use?"

"I dunno, just looked one up on the internet." He took a bite of the waffle. "I'm a pancake man myself, but this is pretty good."

"*Pretty* good? It's a slice of heaven."

"Just like you."

Though she attempted to roll her eyes, he looked so pleased with himself over the compliment that she got all soft inside. Yes, the man could melt her like butter on this exquisite waffle.

Never before had she indulged in such a hearty morning-after breakfast with a man. She usually either sent them on their way the night before, or she made a quick egg-white omelet and hustled them out the door. Certainly she'd never spent well over an hour lingering with a man over waffles and coffee, skimming the newspaper and glancing up every now and then to find him watching her.

Of course, Warren wasn't any man. He was the only man who knew her, looked out for her, loved her.

He rinsed their plates and put them in the dishwasher, wiping his hands on a towel before picking up the *Before Fifty* list she'd left on the counter.

"Looks like you're making progress." He indicated the blue checkmarks she'd placed beside several of the items.

"I'm just doing a few of them in my spare time." She sipped her coffee and shrugged with nonchalance. "It's not like I'm taking it seriously or anything."

Amusement glinted in his eyes. "Of course not. Why a red balloon?"

Julia took the list from him.

#19: Set a red balloon free.

"Oh." Bittersweet sorrow twisted her heart. "Did Rebecca ever tell you about *The Red Balloon?* It's a French short film, maybe half an hour, about a little boy in Paris who finds a red balloon that starts following him. Like a friend. Then these mean kids come along and destroy the balloon with a slingshot, and of course the boy is devastated. So were Rebecca and I, frankly. I'm pretty sure we both cried.

"But then hundreds of multicolored balloons rise up from all over the city and float over to the boy as he's sitting there with his broken red balloon. He grabs the strings of the other balloons, and they fly him on a magical journey across the sky."

"She never mentioned it to me." Warren sounded mildly surprised, as if he'd assumed Rebecca had shared all her memories with him.

"We loved the movie. We talked about wanting to send a red balloon over the ocean on its own worldwide journey."

He touched her hair, his eyes softening. "You never did?"

"No." She shrugged, setting the list aside. "I guess we grew out of the idea. But obviously I remembered it when I was nineteen."

"It would be an easy one to cross off your list," Warren said. "We could do it right now."

She looked up at him, her gaze roaming over the lines of his face—his wide mouth that did such beautiful things to her, his thick-lashed eyes and cut-glass cheekbones, the straight bridge of his nose.

The words pushed up from her heart, the center of her soul.

I love you.

Her throat closed over them.

The words still belonged to her sister. Every time Julia thought them, she heard Rebecca's voice. What if Warren did, too?

"Thank you, but I should get to work." She squeezed his arm. "One day."

She rose to her feet, setting her mug in the sink before heading to the bedroom.

One day she would tell him. One day before it was too late.

CHAPTER 13

If Julia had been the type of woman to employ teenage-girl terms, she would have been *squeeing* over her *hot AF bae*. Even though she and Warren were keeping it *low-key*, she was *totally pumped*.

Legit.

She walked into the front door of her studio and deposited two trays loaded with tall skinny lattes on the reception counter. Marco looked up from the computer and blinked.

"Are we throwing these at someone today?" he asked politely.

"Don't look a gift horse in the mouth, whatever that means." Julia waved her hand at the coffee. "Distribute those to the others."

"Well, thank you."

"Let's not overdo it." Julia strode toward her office. "I want the Deck the Halls programs on my desk by ten, the Zuzu photo spread finalized by ten-thirty, and the schedule for the lookbook shoot completed by eleven."

"I knew Christmas miracles couldn't last," Marco muttered.

Julia closed the door behind her, shedding her suede coat before she sat at her desk. She opened her Montblanc agenda, pleased to see a number of checkmarks beside her list of action items. She was getting it done. Like she always did.

Her phone rang with a call from Holiday Festival committee member Minnie. For the first time since she'd taken on the task of coordinating Deck the Halls, Julia answered the call without a sinking feeling of dread.

"Hello, Minnie," she said brightly. "This is Julie."

"Hello, Julie. I wanted to confirm everything for this weekend. Santa's Sleigh and the Sugar Rush Kid Zone will be open Friday starting at four for the first night of the festival, then all day Saturday. Deck the Halls will start at six, expected to run for three hours, concluding with the fireworks display over the ocean."

"Perfect."

"It's all set?" Minnie almost sounded surprised.

"Yes, it is. Happy Holidays." Julia ended the call with a smile. Damn, she felt good. All loose and warm, like a marshmallow swimming in hot cocoa.

"Package for you." Marco strode into Julia's office with a box wrapped in brown paper.

Julia opened the box to reveal a 1000-piece puzzle of a London Christmas scene with lighted windows, snowy side-walks, and a double-decker bus turning the corner.

As if she had time to complete a 1000-piece puzzle.

"Gift for my nephew," she said in answer to Marco's raised brows. "I'm leaving early this afternoon. I need to finish orga-nizing the Christmas Day festivities at Warren's. Anything I need to know about Deck the Halls?"

"Sounds like everyone is ready to go," Marco said. "I have the Jingle Belles scheduled to come in at two on Saturday afternoon to get ready for the show. Speaking of which, have you decided what you're going to wear on performance night?"

Good heavens. She'd been so busy thinking of everyone else's costumes she hadn't considered her own. How odd.

"Maybe the green Versace. Take out a few options for me. I'll try them on later."

She spent the morning refining the designs for her "older woman" clothing line, thinking she really had to come up with a better way to describe it. After lunch—Marco brought her a gourmet plate of grilled salmon, wild rice, and an asparagus salad —Julia headed to Ocean Avenue to finish up a few things for the family gathering on Christmas Day.

She turned to the "Xmas Day" page in her Montblanc agenda, where most of the action items were checked off. The Stones didn't exchange extravagant presents during the holidays, given that none of them actually needed anything, but Julia liked giving her nephews and niece personal gifts they would like—a botany book for Hailey, a travel backpack for Adam, a fountain pen for Luke, a wood-carving set for Evan.

For the past few years, she'd bought Warren a model kit, but he'd been getting away from modeling lately. Maybe she needed to get him new hiking boots, given his increased outdoor activities.

She paused to look in the window of a baby and children's boutique. Soft booties and blankets, fuzzy stuffed animals, tiny onesies and jumpers. A shadow of regret passed through her. Was there ever a time in life when *what if* wasn't a question? What if she'd had a baby? What if Sam hadn't left her? What if Rebecca hadn't died?

She opened the door of the boutique. A little bell announced her arrival, and a saleswoman approached.

"Can I help you find something today?" she asked pleasantly.

"Yes," Julia said. "A...friend of mine is expecting a new granddaughter any day now. I'd like to get her a gift for the baby, but I don't know what she already has."

"Oh, no problem. We have so many options, and honestly, it never hurts for a baby to have more than one of something."

Julia spent the next hour perusing all the store's offerings. By the time she left, she had a bag full of organic cotton baby girl clothes, an organic fleece stuffed elephant, a baby rattle made of polished cherry wood, and an untreated Indian-wood play gym with little hand-knit animal toys.

She returned to her car, a bit surprised to realize it was the first time she'd ever bought baby clothes herself. Whenever someone she knew had been pregnant, she'd always sent an assistant to purchase a gift, or she'd ordered something online.

Maybe she should add that to her *Before Fifty* list. *Buy baby clothes.*

She checked her phone, where a text from Warren was waiting.

WARREN: Tonight, put on the black La Perla chemise.
JULIA: How do you know I have an LP chemise?
WARREN: Saw it in your drawer this morning.
JULIA: You went through my lingerie drawer?
WARREN: To pick out what you're going to wear tonight.
JULIA: What if I don't want to wear it?
WARREN: You sure you want to play that game again?

A little tingle of anticipation went through her.

JULIA: Maybe.

She set the phone aside and started the car. Or maybe she'd make up a game of her own. With her own rules.

Knowing he was alone at home, she drove to his house. He was in his office, looking incredibly sexy and rumpled in his white dress shirt, his tie loose and the shirtsleeves rolled up to reveal his muscular forearms.

Julia closed and locked the door behind her with a sharp click. He glanced up, eyeing her over the tops of his reading glasses.

"Remember when you told me you like taking control?" she asked.

"Uh huh." His gaze skimmed over her YSL suede dress and stocking-clad legs. "You like it too, if I recall."

"What would you do if I gave you an order?"

Interest sparked in his brown eyes. "Try it, and you'll find out."

"Move away from the desk."

He pushed his chair back, leaving a space between him and the desk.

"Take out your cock."

He stared at her for a second before a curse broke from his lips. He shifted to unfasten his belt and lower his zipper. Julia's breath increased as she watched him. He had such a fucking beautiful cock—long and thick with that big, smooth tip that she wanted to lick like a lollipop. He held the shaft in his palm, his body tensing with restraint.

Julia pushed away from the door and approached, her blood starting to heat. Even in the short distance from the door to his desk, he grew noticeably harder, his shaft thickening and expanding in his loose grip. Arousal curled through her.

She edged herself between him and the desk, her gaze still on his growing erection. He tightened his fingers around his shaft, a heavy breath escaping him.

"Let go of it," Julia ordered.

He released his cock, which stuck out of the fly of his trousers like an invitation. Julia pushed his chair back a bit more and sank to her knees in front of him. Before he could move, she placed her hands on his thighs and leaned forward to take the tip of his cock in her mouth.

He groaned, fisting his hand in her hair. "Fuck, Jules…"

She gripped his thighs, only touching his cock with her mouth. The taste of him flooded through her. She lowered her head slowly, taking him in inch by inch, as his fist tightened in her hair and his muscles tightened with urgency.

"Lick it," he said.

She pulled back, her breathing fast and her skin hot. "You're not giving the orders."

He groaned and rested his head on the back of the chair. Julia smiled to herself and sucked his cock into her mouth again. She took her time, tracing the pulsing veins on his shaft, swirling her tongue over the damp head, wiggling her fingers down to cup his heavy testicles.

She squirmed and pressed her thighs together to ease the ache in her clit. She pulled back and took a breath, her lust spiking higher at the sight of his wet shaft, the tip now darkened to the deep color of a plum. She rose to her feet, steadying herself on his thighs.

"Take off your...shit." He bit the order back, his glazed eyes on her breasts.

Julia grasped the hem of her dress and wiggled it up past her hips.

"Christ, you're killing me." Warren's gaze snapped to her garter belt and stockings—and complete lack of panties. "You've been walking around like that all day?"

"Mmm. Felt the air tickling my pussy every time I took a step."

"Naughty girl." He straightened, reaching to slide his hand up her thigh.

Much as she craved his touch, Julia slapped his hand away. "God, you are such a control-freak. You have to do *what I say.*"

"Then tell me to touch you."

"You can touch me after you make me come with your cock."

Warren gave a hoarse laugh and leaned back in the chair, working his trousers and boxers down. "I would be more than happy to follow that order."

Julia straddled his thighs, bracing her hands on the back of the chair as she positioned herself. Sweat broke out on her fore-head. She lowered herself onto him, his cock easily sliding through her slick folds and into her. Lower and lower she slid, her body tensing as she took him in until her ass rested on his thighs and the length of his shaft throbbed inside her.

God. Her blood pulsed in rhythm with his. He brought his hands up to either side of her head, bringing her lips down to his. He slid his tongue into her mouth, bit down gently on her lower lip. Heat bloomed inside her, spreading tendrils through her veins.

"Move." His voice was guttural with need.

Deciding to ignore the fact that he'd technically given her an order, Julia lifted her body and brought it down again. Pleasure shot through her. Warren's hot breath rasped against her neck, his hands sliding down to clutch her ass. She rode him harder, straining to find a rhythm, tension spinning and coiling through her blood. His thighs tightened beneath her.

"Fuck, I can't wait much longer." His fingers dug into her ass. He thrust upward as she sank down, creating an explosive heat that made her blood burn.

Julia moved her hand to the slippery button of her clit. One touch was all it took. She cried out, her body convulsing around his shaft as bliss rolled and pitched throughout her entire body. She shuddered, still feeling him pulsing inside her. With a muffled grunt, he drove upward, thrusting deep before filling her with his release.

Julia gasped, draping her arms around his neck as she went slack against him.

"You are the GOAT," she murmured.

He pulled back to look at her. "Did you just say I was a goat?"

"Greatest Of All Time." Julia kissed his nose. "You wouldn't understand millennial slang like I do."

"I guess not." He straightened as she eased off him. "But I defi-nitely 143."

Julia arched an eyebrow. "What does that mean?"

He smirked. "Look it up, dime-piece."

Julia stood behind her desk, studying the sketches her assistant Anisa had placed in front of her. She crossed her arms and frowned, tapping her fingernails on her sleeves.

"So this is what you've come up with now?" she asked crisply.

Anisa nodded. "Um, I was going for trendy and...stuff."

Julia gave her a sharp glare. "You just about put me to sleep with that description."

Anxiety flashed in the younger woman's eyes. "But do you like the designs?"

"Not if that's how you're going to describe them."

Anisa shifted her weight from one stiletto heel to the other and pushed a lock of hair behind her ear. She stared at the sketches she'd put on Julia's desk.

Julia snapped her fingers. The sharp crack jerked Anisa to attention.

"*Look* at me," Julia ordered. "If you want to succeed in fashion, you *must* know how to interact, no matter how intimidating a person is—and believe me when I tell you this industry is filled with people who will kiss you one minute and stab you in the back the next. Now stand up straight, look me in the eye, and tell me what the fuck your vision is for these designs."

Anisa put her shoulders back and took a deep breath. Though her hands trembled, her voice was steady as she said, "I want these designs to appeal to creative people. Artists, writers, photographers. So they have to be comfortable, with fabrics that move and breathe, and styles that are a bit edgy and innovative."

"Now distill that into a few words."

Anisa bit her lip, then said, "Creative...comfortable, and...uh, compelling? No, captivating?"

"Are you asking me or telling me?"

"Creative. Comfortable. Captivating."

Julia studied the designs again, then gave a short nod of approval.

"Well done," she said. "Bring me the prototypes when you've finished them."

Anisa stared at her in shock. "Are you serious?"

"Am I ever *not* serious?" Julia sat back down behind her desk and waved for Anisa to take the sketches away. "Now go away before I do something silly like tell you you have talent."

Anisa scrambled to gather the sketches, clutching them to her chest as she hurried to the door.

"Anisa," Julia called sharply.

The younger woman stopped and turned, her eyes still wide with disbelief.

"You do, you know," Julia said. "Have talent. A great deal, from what I've seen so far."

A radiant smile bloomed over Anisa's face, transforming her from a pretty girl into one of great beauty.

"Thank you, Julia." She backed away, still holding her sketches close. "I mean…really, thank you so much. You don't know what this means to me…*thank* you."

Julia flicked her hand to the door. "Go."

Still smiling, Anisa turned and hurried away.

Julia focused on her emails. If she were the type of person who enjoyed making other people feel good about their talents, she'd have been smiling too.

She glanced at her reflection in the mirror on the opposite wall. Oh, look at that. She *was* smiling.

Her intercom buzzed.

"Gird your loins," Marco advised. "Vincent Peck of Evermore Associates, line one."

Her insides went cold.

"Should I hang up on him?" Marco asked.

"No, I'll take it." She closed her eyes, took a breath, and switched the line.

"Hello, Vincent," she said coolly.

"Julia. I know I'm on your shit list," he said. "But I just heard some interesting things about you through the grapevine."

"What did you hear?"

"That you might be tapping into an underserved and unique demographic," Vincent said. "Maybe I can give you more advice."

"You didn't give me advice. You insulted me."

"Potato, potahtoe. I'd like to take a look at your new portfolio."

"I'm sure you would," Julia said dryly. "But I'm afraid my portfolio will be too *mature* for you."

"Come on, Julia, business is business, right? Don't hold a grudge. Appear didn't work out for us, but that doesn't mean this won't."

"If you're interested, you'll have to do some groveling to get back on my good side."

"If I like what I see, I'll wear a hair shirt to win you over."

Julia agreed to give him access to her online portfolio and hung up the phone. She opened her sketchbook and drew a quick caricature of Vincent Peck wearing a hair shirt. She added it to the portfolio and emailed him the link.

Never let it be said she wasn't a professional.

CHAPTER 14

S tart packing.

The email came at nine in the morning, a group message from Alpine Climbs verifying that the climb was green-lighted. The post-Christmas weather conditions looked favorable, and since the slopes wouldn't be crowded owing to the time of year, their expedition was a go.

"Woo hoo!" The speaker phone on Warren's desk burst with cheers from Rick and Dave. "You ready, boss?"

"I was ready before you were born, kid."

They laughed, the air filling with cheer and excited anticipation.

About damn time, too. They'd waited a long time for this, trained incredibly hard. Standing on the summit of the mountain would be the culmination of everything they'd worked for. Theo would be proud.

Warren stood from his desk, smothering a rush of emotion. He pulled on his coat and headed out to his car. Now he could finally tell the boys, Hailey, and Julia that the start of his retirement didn't mean he intended to sit in his office working on a model airplane. He'd start with the biggest physical challenge of his life.

He'd talk to them all privately after the Sugar Rush party tomorrow night. His retirement announcement would be official, and they'd all be together. The timing was perfect.

He drove downtown, which was jam-packed with cars and holiday crowds. He found a parking spot and walked to Ocean Avenue. Holiday lights twinkled from the lampposts lining the sidewalk, and the massive town Christmas tree presided at the end of the street. Storefronts displayed stuffed Santas, and the smells of roasted chestnuts and hot chocolate drifted from the vendors lined up along the street.

He didn't remember a Christmas he hadn't spent at the Indigo Bay Holiday Festival. It was a tradition almost as old as the town itself, and Sugar Rush had always been one of the main sponsors. In the few days before Christmas, families could shop late, visit the gingerbread houses and the arts and crafts fair, get pictures taken with Santa, and enjoy the Kid Zone.

He checked his texts, but found no response from Julia to his query about where they should meet.

Since Deck the Halls was in two days, this was also supposed to be Julia's "free" night when she could enjoy the festivities with the rest of the family. More than likely, she'd gotten caught up in one crisis or another.

He'd just have to find her and insist that she *delegate* whatever she was doing. He stopped at the Wild Child Bakery, which bustled with customers. Luke, Polly, and Mia were all working behind the counter, packaging pastries, coffee, and towering croquambouches for Christmas dessert.

"Hi, Warren." Polly waved, pushing a lock of hair away from her forehead. "We'll have all the desserts for the Sugar Rush party at the villa by six tomorrow night."

"Great, thanks." Warren took a Declair Luke passed to him. "Have you seen Julia?"

"No. Did you text her?"

Warren frowned. "She's not answering."

"Check Santa's Sleigh," Mia called from the other end of the counter. "She said something about needing to be there tonight."

Warren thanked her and headed out, polishing off the cream-filled Declair as he walked. He made his way to the towering Christmas tree and past the line of children snaking in front of it on their way to visit Santa. The elaborate sleigh, pulled by eight life-sized stuffed reindeer, was situated in a wonderland of miniature lighted trees, snowmen, and a huge gingerbread Santa's workshop. The man himself sat in the sleigh alongside a bag of toys, as children clambered onto his lap or the bench to express their wishes and get their pictures taken. Half-a-dozen elves corralled the children, manned the camera and tripod, and distributed photo packages.

Warren walked to the back of the sleigh near the city hall steps. He stopped, his heart jolting.

No way in...

Dressed in red-and-white striped tights, a green miniskirt dress with big peppermint-colored buttons, shiny black boots, green gloves, and a red-and-green elf hat was...fashion stylist Julia Bennett.

Warren's heart did a crazy somersault. He stopped at the fence and stared at her. She latched her hand around a little girl's and guided her toward the steps leading up to the sleigh. Though Julia was smiling, Warren could see the irritated tension simmering just beneath her surface.

He bit back a laugh of both amusement and affection. This was exactly the kind of task she hated, and yet...here she was. He waited until she'd guided the girl up to Santa's platform.

"Jules."

She startled, turning toward him on her way back to the camera. "What are you doing here?"

"Looking for you."

She frowned. "So you found me."

"Indeed I did. Well worth the search, I might add." His gaze slid admiringly over her form-fitting dress and shapely legs.

Her frown deepened, even as amusement flashed in her eyes. "One of the elves called in sick, so guess who had to take over?"

"Looks like you're doing a great job," he remarked. "When do you get off?"

"Not for another two hours, if not longer." She waved him away and turned back to the camera. "Go on without me. I promised all the children would get a chance to talk to Santa, which means this could take a while."

Warren stepped away from the fence. He'd spent the past thirteen years at the Holiday Festival with Julia. Tonight would be no different. He made a couple of phone calls, then met Tyler and Kate two blocks away at the Indigo Bay Theater. After the costume director hooked them both up with elf costumes—which made his son oddly happy—they returned to Santa's Sleigh.

"Julia, your relief crew has arrived." Warren opened the gate in the fence and ushered Tyler and Kate through.

Julia straightened from the computer, her hat askew and her skin flushed. "What?"

"We're here to take over." Tyler went around to where she stood, pausing to admire himself in the mirror.

"Warren said you haven't had a chance to do anything yet," Kate explained. "So we'll take over your final shift."

Julia opened her mouth—to protest, Warren knew. He maneuvered past his son and grabbed Julia's hand. "No arguing. We're going."

"But I should explain the procedure for…"

"Julia, we got this." Kate took her place behind the camera. "Have fun."

Warren managed to get Julia out of the fenced area, taking her coat from the stash piled behind the sleigh. He slipped it over her shoulders, belatedly regretting the fact that it covered her so thoroughly. Because Julia Bennett in an elf costume was about the hottest thing he'd seen in ages. He led her away from the crowds of children and parents.

"Warren, I really have to make sure the—"

"You listen to me." He grabbed the lapels of her coat and hauled her closer, lowering his head to look her in the eye. "You've done more than enough for this town. You've worked your ass off to organize Deck the Halls, and you've succeeded tenfold. This is your last free night of the festival, and it's time for you to enjoy it. We are going to eat roasted chestnuts, sing Christmas carols, ride the Jingle Bus, do last-minute shopping, and, if you're good, I'll let you sit on my lap at the end of the night. Understand?"

She opened her mouth, her eyes darkening with unmistakable heat. "Er…yes, sir."

"Good. Because you're so fucking hot in that little costume that I doubt I'll last beyond midnight."

"Hmm." A pink flush colored her cheeks, her eyelashes fluttering. "So what are you waiting for?"

Warren didn't think. He pulled her around the side of the city hall, past a row of art galleries and boutiques, and into one of the many isolated little courtyards tucked around town. Without preamble, he pushed her up against a stone wall and crushed his mouth down on hers. His head filled with the taste of candy canes and gingerbread, the sweet-spicy combination going straight to his blood.

He lifted his head for an instant, his eyes burning into hers. "Sugar? You?"

"Elves eat candy canes and gingerbread." She parted her lips, her breath puffing hotly against his mouth. "I was doing some method acting."

Whatever she was doing, he liked the result. A rumble of appreciation rolled through his chest as he slanted his mouth over hers again. She moaned, curling her fingers into the front of his coat, her head falling back against the wall. She fueled his lust hotter with each second, flames licking at his skin. He slid his hand around her nape, tilted her head to just the right angle so he could devour her.

Only when the noise of conversation drifted past on the sidewalk did he force himself to break away from her. Julia groaned, her hand still fisted in his coat and her eyes dark.

"I'm already wet," she whispered.

Warren clenched his jaw in a supreme effort not to hike up her little elf skirt and find out for himself just how wet she was.

"You can show me later," he said.

"I can show you n…"

Before he could give in to the temptation—much as he wanted Julia, he wasn't a hormone-driven teenager who couldn't see the repercussions of getting caught fucking in a public courtyard. Even worse if you were the president of Sugar Rush.

"Come on." He straightened his coat and took her hand. "I told you what we're going to do, and I intend to do it."

Though suppressed lust continued to heat his blood, he guided her back to the festival. They rejoined the crowds milling around Ocean Avenue and the Christmas tree. Warren bought bags of roasted chestnuts, which they ate while looking at all the window displays. They paused to watch kids playing in the Kid Zone, toured the Victorian open house, admired the light displays in the park, shopped at the crafts fair.

Through it all, they exchanged glances simmering with both heat and affection, and Warren realized the emotion filling him was happiness. Personal happiness, not just happiness related to his children or his work. He was happy for himself, being with the woman he loved, knowing he'd live the rest of his life without regrets.

Once they'd had their fill of Christmas cheer, they returned to Julia's house. She started to pass him, unfastening her little elf vest. He grabbed her arm to stop her. She met his gaze, her eyes widening at his expression.

"Leave it on," Warren ordered gruffly.

Julia laughed. Less than a minute later, they were in the bedroom and she was working the buckle on his belt. His dick, already primed after their courtyard kiss, sprang out of his trousers and into her warm hand.

"Jesus, Warren," she breathed, her eyes glazing over as she stared down at his cock. "Do you just walk around with a hard-on all the time?"

"When I think about you, yes. Why do you think I spend so much time behind a desk?"

He pushed off his trousers and boxers, then tumbled her onto the bed, his mouth on hers, his head filling with the taste and scent of her. Flames licked at his blood. He fumbled to get her tight stockings off and skimmed his hand up her smooth thigh. His fingers encountered the dampness of her pussy. Pleasure bolted through him. He slipped a finger into her, loving the way she writhed and twisted underneath him, the way she arched her hips as if begging him to penetrate her deeper.

He shifted them around so he was lying on his back. He fisted his cock, his nerves firing with heat.

"Ride me," he ordered.

Julia shot him a grin and tugged her miniskirt up to her hips. Still fully clad in her costume, minus the hat, she straddled his thighs and positioned herself over his shaft. Warren guided his cock into her slit, the heat in his blood rising to a boil as her tight pussy enclosed his shaft. She gasped, leaning forward to brace her hands on his chest, her cleavage spilling out of the scooped neckline of her blouse.

"I didn't know you had an elf fetish," she murmured, wincing a little as he pushed deeper inside her.

"Only thing I have is a Julia fetish. Ah, *fuck*, you feel so damned good…"

He thrust upward, jolting her body as he sank balls-deep into her. Julia closed her eyes and pulled in a breath. Sweat glistened on her throat.

"God, I feel you all the way up here." She pressed a hand to her belly and swiveled her hips, rubbing her clit against him.

Tempted as he was to fondle the little button of her arousal, he wanted to see her come by stimulating herself. He grasped her hips.

"Move," he ordered gruffly.

She obeyed, lifting her hips and bringing them down again in an increasingly fast rhythm. Her ass hit his thighs, her body bouncing as inarticulate moans and whimpers emerged from her throat.

Lust submerged them both. Heat crackled in the air. The world disappeared, leaving only the drive for release and the fucking gorgeous sight of Julia riding him, her blonde hair tousled and her elf skirt flouncing up and down with every stroke of her body around his.

When he couldn't take it any longer, he clenched his hands on her hips to stop her. "Turn around."

Her breath caught, her eyes sparking with excitement. She got on to her hands and knees, He moved behind her, his gaze roaming hungrily over the rounded curves of her ass. He flipped the skirt over her back and plunged into her from behind. Julia cried out, her body jerking forward as she fisted the bedcovers.

"Oh my God, Warren…"

He thrust deeper, her ass hitting his stomach with the wet, smacking sound of sex. She pushed back to meet his increasingly hard penetration, her moans adding to the pressure coiling through his entire body. She came with a cry, her pussy tightening around his shaft so intensely his own control snapped like a thread. He thrust inside her with a groan, pleasure exploding through every nerve.

"Oh, fuck." Julia collapsed on the bed, her chest heaving. "I think I need to keep this costume."

Warren eased off her, and she snuggled against his side in a sweet, warm bundle of Christmas smells and colors. He'd need to buy her a dozen more costumes. He wanted to see her dressed as a sexy pirate, a fairy, a witch…well, hell. He'd never ventured into costumed roleplay in the bedroom. That was about to change.

Julia lifted her head to press a warm, wet kiss against his mouth before clambering off the bed and going into the bathroom.

He hauled himself to his feet and went to clean up in the guest bathroom before going to the kitchen. He'd left his phone on the foyer table, and it buzzed with messages and reminders about the climb—the itinerary, the packing list, the flight schedule.

"Hungry?" Julia came out of the bedroom in her silk robe, her skin still flushed. "I can make waff…er, something."

Warren shook his head. She gave him a quizzical look, pausing as she started to pass him to the kitchen. "Are you okay?"

"Yeah." He set his phone down and dragged a hand through his hair. "There's just something I need to tell you. It's not bad," he added hastily when her eyes clouded. "It's a trip I've been planning for a long time. I just received word that it's actually a go."

"What kind of trip?"

"You remember we had that conversation about Amelie?" Warren asked.

"I know you didn't just bring up another woman right now."

He smiled faintly. "I told you she's just a friend. She works for a Swiss company that specializes in Alpine climbs. She's helping me organize a mountaineering expedition."

Julia blinked. "A *mountaineering* expedition?"

"You remember my friend Theo? He died about a year ago."

"Yes." Wariness darkened her expression. "He'd been planning a big road trip."

"His *finale*, as he called it." Old sorrow twisted through him. "One of his dreams had been to climb the Matterhorn, but he never made it. After he died, I couldn't stop thinking about him, about how he lost the chance to fulfill his last goal. So I decided I needed to complete the climb in his honor. I asked a few of our mutual friends, and we've been training for most of the year. That's part of the reason I've been going to Switzerland so often. I've been doing some smaller scale climbs, learning ice and glacier techniques, extra training."

Julia shook her head, disbelief diluting the blue of her eyes. "And you were planning to tell me this...when?"

"When we got the green-light, which we did this morning."

"What?" She stalked past him into the kitchen. "You should have told me weeks ago."

"We didn't know if we were going to go." He paused in the doorway and leaned his shoulder against the jamb. "The Swiss weather service had issued some warnings. Heavy snowfall and mild temperatures. We had to wait until we knew the conditions would allow us to climb. Often you don't know until a few days before."

"I can't believe it." Julia pressed her hands to her temples. "I mean, I knew you were stepping up your hikes and bouldering, but you're planning to climb the *Matterhorn*? One of the most difficult routes in the world?"

"That's why we've been training," Warren said. "A few preliminary climbs to acclimatize ourselves, then a final hike to the summit of the Matterhorn."

"When is this supposed to take place?"

"After Christmas."

Shock flashed in her eyes. "Warren, Christmas is on Sunday. Do the boys and Hailey know about this?"

"Adam has been helping me train. I was going to tell the others, but then with the pushback over retiring, I decided to wait. And given the weather situation, I didn't see the point of worrying everyone needlessly."

"Right. Might as well give us a *reason* to worry." Julia muttered something under her breath and pinched the bridge of her nose. "Is Adam going with you?"

"He wanted to. I won't let him. This is all for Theo. I don't want to put Adam at risk."

"But you'll put yourself at risk? *That's* okay with you?"

"Julia." He steeled himself against her distress. Part of the reason he hadn't wanted to tell her, of all people, was that he knew she'd be upset and he couldn't let that stop him. "I have to do this."

"A safari or even a rock climb aren't enough for you?" she asked. "Why a mountain? Because it's there?"

"No." He closed the distance between them in a few strides. "Because *I'm here*. And because I've spent years doing the right thing, doing what was expected of me. I'd do it all over again a thousand times because I couldn't have asked for a better life, but if Theo's death reminded me of anything it's that time is *short*. It feels like yesterday that Luke was an infant, that Evan was having his first surgery, that Adam wanted to be an astronaut, that the twins were playing tricks on their teachers, that Hailey won first prize in the science fair. It feels like yesterday that a twenty-one-year-old girl kissed me and then disappeared."

A hot flush colored her cheeks. She looked away from him.

"Julia." He put his hands on either side of her head, turning her back to face him, hating the dark gleam in her eyes. "Do you want to know why I love climbing? Because it's so damned hard. It takes everything I have—every ounce of concentration, strength, endurance. It hurts. It can be terrifying. It's dangerous. I think I'll never make it. Then I do. I'm at the top. The view is sweeping out from all sides, the air is so clean and clear I can taste it, and suddenly I'm not hurting anymore. Everything is so *good*. I did what I set out to do. I feel like I could climb every mountain in the world."

Her lips tightened. "And when you're up there drinking in the view and feeling invincible, do you think about the people at the bottom of the mountain who are worrying about you and hoping you come back alive? Oh, wait a second. No, you don't, do you? Because otherwise you'd have told us you were training to climb the fucking *Matterhorn*."

She tore herself away from him and stalked to the other side of the kitchen. Warren took a breath, hating the sight of her bent head, her hair falling forward to conceal her profile, the trembles rippling through her.

"I hate it every time Adam goes off on one of his *adventure* tours," she confessed, wrapping her arms around her midriff. "But I don't tell him that because he's thirty-one years old and I don't want him to stop doing what he loves because of me. I don't want that for you either. But Jesus Christ, Warren…really? People die every year trying to reach the summit of a mountain. *Young* people. And you want to do it so you can feel like a damned superhero? No. If you're having a mid-life crisis, go buy a fucking Ferrari, but don't go running off to climb a mountain just to prove you're all-powerful. Because I have news for you. You don't have to prove it. You just *are*."

His throat tightened. "I love you."

She didn't say it back. She turned away and shook her head.

He approached her from behind and wrapped his arms around her. Her body was tense, her spine stiff. He closed his arms harder around her, pressed his face to her sweet-smelling hair. A long sigh shuddered through her.

"Damn you, Warren Stone."

"I love you. I have to do this."

Julia gave a hoarse laugh. Her body relaxed back against his, her hand curling around his forearm.

"I know," she murmured. "Oddly enough, your determination

to finish what you start is one of the things I…admire most about you."

Warren tightened his hold on her even more. "Say it."

Julia turned in his arms, her eyes clouded. "I wish I could."

"Why can't you?"

"Because of Becca." She swallowed and averted her gaze. "I know it's stupid, but I feel like those words belong to her. How many times in your life did she say them to you? How many times did you hear them?"

"Countless. And is every one of those times part of my heart? Yes." He put his hand under her chin and lifted her face to look at him. "But those words don't belong to any one person. Every time someone says them to someone else, it's private. Personal. Exclusive. It's as if no one has ever said them before in the history of time. Because love is different for everyone."

She gave him a smile tinged with sadness and eased out of his arms.

"One day," she murmured.

One day. They both knew that day might never come. It might be too late.

"Warren! Oh my god, Warren!"

Julia's scream flooded him with panic. He leapt up from the desk chair in Julia's bedroom and ran out so fast he banged his leg against the corner of a table. Ignoring the twinge, he raced to the kitchen, his heart hammering.

"Julia! What happened? Where…are you?"

He skidded to a halt, his voice fading. She was sitting at the kitchen counter in one of his wrinkled shirts, her legs bare, her hair a mess and a huge, triumphant smile on her face.

"Look." She held up a Rubik's Cube.

He took a breath and grasped the doorjamb. "Uh…what?"

"I *solved* it!" She twirled the cube around to show him each side covered with the same color—white, yellow, orange, green, red, and blue. "I solved the Rubik's Cube. By *myself*. I didn't even look up any solution techniques or anything. I just did it!"

She jumped off the stool and hurried around to throw herself into his arms. He caught her, his panic replaced with pleasure over her happiness—though he realized this was an accomplishment, he still didn't get what the big deal was.

"Congratulations," he said, taking advantage of her closeness to kiss her. "Even though your scream just took two years off my life."

"Sorry." She wiggled away from him and opened her handbag, which was resting on the counter. "I've just been working on it so hard. I really had no idea it was so complicated."

She took out her crumpled *Before Fifty* list and unfolded it. "Now I get to check it off my list, which means I have…"

She paused and counted. "Thirty-two items left. But the vodka gummy bears will be ready tomorrow, so that means thirty-one."

She shot him a smile and made a checkmark on the list. She put the list back in her purse. Warren grinned.

Julia lifted an eyebrow. "What's so funny?"

"Nothing. You're amazing. C'mere."

She approached him again, a flush rising to her cheeks. He slid his hands around her waist and pulled her to him for another kiss.

"I'm just doing some of the stuff in my spare time," Julia said hastily, resting her hands on his chest. "I mean, I'm not taking the list seriously or anything."

"Of course not."

"It's just a stupid list," she continued. "I mean, I was nineteen. What nineteen-year-old girl thinks making vodka gummy bears is a rational goal in…well, okay, maybe I get that. But I'm just doing it because I want to finish what I started. Not because I'm enjoying it or anything."

"I know." He tugged a lock of her hair. "You might need a partner for some of the stuff. Salsa dancing. Having sex in the rain."

Her eyebrow rose. "You read my list."

"Read it? Hell, I memorized it. I think we should redo some of them too, like the skinny dipping."

"Hmm. I can get behind that. Or in it, as the case may be." She wound her arms around his neck as their lips met in another kiss.

Heat simmered in his chest. He slid his hands down to cup her ass and backed her toward the counter. As soon as she was seated, he pushed himself between her legs and ran his hands up her smooth thighs. She murmured her pleasure and wiggled closer. He eased his tongue into her mouth and moved his hand up higher...higher...

Helen Reddy's "I Am Woman" burst from Julia's phone. With a groan, she pulled away from him, her breath puffing against his lips.

"Sorry," she murmured. "But that's a two o'clock phone appointment I have to take. And it is a workday."

"We're playing hooky, remember?" He stroked his hand up between her legs and found what he'd suspected—she wasn't wearing panties.

Julia squirmed at his touch and reached for her phone. "This call was on my schedule. I promise, it won't take long. It's Vincent Peckerhead from Evermore calling to tell me I'm older than Cleopatra."

Warren frowned, his hackles rising. She winked and kissed his chin before accepting the call.

"Vincent? Julia Bennett."

She pushed Warren away and jumped off the counter, the phone to her ear. He contented himself with looking at her— such a *woman* with her long-legged stride, her perfect-sized breasts jiggling under his white shirt, her smooth hair swishing back and forth.

But before he'd loved everything physical about her, he'd loved her outright grit, the strength that ran like steel through her spine. And after he'd loved her grit, he'd loved the soft side of her that he—and only he—had ever seen, the woman who curled against his side, who turned to him when she cried, who let him help her fight her pain.

He had no idea what force in the universe had brought her to him and kept her there, but he was forever grateful for it.

Julia set her phone down, a sudden stillness descending over her.

"Everything okay?" Warren asked.

She turned to face him, surprise and a touch of disbelief registering in her eyes. "That was Vincent Peck."

"You told me." He frowned. "Did he insult you again? I'll deal with him myself if he did."

"No." She waved her hand dismissively. "I emailed him my new portfolio of clothing designs for older women. Turns out he and his team are so impressed that they want to fly me out to New York for a meeting."

Warren's response to that news was mixed. Much as he wanted her success, he didn't like the way Peck had treated her. "What did you tell him?"

"Well, I said yes." She spread her hands out, a sudden laugh breaking from her. "He was an asshole, but Evermore owns the biggest luxury department store chain in the country. *And* they own Kingsley Bishop on Fifth Avenue, which is an iconic store. If Kingsley Bishop sold my clothing line…every designer and stylist in New York would know about it. It would launch my brand into a whole other stratosphere."

"Then you're doing the right thing."

"It's just a preliminary meeting, but maybe it's a step in the right direction. Funny how I thought I was done not too long ago, and now I might have another shot."

"When are you going?"

"He wants to know if I can come right after Christmas. He has some marketing ideas he wants to discuss for the new year."

"But the line is yours, not his."

"If he wants to partner with me, I'm willing to listen to what he has to say." Julia picked up her phone and studied the screen. "I haven't come up with a name yet. I used Appear because that line was geared toward younger women just starting out, but I can't flip the name the way I flipped the demographic. Disappear?" She shook her head with a grimace. "Unfortunately, adjectives about *decline* are not the vision I want to convey. Neither are synonyms for older women. Spinster. Old Maid. Crone. Witch."

She put her phone down with a huff of annoyance. "Why is society so shitty to older women? We should be worshipped."

"I couldn't agree more." He would have been more than happy to worship Julia Bennett in multiple ways. "What about a regal term like *countess*?"

"I like regal, as long as it doesn't sound too upscale. These clothes should appeal to women who want to feel confident and sexy, even when they're going to the grocery store or taking care of their grandchildren. Those are the women who have been ruling the world, even if the world has yet to acknowledge it. The queen bees. I..."

She stopped, looking up at him in astonishment. "Queen Bee."

He nodded. "That's perfect."

Julia laughed, the sound warming him to his bones. "I love it. I need to add that to my portfolio. I'll be right back."

She hurried out of the kitchen. Warren took a sip of coffee and looked out at the backyard, the manicured grass and rows of hedges. A low ringing started in his ears the second before dizziness struck him.

He put his hand on the counter and gritted his teeth, fighting the sense that he was about to fall. When it finally passed, he realized he was sweating. He wiped his forehead and took a breath, hating the sense that he wasn't in control of his own body. Hell, his own *mind*.

He'd always been in control. He wouldn't let that change now, especially not when he had everything he both wanted and needed to start the rest of his life.

CHAPTER 15

"Holly Rocks, you're next," Julia called, her pointed-toe Manolos clicking as she descended the stage steps.

Tomorrow night was Christmas Eve. The final Deck the Halls show was scheduled to start at six p.m., and tonight's dress rehearsal was onsite at the outdoor town stage.

Hundreds of seats had been arranged in a semi-circle around the stage. Julia sat in the front row as three women dressed as gift-wrapped presents with wreaths of holly in their hair came out with guitars. Their rendition of "Santa Baby" was followed by a comedy skit *("Where do snowmen keep their money? In a snow bank!")*, a ballet dancer, and a group of bell ringers.

Julia found herself actually enjoying the acts—not only because the performance was going smoothly but because they were finally reaching the culmination of all their hard work.

Metaphorically, organizing Deck the Halls had been a bit like climbing a mountain. Not exactly the Matterhorn, but still…

She shook her head. Warren had been right. Time was short, and dwelling on the past or overthinking ones choices was a waste of that precious time.

Of course, she didn't know what would happen when they

told the boys and Hailey, but she and Warren had agreed to keep their new relationship to themselves at least until after Christmas. Maybe even until his climb was over.

Not that she wanted to think too much about that either. Clearly he was determined to go and finish what he'd started—a philosophy Julia had developed a whole new appreciation for in recent days. And she would never try and convince him to not go simply because she was scared for him. He would never try and stop her from doing what she wanted to do.

Yet another mature lesson she'd learned. Life was about both compromise and learning when to STFU and just deal with it.

When all the Deck the Halls acts had finished, they came out one by one for their individual bows and then a big group bow.

Julia glanced at her watch, pleased that the entire show had ended on time. Aside from one final light and audio check, they were ready to go.

"Thank you all," she said into the wireless mic Marco handed her. "You've worked so hard, and you should all be proud of what you've done. We'll see you tomorrow night for the final performance. Call time is four-thirty."

As the performers began dispersing, she picked up the bag loaded with the wrapped gifts for Gail's soon-to-arrive granddaughter and went backstage. The four Jingle Belles stood in the wings, assessing their rehearsal performance. They all wore their custom-made gowns, which had generated a number of compliments from their fellow performers.

"Julia, we're going out for drinks as soon as we change," Connie said. "Can you join us?"

"I'm sorry, I have to attend the Sugar Rush holiday party tonight." Julia glanced at her watch, disappointed at having to decline a second invitation.

"What time does it start?" Sharon asked. "We want to get to Asante by five. Connie is going to her daughter's piano recital tonight, so we're not going to stay long."

Julia calculated her timing. Since Warren had…dismissed her from organizing Sugar Rush's party, she didn't have to be there early to set up and ensure everything was in place. For the first time in ten years, she could actually arrive at the party when it started. Heck, she could even be fashionably late.

"I'd be happy to join you," she said. "If I leave by six-thirty, I'll have time to go home and get ready before the party."

"Great." Connie smiled. "We'll go get changed right now."

Julia handed Gail the bag of gifts. "These are a few things I picked up for your granddaughter."

"Oh, Julia, you didn't have to do that." Gail's eyes widened as she peeked into the bag at the elaborately wrapped gifts. "How incredibly thoughtful of you."

"I was happy to do it." Not wanting any gushy thanks, Julia started back to the seats. "I'll meet you out front, and we can walk to Asante."

Half an hour later, the Jingle Belles were dressed in their regular clothes, they'd procured a table at the upscale bar, and were ordering cocktails.

"I'm getting us tickets for a January tour of Filoli, the estate up in Woodside," Beverly told Julia. "Have you been there?"

"Once or twice." Julia didn't find it necessary or desirable to tell them she'd attended many private events and organized several photo shoots at the historic mansion set in an eighteen-acre garden. "It's lovely."

"Would you like to go with us?" Gail asked. "We're hoping to reserve a table for their afternoon tea, but if we can't, we'll pack a picnic lunch. Maybe a Saturday toward the end of January. Are you interested?"

If Gail had asked her a month ago, would Julia have even considered it? For so long, her socializing had consisted of charity dinners and events for the Rebecca Stone Foundation or high-society galas. Aside from occasional dating, she'd either spent her spare time with the Stones or used it to catch up on work. She certainly didn't get together with a group of girl-friends for drinks or to picnic at a historic mansion.

"I'd like that," she finally said. "Thanks for asking me."

The other ladies inputted Julia's contact info into their phones so they could keep her informed. The conversation turned to Beverly's son's new girlfriend, Sharon's difficulties in hiring a new children's librarian, and Gail's boot camp clients. Julia found herself enjoying the conversation. She'd never be "one of the girls," but she decidedly liked the idea of being "one of the women." Of having friends.

Friends. It wasn't a word she used often or lightly. While she'd had numerous close acquaintances, and even friends, when she was younger, the cutthroat fashion industry had made her wary of people who used friendship as a way to get what they wanted. Her ice-queen armor had successfully fended off anyone who might have had ideas about getting close to her.

But the Jingle Belles didn't care who she was or what she could do for them.

Yes, they'd enjoyed the glamour of custom-made gowns and cosmetics, but they'd never asked her for anything. Certainly they'd never try to finagle their way into a career boost or free clothes and accessories. They'd never even asked her opinion on their wardrobes. And though they knew of her connection to Sugar Rush, they hadn't hit her up for donations or fund-raiser requests like so many other people did.

The Jingle Belles seemed to like her just because...they liked her.

"I've heard they have Christmas peppermint martinis here." She stood and reached for her handbag. "I'll get us a round."

She went to the bar for the martinis and distributed them to the other women. She stayed for a few more minutes, then apologetically explained that she had to leave for the Sugar Rush party. After telling the Belles that she'd see them on Christmas Eve, she headed back to her car.

She texted Hailey that she was on her way and drove to Warren's house, where she'd agreed to help her niece get ready before returning to her studio to dress. She pulled into the driveway, mildly surprised to see only Hailey's car parked by the garage. Warren must have already left for the party.

She knocked and went inside when there was no response. The house was oddly still and silent, the Christmas tree and decorations glittering in the dim light.

"Hailey?"

No response.

Alarm flickered inside Julia. She walked upstairs to her niece's old bedroom, where Hailey still stayed when she came to visit.

"Hailey?"

She pushed open the door. The light was on, and Hailey's dress lay on the bed but there was no sign of the girl. She hurried back downstairs and checked the kitchen. Nothing. As she started through the great room, a light shining in Warren's office caught her eye. She swiveled on her heel and walked down the corridor.

The door was partly open. She knocked and pushed it the rest of the way.

"Hailey?"

Her niece sat at the long table where Warren worked on his models, the work light illuminating her face. The parts of an airplane were strewn on the table, and she was turning the propeller around and around.

A weight whose source she could not place settled over Julia's heart. She stepped into the room.

"Hailey."

The girl looked up, her expression shadowed. Julia approached with caution, sensing that whatever was the matter had something to do with her.

"Are you all..." Dread knotted her stomach.

Oh no.

A creased piece of paper rested on the table beside Hailey. The large, looping cursive burned through Julia like a brand, searing her insides.

"Oh, Hailey. I'm so sorry."

"This was the letter." Hailey nudged the paper with her elbow.

"I...I made a terrible mistake." She stopped in front of the table, curling her fingers into her palms in an attempt not to reach for her niece. "I was struggling with the end of a short-lived marriage, and I'd had too much to drink...I mean, that's not an excuse and I behaved badly, but I want you to know your father did nothing wrong. Ever. He was trying to help me. It was totally my fault."

Hailey focused on the propeller. Her eyes were dark, even in the brightness of the work light.

"This is the letter they were fighting about," she said.

The world seemed to shift under Julia's feet. "What?"

"I once heard Mom and Dad fighting," Hailey said, her voice quiet. "I noticed it...I *remembered* it...because they never fought. They argued, but they never had big explosive fights. But once when I was maybe ten or something, I heard Mom yelling. Loud enough that I could hear her from upstairs. I got worried so I came down to see what was going on. The office door was partly open, so I peeked inside. They were over there..." she gestured to Warren's desk, "...and she was holding a piece of paper and shouting about *this letter* and *why didn't you tell me*. And Dad kept saying that it didn't matter, it was nothing, he didn't want it to ruin anything.

"Of course I had no idea what they were talking about. Mom dropped the letter back onto the desk and said, *'That's just the kind of thing she would do.'* Then she went to Dad and he took her in his arms. And they stayed like that."

Julia couldn't move. Everything inside her was cold, like she'd been turned to ice.

"I went back to my room," Hailey continued. "Later that

evening, everything seemed normal again. Neither one of them talked about *the letter*. I forgot about it until…"

She dropped the propeller, her shoulders straightening. "I needed scissors to cut the tags off my dress, so I came to get some from Dad's desk. The letter was sitting by his computer. I didn't intend to read it, but it caught my eye because it looked old and I didn't recognize the handwriting…so I read it and suddenly remembered that argument. This was the letter. You wrote it to Dad, and Mom found it."

Julia pressed her hands to her hot cheeks. Her stomach roiled with nausea as she tried to process the stark fact that Rebecca *had known* what she'd done. Now Hailey knew.

"Hailey, I'm so…so sorry." Her voice cracked. "I didn't know if your mother knew what I'd done. I assumed your father had told her, but…all I wanted to do was apologize. I was a foolish young girl who behaved badly, and I'm sorry. I was sorry then, and I'm sorry now."

"I just can't believe you did that." Hailey pushed the letter away and stood, anger flashing in her eyes. "He was married. To your *sister*. And yeah, I get that you were upset and drunk and that people do stupid things, but…*really*? And it's the one thing I heard them fight about, like *you* were this…this thorn between them."

"I don't…" A lump stuck in Julia's throat. "I don't know what to do to make this right for you. Whatever it is, I'll do it. I'll do anything."

"I need some time." Hailey shook her head and walked toward the door. "I'll get ready for the party by myself."

"I love you." Julia turned, her heart cracking in half at the thought that a thirty-year-old mistake could drive her niece away. "I love you so much. Not because I'm trying to make up for what I did but because I just do."

Hailey hesitated at the door, turning for half a second. Julia's heart surged with hope, but then Hailey turned away and went upstairs.

Julia stood in the office for a long moment, her heart pounding and her insides still frozen. She picked up the letter and tore it into little pieces, dropping them into the trash. She walked back out to her car. Pain stabbed her behind the eyes.

CHAPTER 16

W*here was she?*
Warren checked his phone for the hundredth time. Nothing except for a dangerously low battery. He shoved the phone back into his pocket, attempting to keep his expression neutral as he made his way through the crowd of Sugar Rush employees all decked out in their holiday finest. The party had been well underway for the past two hours, and he'd spent most of it attempting to be politely social while also trying to figure out where the hell Julia was.

And why she wasn't answering his calls and texts again.

He caught sight of Hailey. His unease intensified. His daughter had arrived an hour ago with Carson, but she'd been subdued and quiet, only shaking her head when he'd asked if she'd seen Julia.

He crossed the foyer to the courtyard of the Spanish-style villa. Colorful lights twinkled around the exterior trees, and music from the live band drifted through the window. People talked, laughed, danced, and mingled, moving from the open bar to the buffet tables. Mia Donovan had done an excellent job with the party planning, incorporating an "around the world" theme that included roaming mimes and magicians.

Warren scanned the crowd yet again. Though Julia had been upset that he'd taken the party away from her, she wouldn't boycott the event out of spite. Especially not when he was about to announce his retirement to the whole company.

Would she?

He hadn't even realized until now that he'd simply expected she'd be there. At his side, like she always was. He didn't want to stand on the stage without her, much less tell his incredibly loyal and devoted employees that he was leaving. He *couldn't* do it without her.

Had he taken her for granted all these years? He'd never asked her for anything—not to stay in Indigo Bay, to help raise his children, to be there through thick and thin. But damned if he hadn't come to rely on her more than he'd ever relied on anyone.

Thirteen years ago, he'd been sitting beside Hailey's bed in the hospital, wrecked by the sight of his beautiful daughter with her head wrapped in a bandage and an oxygen mask covering her face.

Something had made him look up. Julia had been standing in the doorway, her eyes haunted, her face pale, her hair limp. She'd been wearing an old T-shirt and sweatpants, and for an instant all he could do was stare at her and wonder if he was seeing things. Last he remembered Julia Bennett was a gypsy girl who wore flowered dresses and sandals.

"Hello, Warren."

She'd stepped into the room and walked around the bed to his and Hailey's side.

And she'd never left. For thirteen years, *she'd never left.*

Warren swiped the screen on his phone again. No message. Had something happened? She'd had the Deck the Halls dress rehearsal this afternoon, but she'd said there was plenty of time between the two events.

He started back to the dining hall. Mia and Polly crossed the foyer in front of him, both of them sparkly visions in red and green gowns.

"Hi, Warren." Polly stopped and smiled. "What are you doing out here instead of cutting a rug on the dance floor?"

"I'm looking for Julia. Have you seen her?"

"No, but she said she'd be here." Polly glanced back at the courtyard. "Do you want me to ask Luke?"

"I already did. If you see her, please tell her I'm looking for her."

"Sure."

He strode into the dining hall, still scanning the crowd. Evan approached from one of the tables near the window.

"You ready, Dad?" he asked. "Luke thought you'd make your speech half an hour ago."

Warren's chest was tight, both because of Julia's absence and because he suddenly couldn't stand the thought of telling everyone he was walking away from the company. He'd thought it was what he'd wanted, but now that he had to make it official…

"Give me fifteen minutes," he told his son.

He needed to talk to Julia. Needed *her*.

He crossed the foyer and returned to the crowded courtyard. He made his way through the crowd, pausing to be polite to the guests who stopped to wish him happy holidays and thank him for hosting the party.

He turned just as the courtyard doors opened. His heart slammed against his chest as Julia stepped out onto the tiled terrace. Resplendent in a dark blue crepe gown that hugged her figure and showed off the elegant lines of her shoulders, she looked like a sculpture come to living, breathing life.

Several people paused in mid-conversation to look her way. He wasn't surprised. It was like she'd stilled the air with her presence alone.

He started forward, then stopped. Her ice queen shield was in place, shimmering around her like a force field.

"Julia."

Her eyes grazed his.

Something was wrong.

He walked up the terrace steps, not taking his eyes from hers. Her lovely features were a mask of perfection—red lips, black lashes, shaded eyes. He almost felt the cold radiating from her.

You're beautiful.

That was what he meant to say. Instead, his frustration throughout the evening, his unsettling need for her, rose to the surface.

"Where were you?" he asked instead.

"Busy. I can't be at your beck and call, much as you'd like me to be."

Irritation prickled his neck. A woman standing near the railing glanced in their direction.

"You couldn't answer my calls?" he asked.

"I had a commitment."

"You had a commitment to be here too," he retorted.

"Right, before you fucking *fired me*." Her voice rose, tense and strained.

More people glanced in their direction. His fists clenched. He forced himself to lower his voice.

"What the hell is going on?" he hissed.

Julia stepped closer to him, tension evident in every line of her body. "I can't believe you kept that from me."

Wariness twisted through him. He'd thought she'd come to terms with his Matterhorn climb. She didn't like it, but she wouldn't try and stop him.

"I explained why I didn't tell you. We didn't know if we'd be able to go."

Julia blinked. "Go where?"

Warren frowned. Unease pushed at his chest. What the hell were they talking about?

"Dad, we're ready for you." Luke came onto the terrace, followed by Evan. "Carson is asking everyone to come back into the dining hall."

Warren didn't respond. His sons looked from him to Julia and back again, clearly sensing the tension.

Julia's mouth compressed. She slanted her gaze to her nephews. A frost descended over her expression, silencing whatever she was about to say. "I need a drink."

Warren stepped closer to her. Beneath her makeup, lines of stress bracketed her mouth and pain tightened her jaw.

"You're getting a migraine," he said. "You shouldn't have alcohol."

Julia's eyes hardened into cobalt. "Don't you tell me what I should or shouldn't do."

She started to sweep past him, her spine stiff.

He grabbed her arm to stop her. She turned, her gaze colliding with his. Suddenly he knew everything was about to change.

The ache intensified behind Julia's eyes, the sharp crystalline aura poking at the edges of her vision. Carson's voice sounded from a distance away. The guests in the courtyard began rising from their seats and walking to the steps. She registered a blur of movement, voices, but only Warren was clear and in focus.

Why didn't you tell me? Why didn't you tell her?

"What?" The single word was laced with urgency, his grip tightening on her arm.

"Rebecca." Her sister's name escaped on a breath. "You didn't tell her."

A muscle ticked in his jaw. "Should I have?"

"I don't...I don't know."

What would he have said? *Julia was drunk and she kissed me and that was it?*

But that *was* it. She'd been in the wrong, not him, no matter what he thought he'd felt.

For God's sake. Thirty years ago, and she was being punished all over again.

"I can't do this anymore." The words pricked her like needles.

Warren's expression darkened.

"Everyone back inside, please." Luke's voice, a sharp order.

Her nephews blurred in front of Julia's eyes. Too many people were standing around them, watching and listening. They knew Warren Stone as the stoic authoritarian, the president who kept his cool in all circumstances, the man who rarely showed emotion. She had to...

Warren hadn't taken his eyes off her, rooting her to the spot. She was trapped, the pressure squeezing her head from every side, her breath choking her throat.

"Why didn't you tell her?" she whispered.

"I wanted to protect her. I wanted to protect you."

"Why me?"

"Because you were my wife's little sister, and she was worried about you."

"And why didn't you tell me she *knew*? That she'd found the letter?"

Something shattered in the air between them, like a pane of glass. Warren flinched—a barely visible movement that no one except Julia might have noticed. Her heart closed down. Everything she'd done to try and amend for her mistakes suddenly seemed meaningless, as if her whole life had been defined by one ill-conceived choice.

"What she must have thought of me when she found the letter..." Julia shook her head. She heard the words in her sister's voice—*just the kind of thing she would do.* "She never stopped thinking I was just a useless little hippie girl, did she?"

"She *didn't* think that," Warren argued. "She knew what a success you'd become. She always knew."

"I never wanted to come between you and her." The ache intensified, pounding against her head, clawing at her eyes. "Never."

"You didn't. No one could have." Frustration and deep pain etched his features. "I loved Rebecca. I loved everything she was —my wife, the mother of our children, my best friend, *your sister.* I thought my life was over when she died. There couldn't be anyone else, I couldn't love anyone else. She'd taken it all with her when she died.

"But *you...*" He pulled her inexorably closer, his gaze holding hers like a magnet. "You saved me. After the accident, I didn't know how I'd ever be there for the boys again. Then you walked into Hailey's hospital room and reminded me I had seven reasons to keep living. You gave me an eighth reason. Like you were a light showing me the way out of the dark. You proved that love doesn't stop when someone leaves you. I'll always love her. And here, now, in this life, I love you."

His mouth descended on hers like an eagle capturing prey— swift, hard, possessive. Shock ricocheted through her in the instant before her body fell against his. Fragmented thoughts broke in her mind—he shouldn't be doing this, not here, a crowd had gathered, she didn't know how many people were standing on the steps, how much they had seen, what they were thinking—

But his *kiss*, my god, his kiss—a hymn to soothe her soul, a potion to ease her pain, a force to steady the ground beneath her feet. She fisted her hands into his jacket, surrendering to the sheer power of him, the unbreakable knowledge that no matter what life threw at them, he would *always* be there. Like the rocky cliffs battered incessantly by the sea, worn to a polish but enduring, invulnerable. *Eternal.*

He spread his hand over the back of her head in the way she loved—a cradle, like she was meant to be cherished—and deepened the kiss. She let him in, drank in the taste and feel of him, the here and now rather than the long-gone past. The solid strength of his body pressed against hers, his arm a band of steel wrapping around her lower back. She never wanted to leave the circle of strength and certainty in which he'd enclosed her.

Tears stung her eyes. She'd had a first love once upon a time, one she'd thought would last forever. She would never deny that her nineteen-year-old heart had truly loved the guitar-playing, rakish boy with whom she'd shared so many youthful experiences.

But *this*? This was time stopping, the air stilling, the world coming to a slow halt. This was infinity and a second wrapped into one. She spread her hands over Warren's chest. His heart beat forcefully against her palm, radiating warmth through her arm as if sending a direct signal to her soul. She never wanted this kiss to end. Everything inside her melted.

Then an unfamiliar voice broke through her consciousness, a man asking, "Is this part of a show?"

Warren's grip on her tightened. He'd heard the same voice. He lifted his mouth from hers, his darkened eyes catching hers briefly before shifting to the terrace steps. Guests lingered, caught by the spectacle that had lasted no more than five minutes. Julia's heart raced. Alarm coursed through her veins.

Warren released her slowly. He stepped in front of her, shielding her behind his back. Voices rose again. Julia tried to breathe. Pain knifed between her eyes.

Warren was speaking, telling everyone to go back inside. Her nephews' voices rose around them. She had to get herself together, to try and mitigate whatever damage had just been done.

She was in control. Stepping out from behind Warren's back, she forced herself to cross the terrace. The guests were moving slowly back into the foyer, their expressions ranging from shock to confusion and even amusement.

She caught snippets of conversation floating on the air like leaves. *I can't believe it. I had no idea they had a thing going on. Did you know? I'm surprised she didn't move in on him sooner.*

Nausea roiled in the pit of her belly.

"The show is over, everyone," she called. "You can consider that a new form of performance art."

A few laughs rippled over the crowd. Evan and Adam stood among the others, both of them businesslike and firm as they corralled guests inside. Luke strode up the steps toward her, his eyes dark with concern.

"Aunt Julia, are you all right?"

"Of course. I…"

Her voice cracked. Just past his shoulder, Hailey stood on the lowest step, her gaze on Julia and her lovely face devoid of expression. Empty.

A black pit opened in Julia's heart. Sudden zigzag flashes splintered her vision.

Warren caught her the instant before she fell.

CHAPTER 17

P ain and Warren's arms were the only real things in the
world. She was aware of him barking orders at his sons,
then lowering her into the passenger seat of his car.

He got into the driver's seat and dug through her bag for a
bottle of pain meds. Though they both knew it was too late for
the meds to be effective, Julia accepted the two pills he held out
to her. He cracked open a bottle of water, handing it to her before
he started the car.

Blissful silence followed. He didn't speak, knowing noise
exacerbated her headaches. He drove to her house and helped her
into the bedroom. Julia barely managed to kick off her shoes
before falling onto the bed.

Her nausea worsened, pitching in her stomach like a stormy
sea. The headache had won, killing off any relieving effects the
medication might have had. Excruciating pain stabbed both her
eyes, radiating into her neck. She pressed her face into the pillow
and tried to breathe past the sobs choking her throat.

"Julia."

His voice washed over her. She gripped the pillow, tried to
speak, both desperately relieved that he was here and wishing

he'd go away. The bed shifted with his weight, and then his hands settled on her hair, his fingers resting against her temples.

"Do you have any other meds?" He spoke quietly.

She managed to shake her head. The stroke of his fingers on her temples didn't ease the pain, but the rhythmic movement soothed her. He moved his hands down to her neck, finding the pulse points at the base. He applied a steady, hard pressure, even when she moaned in protest.

Part of her welcomed the different kind of pain; it might provide even a slight relief. Two years ago, when her headaches had worsened with the onset of menopause, Warren had researched alternative therapies and taken classes on acupressure and massage in the hopes of being able to help her.

Tears leaked from the corners of her eyes. Even through the black cloud of her headache, she couldn't bear the thought that their public debacle might have ruined everything. That they could never go back to the way things were. Everyone knew. Hailey's expression burned Julia like a hot iron.

Warren dug harder into the points of her neck, then moved to her shoulders. He pushed and kneaded her strained muscles hard enough to hurt, though she continued to bear the pain in the hopes that it would loosen the grip of the headache.

"I'm taking your clothes off." His voice spilled into her, his lips close to her ear. "Try not to move."

He worked the zipper of her dress and slipped it off her shoulders. With a few quick, efficient movements, he removed her bra and panties, then pulled a cotton blanket over her. The relief from the constriction of her clothes made Julia curl into a ball like a cat. She pressed her hand to her head.

He massaged her spine, the warmth of his hands easing the dull, icy throb. She gave up, stopped thinking, let him take over. He threaded his fingers into her hair, rubbed her scalp with slow, deliberate strokes, then stroked her temples again, her cheekbones, her jaw. The certainty and strength of his touch alleviated the headache's sharp edge, but the pain was relentless, stabbing her eyes, her forehead, clawing through her whole body.

He moved away from her. An inarticulate cry spilled from her throat. The shower started. He returned to lift her into his arms, carrying her into the shower. Fully clothed, he got under the spray with her and sat on the ledge. Cradling her against him, he directed the shower spray to the back of her head and neck. The full force of the hot water pounded against her muscles and tendons, loosening some of the awful tension.

She huddled against him, taking the strength he gave her. She lost track of how long they sat there, but eventually the water cooled. Warren lifted her again, dried her with a towel, and settled her back into bed. He tucked the blanket around her and rested a hand on her head.

"Try to sleep."

He started to take his hand away. Panic shot through her. She managed to grab his wrist.

"Don't go."

"I'm not going anywhere. I'll be right back."

A thousand painful years seemed to pass before he was climbing under the blanket behind her. He pulled her back against his bare chest, wrapping both arms around her as if he were protecting her from the onslaught.

Relief unfurled through Julia like ribbons. Her headache still had control, stifling her into immobility, but Warren was stronger than the pain. His warm, powerful presence calmed her fear, soothed her shattered thoughts, and finally sent her into the blissful oblivion of sleep.

Gray sunlight shone through the blinds. Julia blinked, wary of pulling herself into consciousness lest the pain was lurking and waiting again to attack.

But no. Aside from a slight lingering throb, the headache had retreated—conquered by time, her own defenses, and Warren's forceful intervention. She shifted cautiously. Her body was sore, but the after-effects were a relief after the attack. Her back brushed against Warren's solid chest. She turned to find him watching her, his brown eyes hooded, his expression grave.

Julia swallowed. Her throat was parched.

"Hi," she whispered.

He ran his hand over her hip. "How do you feel?"

"Better."

"I want you to see my doctor," he said. "Find out about other medication options. The one you're taking doesn't work nearly well enough."

"It works better if I take it sooner than I did." She recalled why she hadn't taken the meds sooner—because she'd been caught in the disaster of a public spectacle.

He frowned, as if he could see the memory descending over her. Was there anything he didn't know or couldn't sense about her? A dozen other questions crowded her mind—if he'd talked to Hailey and the boys, what had happened after they'd left, was everything okay…

She didn't want answers. Not yet. She rose on one elbow and pressed her lips to his, wanting him to make the world disappear before everything else crowded back in on them.

Her heart clenched like a fist. She kissed him again, urged his lips apart. Crisp mint toothpaste and the warm, familiar taste of *him*, a comfort like no other.

Tension laced his shoulders. He lifted his head. She put her hand on his cheek, rubbed the coarse stubble of his beard.

"It's okay," she whispered. "I want…no, I *need* you."

And she did—in more ways than she could name. She needed his strength, his loyalty, his concern, his friendship, his love. She needed the way he was the only person in the world who understood her even when she was being caustic and difficult.

She needed him to turn her failures and disappointments around in his big, capable hands, to help her look at them from different angles, listen to possible solutions. She needed the way his eyes crinkled at the corners when he smiled, the warm pleasure of the secret winks he sent only to her. She needed him always answering her calls and assuring her she could handle anything.

She needed their shared past. His knowledge of everything she'd been and everything she was now. She needed him knowing her better than anyone, better than she knew herself.

"Please," she said.

He put his hands on either side of her head, spreading his fingers against her scalp. His eyes darkened to the color of the earth. Exactly like him—solid, unshakable, enduring. A mountain.

He pulled her closer, the touch of their lips warming her slowly, the burn of a candle. She stroked his chest, absorbed his strength. He trailed his lips over her cheek and ear, down to her neck, flicking his tongue out to lick the hollow of her throat. Pleasure streamed through her, banishing the last threads of pain. He rubbed her breasts, his breath hardening her nipples, awakening her arousal.

Erotic tension began to wind around them both. The air thickened. She ran her fingers over the map of his chest—the hard slopes of his pectoral muscles, down to the ridges of his abdomen and the trail of hair leading to his groin. She rose, pushing him gently onto his back and bringing her mouth down on his.

He tangled his hand in her hair as their lips met in a warm, lengthy advance and retreat—nibbling, tasting, licking. She slid down to kiss his neck, his chest, stroking her tongue down the indentation bisecting his abdomen. When she moved lower and took his half-hard cock in her hand, his fist tightened in her hair.

"Jules, you don't have to…"

"I want to." She opened her mouth and took him in, her body firing with heat at the purely male taste and scent of him.

"Ah, shit, that's good…" A groan rumbled through his chest. His head fell back on the pillow.

Emboldened, Julia got to her knees and sucked him in deeper, tightening her lips around the base. He swelled deliciously in her mouth, the growing thickness of his shaft eliciting a surge of lust. She pressed her thighs together as her own body tingled and dampened in readiness for him. Oh, how she loved their responsiveness to each other, the way their bodies synced as if they knew instinctively what the other wanted and needed.

She licked his shaft, swirled her tongue around the swollen, damp head, and sucked him in again as far as she could. He stroked his hand over her back to her ass, then between her legs. Julia gasped, startling briefly at the sensation of his fingers probing her.

"Keep going." With his other hand, he gently returned her attention to his cock.

She obeyed—because she liked obeying him—and tried to concentrate on pleasuring him even while he fingered her pussy with expert precision, fondling her labia, slipping his forefinger into her slit. She closed her eyes, opening her mouth to pull in a breath.

"I love that you get so fucking wet so fast." His voice was rough, his body tense.

"It's only…" she let out a moan and pushed her hips back to encourage the deeper penetration of his finger, "…only because of you. Oh, that feels good…"

"Your turn. I need to taste you."

He shifted them so she was lying on her back, her legs open. Even now, she was astonished by the sense of freedom that came from being with him. They knew each other so well that, with them, there was only desire, excitement, love.

He moved between her legs, flicking his tongue over her clit, his breath puffing against her sensitive folds. Her breath caught, her body twitching and aching at the touch of his tongue. His chuckle vibrated through her as he clamped his hands on her thighs to hold her in place.

And then his tongue pressed harder, licking at her like candy, down and up, swirling over the pulsing knot of her arousal. Julia could hardly lie still, her hips thrusting like she wanted to impale herself on his tongue. Excitement flooded her with the force of a storm, filling her with heat and passion and that delicious, aching climb toward shattering release.

He pushed her legs farther apart, his movements increasing as if he sensed the tension wrapping around her like ribbons. Her thighs trembled, her body beginning to shake as her arousal reached an unbearable limit. One more sweeping flick of his tongue, and she splintered into a thousand pieces, a high wail emerging from her throat.

"There." His voice filled with satisfaction, Warren lifted himself over her and brought his mouth down for a kiss.

The taste of her own body on his lips fired Julia with fresh heat. She wrapped her legs around his hips as his cock rubbed with delicious intent against her cleft. He covered her like a blanket, making her feel both overwhelmed and protected all at once.

His muscles were taut and slick with perspiration, his breath hot. He lowered his head and sucked her nipples, causing her to gasp and arch against him. The ache in her lower body intensified, her nerves stretched to breaking point. He reached down to grasp his cock and position it at the entrance of her body.

Julia clutched his shoulders, her legs spread wide. Anticipation flared through her. He pushed slowly into her, and she let her body relax and accept the exquisite invasion.

"Ah, tight." Warren groaned as he eased forward, holding himself off her, his muscles straining with the effort of self-control. "Like a fucking glove."

Julia lifted her hips, pulses of need surging through her. She hooked her legs around his thighs to open herself even wider. He pushed forward until he was seated completely within her, and then he stopped and looked down at her, his eyes burning with a thousand emotions all directed only at her.

His cock throbbed inside her, sending heat to her every nerve ending. She felt stretched, full, deliciously taken. She moaned, shifting underneath him, her body craving more.

Warren pulled back a little, pushed forward again, but gently —too gently, as if he were afraid of hurting her. She tightened her legs around him and gripped his big arms.

"Harder," she gasped, her breath scorching her lungs. "Do it harder. Oh, *please*."

He emitted a low groan, his jaw clenching. He eased out of her almost completely, and then pushed forward with a forceful thrust that made her cry out in pleasure. Before she could absorb the sensation, he surged again, creating a friction that coiled her arousal tighter and tighter.

Her mind fogged with the intensity of all she was experiencing—the thick cock plunging in and out of her, the weight of Warren's body above hers, the waves of heat spreading from their naked skin. She clutched him to her, rolling her hips upward to accept every hard plunge of his shaft, reveling in the sensations flowing through her body. He grunted with each thrust, his breath heating her bare shoulder, his hands gliding over her skin.

His pace increased, driving her into the mattress, her body trembling and shuddering beneath him. She came again, vibrating around his cock with an intensity that surpassed the first. He gave a rough shout, his muscles stiffening as he swelled inside her, and her sex flooded with the warm, wet current of his seed.

Panting and sweaty, they rolled apart to catch their breath. Julia closed her eyes. Her love for him was an enormous force inside her, like the intangible power that caused the stars to shine and the earth to rotate. Whatever made the oceans flow and the seasons change.

But for the first time, she didn't turn toward him and tuck herself against his side. He didn't reach for her either. A cold breeze prickled her skin.

CHAPTER 18

W arren woke the next morning with only the haziest realization that it was Christmas Eve. For years, he'd followed the same morning routine, and he did so again, hoping the sameness of brushing his teeth and making coffee would prevent him from thinking too hard.

His phone was overloaded with texts and voicemails. He checked the ones from his children—all asking if Julia was okay, if he was okay, if they needed anything. He texted them with reassurances and promised he would talk to them later.

He couldn't respond to his daughter. Given her standoffish behavior at the party, he had a sick feeling that last night had had something to do with her.

The rustle of stockinged feet sounded behind him. He turned to see Julia in the kitchen doorway, looking soft and fragile in a pink fleece and black pants, her eyes smudged with dark circles and her skin pale.

"How do you feel?" He poured a cup of coffee for her and approached, reaching out to brush a lock of honey-blonde hair away from her forehead.

"Better." She lowered her head to sip the coffee, her expression tensing. "Have you talked to the boys? Hailey?"

"Not yet. I texted them that you're all right." He took a breath and forced the question past his tight throat. "What happened with Hailey?"

Julia shook her head. Tears shone in her eyes.

"She found the letter. You'd left it on your desk, and she went in to get something…and she found it."

Warren kept the intellectual part of his brain focused on that revelation, ignoring the emotions bubbling under the surface. His past wasn't a secret from his children—God knew they'd all made mistakes—but he didn't like the thought that this would change Hailey's relationship with Julia.

"She heard you and Becca fighting about it." Her lips compressed. "Honestly, I always thought you'd told Becca. But Hailey will never look at me the same way again. Not after knowing what I did."

"I'll talk to her." His daughter wasn't vindictive or one to hold a grudge. But she'd also been close to her mother, especially in a family of boys. Rebecca had occasionally been exasperated by Hailey's tomboyish ways, but their daughter had been special to both her and Warren, and everyone knew it. Losing her mother had been the most devastating thing that could have happened to Hailey. To any of them.

But if Julia hadn't stepped in, Hailey never would have recovered as well as she had. Of that Warren had no doubt.

"I love you." There was nothing else he could say.

She looked at him, her eyes glittering. She loved him too. He knew it. Felt it down to his bones, the center of his soul. But she had yet to say it.

"Tell me," he said.

She shook her head, dismay etching her fine features. "I can't."

He slid his hand over her smooth hair to the back of her neck.

The scent of her filled his blood—lavender soap, Julia. Gypsy girl, fashion stylist, ice queen, kitten.

"You can still tell me everything," he said.

But she didn't.

He felt her surrender in the instant before she leaned into him, pressing her face to his shirtfront. A tremble rocked through her. He tightened his arms around her. Breathed her in.

"I have to go," she mumbled. "Deck the Halls is tonight, and there's a ton of stuff left to do."

He forced aside his unease, his frustration with her inability to tell him she loved him. Now was not the time to unpack all the reasons she couldn't say the words.

"I'm helping you," he said. "What do you need me to do?"

"Talk to your children." She pulled away from him. "Because if I tried to talk to them right now, they'd probably tell me to *exit stage left.*"

The clock on the mantel ticked so loudly it echoed in the silence. The bright Christmas decorations, the glittering tree, all were a stark contrast to the somber mood that hung over the room. Warren stood by the fireplace, studying his children. The boys sprawled on the sofa and chairs, none of them making eye contact with either each other or him.

"Where's Hailey?" he asked.

"At my place." Adam rested his elbows on his knees. "She wanted some time alone. Is Aunt Julia okay?"

"She suffers from migraines." Warren dragged a hand down his face, suddenly feeling older than he had in ages. "Often severe. One hit her last night. She's all right now, but the headaches can be incapacitating. She hasn't wanted anyone to know because she...she always wants to be strong."

"She is," Luke said. "I mean, she has been."

"Yes. And I want to remind you all that Julia has been an invaluable part of this family for many years," Warren said. "After your mother died, she helped us in ways we'll never be able to measure. So whatever you think of us as a couple, please remember that she gave up her life in London to move here and be with us. Everything that's happened—good and bad—she's been there. Not only that, she's never wavered. So if any of you have any reason to object to us being together, then you direct those objections to me and me alone. I will not stand for anyone confronting Julia."

The boys shuffled and exchanged glances.

"I don't actually *object*," Luke muttered. "I mean, it'll take some getting used to, but…I can't imagine what we would have done if she hadn't been there."

"It's just a surprise," Evan added.

"Oh, please." Tyler rolled his eyes and put his feet on the coffee table. "You're seriously surprised that Dad and Julia have finally gotten busy? I can't believe they didn't start banging years ago."

"Thank you for your incredulity, son," Warren said dryly.

"But Julia is Mom's sister," Carson added.

"*Mom's* sister," Adam said. "Not *Dad's* sister, for God's sake."

Carson shrugged. "It's still a little strange."

"No it's not," Tyler argued. "They've known each other forever. Objectively speaking, Aunt Julia is incredibly hot. Why wouldn't Dad want to hook up with her?"

"There's a lot more to it than a hook-up," Warren said. "But yes. Julia is indeed *incredibly hot*."

"Right?" Tyler gave Carson a pointed look. "And what better way to start a relationship than as friends? That's exactly what Kate and I did, and look at us. We're so freaking happy together the bluebirds should start singing whenever we kiss."

"What bluebirds?" Spencer asked.

"The *bluebirds*." Tyler scowled and nudged his brother. "Of happiness or whatever. Are you really such a nerd you don't know about the bluebirds?"

"Forget the fucking bluebirds." Luke rubbed his hands over his face. "Dad, this is your business. We want you to be happy."

"What if it doesn't work out?" Spencer asked.

The logic of the question quieted everyone for a second.

"Why wouldn't it work out?" Adam said.

"Well, how long have you been together?" Spencer asked Warren.

"Two weeks."

"So what if a month from now you decide you made a mistake?" Spencer asked. "Not to be grim, but wouldn't that be a problem? Isn't that part of what Hailey is worried about?"

And what Julia had worried about.

"We've been romantically involved for two weeks," Warren said. "But we've been together for far longer than that." He cleared his throat, deciding that now was as good a time as any to tell them the complete truth. "I love her. I hope to marry her one day. Your blessing...all of you...would mean everything to me."

The boys fell silent again, several of them glancing at Luke.

"I don't want or need an answer now," Warren said. "We could all use some time to think. I hope you all still plan to support Julia at Deck the Halls tonight. She needs you."

They all nodded and muttered that they would be there, carrying out their assigned volunteer duties.

After thanking them, Warren went into his office. His gaze skimmed over the unfinished airplane model he'd left on the worktable. He started toward his desk. The room spun around him, almost knocking him off his feet.

A curse blistered through his head. He grabbed hold of a chair and shut his eyes. A heavy tone resounded in his ears, blocking out sound, pressure filling his head. The attack felt as if it lasted an eternity, though when the sick sensations finally began to fade, only a few minutes had passed.

A few minutes too long. On the mountain, in winter, he needed to be capable of making split-second decisions. He couldn't even think when a spell hit, much less *decide* anything.

What if...

He picked up his phone and called the ENT's office. The specialist was available for emergency appointments until one, and the receptionist promised to fit Warren in.

He sank into his desk chair, his insides churning.

"Dad?"

Warren looked up. Luke stood in the doorway, his hands in his pockets and his expression shadowed.

"Come in, son." He straightened, gesturing to a nearby chair.

"Just wanted to tell you I'm okay with everything." Luke sat down, a troubled gleam appearing in his eyes. "I mean, you and Aunt Julia. She drives me crazy, but I know how much she's done for us. So you have my blessing no matter what. And obviously we all want you and Julia to be happy."

Warren's chest tightened. "I appreciate that."

"Okay." Luke nodded, tapping his fingers on the chair arm. "I...uh, I also wanted to apologize."

"For what?"

"For being an asshole about you retiring. I don't want to be that way about Julia."

"You haven't been. You won't be. I get that my retirement is a rough transition. Have you thought any more about a replacement?"

"Yeah, actually. Can I ask your opinion?"

"Sure."

"What do you think of Kate Darling as a candidate for Sugar Rush president?" Luke asked. "She's young, but she's proven herself in countless ways, she's excelled at whatever task she's been given, everyone respects her, and she and I already work really well together. Out of everyone, she might be the best fit."

"I agree." Pride rose in Warren, banishing the lingering unease of the dizzy spell. "In fact, I was waiting for you to figure that out."

"Great." Luke let out his breath, clearly relieved. "It's still going to take a long time to get use to the idea of you retiring. When you first mentioned it, I had this flashback to the months after Mom died, when we were just struggling to keep the company afloat. And with Hailey in the hospital, every night before going to bed I thought we wouldn't make it.

"Then I'd get up in the morning and go back to work. Because I thought, *Well, this is what Dad would do.* I've made a lot of decisions that way, either asking you or thinking about what you would do. So when I realized you wouldn't be at Sugar Rush anymore...well, I felt about five years old, walking into kindergarten for the first time and knowing you couldn't stay there with me."

A smile tugged at Warren's mouth. "I didn't want to leave you at kindergarten. Spent the whole day watching the clock for when I could leave to pick you up."

"Yeah, well..." Luke looked down, rubbing his hands on his thighs. "I just wanted to tell you that I'm the thirty-five-year-old CEO of the Sugar Rush Candy Company, and I can...*probably* handle the transition of the president's retirement."

"I know you can."

"Okay." Luke rose to his feet. "Good. I'll see you later, then."

He started toward the door.

"Luke."

His son turned to look at him.

"I'll still always be there to pick you up."

CHAPTER 19

Christmas Eve dusk in Indigo Bay was bright, cool, sparkly. A marine layer spread across the sky, but thousands of multicolored lights twinkled through the gray fog. The town Christmas tree presided over the square like a king watching his charges, and a lighted banner proclaiming *Indigo Bay's 20th Annual Deck the Halls Show* spanned the stage.

Hundreds of seats had been set up around the stage, with the tree at one side and Santa's Sleigh and village on the other. A line of children waited with varying degrees of patience for their last chance to visit Santa before Christmas Day, and crowds wandered the streets for more last-minute shopping.

"Lady, you have got to get dressed." Marco wove his way through the chairs to where Julia stood near the stage, going over the final details with the lighting technicians. "We have two hours to go, but people are going to start taking seats in an hour to get the best ones. And the poodles are arriving soon, which means backstage is going to the dogs."

Julia smiled at the bad joke, but Marco's shadowed expression told her he knew something was wrong.

"I'll head back now." She glanced at her watch and started toward her car. "Text me if anything comes up."

"Don't you need my help with your makeup and hair?"

"No, I'm good."

Ignoring his puzzled look, she drove to her darkened studio. Everyone was downtown getting ready for the show. She dressed quickly in the dark green, fitted dress she'd chosen for the event. The dress skimmed her torso before flaring out into a full skirt around her calves, and the sweetheart neckline showed off her emerald necklace and earrings. She left her hair loose, brushing it until it shone in a curtain to her shoulders, and reapplied her makeup.

The whole process took her less than an hour, which accounted for Marco's surprise when she returned to the stage.

"Well, fabulous, but what is going on with you?" His gaze skimmed her up and down. "You're a little off."

"Just a migraine yesterday. I'm fine now."

"I didn't know you suffered from migraines."

No one had, except Warren.

She turned her attention back to the last minute details, though part of her mind remained on her worries about the boys and Hailey. A tight knot had formed in the pit of her stomach. She tried not to imagine all the possible consequences as she headed backstage, where the acts were busy warming up and getting increasingly jittery with nerves and excitement.

Jugglers juggled, magicians reviewed their tricks, singers vocalized, poodles barked, and musicians tuned up their instruments. Julia checked attendance to ensure everyone was ready to go and reminded them of their place in the line-up.

She found the Jingle Belles near the stage doors, looking resplendent in their deep red gowns and gold jewelry, their hair and makeup done to perfection. The sight of them eased Julia's tension considerably.

"You all look lovely." She stopped and gave them a genuine smile. "I can't wait to hear you sing."

"We are so grateful to you." Sharon stepped forward to hug her, her own smile wide. "Thank you so much for your time and help."

"We feel like queens." Connie did a little twirl, letting her dress flare out. "Beverly has a—"

"I don't wanna!" A sudden screech broke through the air.

Julia turned, her heart sinking. The Wee Tinsel Dancers clustered in the wings, a tapestry of adorableness in their sparkly red skirts with white ruffles and candy-cane striped bodices. A couple of them were busy practicing their tap dancing routine, but the rest were united in a Wee Tinsel pout.

"We all have to cooperate," Miss Sarah was saying, her arms extended for emphasis. "And we *have* to do a run-through to warm up. We're a team, remember? There's no I in *team*."

"There's a T, though," called the blonde angel.

"And an E," added a curly-haired pixie.

Julia stopped beside them. "What's the problem, girls?"

"Candy canes!" yelled the cinnamon-haired sprite.

"I don't want to do it with Mark," announced a pony-tailed peanut. "I don't like his Gingerbread Man costume."

"Candy canes. Candy canes." The others started a loud chant and marched in a circle.

Sarah sent Julia a weary look. "Maybe we should just bow out. I really don't think they're going to do it. I can't even get them to do a run-through."

Julia groaned inwardly. If the dancers dropped out, she'd have to reorganize the whole timing of the show.

"Did I hear something about candy canes?" boomed a sudden male voice.

Julia and Sarah turned to see Adam approaching in jeans, a red sweater, and a Santa hat. He held a cloth bag in one hand.

"Candy canes!" shouted the sprite.

Adam stopped beside the girls and gave them his sternest look.

"What I have here in my hand…" he gestured to the bag, "…are not only candy canes, but Sugar Rush Chocolate Crunchies, Sparkle Pops, and Honeybee Toffee. They're for the Deck the Halls performers *after* they've finished their act. Kind of like rock stars who return to their dressing rooms for hamburgers and M&Ms."

The girls furrowed their brows and glanced at each other in puzzlement. Adam cleared his throat.

"My point is that they're for after the performance. Now after your magic act, you can—"

"We're not magicians!" yelled the pixie.

"Oh, sorry. After your poodle act…"

The girls burst into giggles. "We're not the poodle act!"

"You're not?" Adam frowned in puzzlement and scratched his head. "Okay, after you finish juggling…"

The girls shrieked with laughter.

"We're tap dancers!"

Adam widened his gaze. "You are? I never would have guessed. I don't believe you."

"Really!" The cherub got up and did a little shuffle to demonstrate. "See our tap shoes?"

"Those are tap shoes?" Adam squinted at their shiny black shoes. "I think I need to see this whole routine to believe it."

"We'll show you!"

The girls scrambled to get into position to perform their act. After giving Adam a relieved and adoring smile, Miss Sarah hurried over to supervise. Within seconds the girls were tapping away.

Julia approached her nephew with wary gratitude. He glanced at her, his expression shuttered but not angry. Awkwardness crackled between them.

"Thank you," she said.

"No problem."

"I...I'm sorry," Julia confessed. "We should have told you from the start."

He shrugged. "Luke said it was none of our business. I guess he's right."

"It is your business. He's your father. And I was..." A stab of guilt hit her. "I'm just so sorry."

"Look, don't worry about it right now, okay? We all know how hard you've worked for this show. You need to focus on it now. We'll talk later."

"Okay." She hesitated. "Have you seen your father?"

"He said he had an appointment this afternoon." Adam glanced at his watch. "But that he'd be here as soon as it was over. Good luck with the show."

As he turned to go, Julia grabbed his arm to stop him. "He said you've been helping him train for the Matterhorn."

"Yeah." Adam looked at her, his blue eyes serious. "Whatever else you're upset with him about, don't be mad about that. There's a reason he's been planning for so long. Dad doesn't do anything half-assed. He and his buddies have been training to the limit. There's no way he'd let any of them set foot on the mountain without knowing exactly what they were doing. And he'd never take any unnecessary risks."

Her nephew's certainty eased Julia's discomfort, as did the knowledge that he was right. Warren's risks were always calculated.

Even the one he'd taken with her.

She let Adam go and got back to work supervising the acts. The crowd outside grew increasingly bigger as it neared six o'clock, the seats filling and the air charging with excited anticipation. As the exterior lights dimmed, Julia forgot about everything but the show.

Adam was right. She had worked so hard for this production. Now it was finally time to celebrate both Indigo Bay's talent and the holidays. The spotlight glowed onstage. The speakers burst out "Deck the Halls." Applause rose from the crowd.

Julia took the wireless microphone from a stagehand and started to the stage for a welcoming announcement.

Marco suddenly grabbed her arm, pulling her to a halt.

"Houston," he said. "We have a problem."

&

"The contractions are three minutes apart." Gail paced back and forth, fidgeting with her phone. "Peter said he'd text me after they check her dilation."

"You need to go." Sharon put her hand on her friend's shoulder. "Laurie needs you there."

"But the show…" Gail glanced at the other Belles, her face tightening with distress, though it was clear her thoughts were with her daughter and approaching granddaughter.

"We can handle it," Beverly said unconvincingly.

Julia glanced at Marco, who shrugged. The Jingle Belles could certainly still perform, but it wouldn't be the same.

"I can't abandon you all right before the final performance." Gail gripped her phone. "I'm the contralto. The harmony will be top-heavy."

"So am I, but I've always managed fine," Beverly remarked, eyeing her own abundant bust.

The women all chuckled, easing the tension for an instant before Gail's phone pinged with a text. Her hand shaking, she swiped the screen. "She's five centimeters dilated."

"Gail, Laurie needs you far more than we do," Sharon told her firmly. "And if you miss seeing your granddaughter in her first moments in the world, you'll regret it forever."

"Go." Connie clasped Gail's shoulders and looked her in the eye. "Get in your car and go to the hospital *now*."

"But what are you all going to do?" Gail asked.

Marco nudged Julia in the side. "Julia is a contralto."

"That has nothing to do with anything," Julia said.

"Well, yeah it does. You could take Gail's place."

"Oh." Gail turned wide eyes on Julia. "*Would* you? That would be fantastic."

When Sharon, Beverly, and Connie turned to Julia with the same, hopeful expectant expressions, her heart plummeted to her toes.

"I most certainly cannot," she said. "First, I can't remember the last time I sang in public. Second, I've never practiced with you three. Third, I am *not* a singer. Fourth—"

"She can sing," Marco told the Jingle Belles. "Really. I've heard it with my own ears."

"Well, it doesn't much matter if you haven't practiced with us, as long as you know your role and hit the notes," Sharon said. "And they're all Christmas songs."

Oh my God. She was going to go onstage and sing. The Jingle Belles were looking at her with such hopeful expectation on their perfectly made-up faces, and they looked so pretty and sweet in the dresses she'd designed—and if she didn't, they might not perform at all, and wouldn't that be a shame because their voices were extraordinary.

"I'll mess up the whole act," she said. "I'm not a *singer*."

"You won't mess up anything." Sharon waved a hand dismissively in a gesture Julia recognized a little too well. "But if you do, we'll be there with you."

Julia turned, her heart squeezing uncomfortably. She shot Marco a glare.

"You're fired," she hissed.

"Hah." He fell into step beside her as she started back to the stage. "I'm like a stubborn zit. I always come back."

CHAPTER 20

"I strongly suggest you don't go. But ultimately it's your call."

The ENT specialist's words rang in Warren's ears as he left the office. Though he was grateful for the last-minute check-in on Christmas Eve, part of him wished he'd never bothered making the appointment. He should have gone with Julia to help her get ready for Deck the Halls. He should have stayed by her side, the way she'd always stayed by his.

He felt weighted, his insides knotted. His call. He was the one who made "the call" after Theo died. The one who'd set the plan into motion. He couldn't quit now. Not after all the work, the preparation, the training they'd done.

But fear pushed at the back of his mind—a fear that had been planted when he'd first realized that his spells of intense vertigo weren't going away.

What if one struck him on the mountain? What if he was scaling a rock face or hit a patch of ice on a slope? What if he made the mistake of looking down at the drop-offs? One slight miscalculation could be fatal—not only for him, but potentially for the other men in his party.

He'd never forgotten the story of the first ascent of the

Matterhorn, during which a rope had broken and four climbers had fallen over four thousand feet to their deaths. Every climber knowingly risked his or her life attempting to reach the summit...but none would risk the life of a fellow climber.

And by not telling his party what was going on, that was exactly what he would be doing.

He parked in the lot of the climbing gym where they'd scheduled an afternoon session, because with the climb so close they didn't even want to take Christmas Eve off.

"Hey, where you been?" Justin called, waving from the spectator area. "Time's almost up."

Warren lifted a hand in greeting and waited for Dave to begin his descent from the wall. He joined them as they packed up their gear, all four of the younger men buzzing with conversation and adrenaline. Warren sat on a bench and tried to muster up the courage to say what he had to say.

"Check it out." Dave dug into his duffle and pulled out five red T-shirts, each emblazoned with the words TEAM THEO. "Figured it would be a way to take him with us."

He tossed a shirt to each of them. Warren caught his. Something stuck in his throat.

"I..." He swallowed, bunching the shirt into his fists. "I gotta tell you all something."

The other men stilled, as if sensing a sudden change in mood.

"What's going on?" Justin asked.

"I've had some health issues the past few months," Warren explained. "Vertigo. Dizzy spells. The doctors haven't found a cause yet, but they're severe enough to make it necessary for me to drop out of the climb."

The weight of stunned silence bore down on him.

"Man, you can't quit," Rick said. "You're the *leader*."

"No. And believe me, I don't want to quit. I'd do anything to get to the summit...except put any of you at risk."

"We can take care of ourselves."

"Yeah, I know. But we also know this climb is more dangerous than high-season climbs. The descent will be brutal. Too many unknown factors. I can't be one of them."

"When the hell did you become an *unknown factor*?" Dave paced a few steps away in frustration. "You've been a fucking rock all this time, man."

Warren shook his head. *Rocks* didn't feel like the earth was rotating too fast.

"I don't know what happened." He tightened his jaw against a sudden stab of fear. "I've never had health problems. My son Evan...That kid's dealt with a heart condition his whole life. Three surgeries before he was ten. And *Hailey*...Jesus Christ. I'm not going to bitch about a little dizziness after what two of my children have gone through."

"Yeah, so you quitting is total bullshit," Justin argued.

Warren leaned his elbows on his knees. "You know why I wouldn't let Adam go with us? Because I knew I'd be too focused on him. Even though he's more experienced than I am, I wouldn't be able to help looking out for him, being concerned. I wouldn't have been able to focus well enough on what I was doing. Which would have put my own safety at risk."

"So Adam's not going with us," Peter said.

"Yeah, but..." He cleared his throat. "I can't let that happen to any of you. I won't."

The other men exchanged glances, their expressions somber and dark.

"Well, that wouldn't happen." Dave spread his hands out, a belligerent note entering his voice. "We know you can handle yourself. We're not going to be concerned about you."

"Yeah," Justin agreed. "We won't give a shit about you on the mountain. Every man for himself, right?"

Affection rose in Warren. He got to his feet and held up the shirt. "I'll wear this when you guys are climbing. I'll always be on

Team Theo. And you'd better reach the fucking summit or I'll kick your asses one by one when you come back down."

He turned and walked away, trying to ignore their voices rising behind him. Like retirement, now that he'd made the decision, he wasn't going to revisit it again. Wasn't going to let anyone talk him out of it.

But damned if it didn't hurt like hell.

He went home to change into a navy suit, knotting a candy-cane patterned tie before leaving for the Holiday Festival. The bright lights and festivities of downtown did nothing to lighten his mood. He maneuvered through the crowd, his thoughts focused only on Julia. He didn't want to interrupt her preparations for Deck the Halls; he just needed to see her.

All the seats around the stage were taken, and more people stood on the perimeter. A salty wind blew in from the ocean. Multicolored lights sparkled and glowed. Throngs of people held paper cups of cocoa and coffee, their faces bright.

The show had already started, everyone's attention focused on a dozen little girls and a Gingerbread Man energetically tap-dancing to "Sleigh Ride." Warren made his way to the side of the stage, scanning the crowd for Julia. He'd have to wait until the show was over.

To tell her the truth. The reason why he'd kept the Matterhorn climb from everyone. Despite all his training, he had never been entirely sure his body wouldn't fail him. Not because he wasn't strong but because he'd lived long enough to know that no one was immune from anything. Evan and Hailey had been his starkest evidence of that fact.

Sometimes you didn't meet the challenges you set for yourself. That was life too.

"Ladies and gentlemen, our next act is Jingle Belles, a marvelous acapella group." Julia's assistant Marco stood on the stage with the microphone, a clipboard in one hand. "We need to announce a slight change in their program. One of their members had to leave and meet her new granddaughter, so the group has a substitute alto for Gail. Please welcome the Jingle Belles. Sharon, Connie, Beverly, and Julia."

Warren's heart jolted. Numerous surprised glances and murmurs accompanied the crowd's applause. Three women decked out in red dresses and one woman in green walked out on to the stage.

God. His heart hammered like that of a fifteen-year-old boy gazing at his movie-star idol. He edged his way to the security rope. One of the Knight Security guards gave him a nod of recognition and removed the rope to let him get closer to the stage.

Julia's hair gleamed in the stage lights, and the green dress flowed over her with the smoothness of a curved leaf. Emeralds winked at her neckline and ears. Even from a distance, Warren detected the nervousness in her expression, even the tremble of her hand as Marco handed her a mic.

He had to suppress the urge not to run onstage and grab her in his arms. Never let her go. The women started to sing "O Come All Ye Faithful," tentative at first and then with greater strength. The audience grew quiet. A chill ran down Warren's spine. Julia's voice—clear, strong—sank into his blood. She transformed when she sang, her face lighting, everything inside her coming through the rise and fall of the notes. Their harmonies were imperfect, but their voices rang together like bells, full of heart and emotion.

The crowd burst into thunderous applause when the song ended. The Jingle Belles consulted for a moment, and Marco stepped out to hand a few pages of music to Julia. The women then launched into "Away in a Manger," "The Holly and the Ivy," and "I Heard the Bells on Christmas Day," concluding with a rendition of "Joy to the World" that had the crowd on its feet applauding before the song ended.

Warren had always been immensely proud of Julia. But this? He didn't think his heart could contain all the pride and love bursting through it.

The women smiled, their eyes bright and their faces glowing. They clasped hands and bowed before one of the women turned to Julia. They spoke for a moment. Julia shook her head. Marco came out again and joined the conversation.

The audience quieted. One of the women, Sharon, turned to the front of the stage.

"Thank you, everyone," she said into her mic. "I think we all know Julia as an incredible stylist and fashion expert. After all, look what she did for us. Miracles can happen, right? But beyond that, she's a truly lovely, kind, generous person and she's become a good friend to the rest of us Belles."

She gave Julia a warm smile. Julia seemed a bit startled, her eyes shifting to the other Belles as if wondering if this was a joke.

"Earlier, Julia's assistant told us that she does an incredible version of 'It Came Upon a Midnight Clear,'" Sharon continued. "We're hoping she'll do a solo. If we can convince her, maybe she'll sing it for us."

Cheers, applause, and whistles rained from the audience. People rose from their seats again, clapping. Julia now had a fixed smile—one Warren recognized as deadly. Marco pointed to the front of the stage. She said something to him through her teeth. He merely shrugged and grinned.

The other Belles stepped back toward the curtain, leaving Julia in the spotlight. Shining like a gemstone. She cleared her throat and spoke into the mic.

"First, thank you for the kind words, Sharon," she said. "I've gotten to know the Jingle Belles as an extraordinary group of women who have inspired me in new ways. As most of you know, I agreed to coordinate this show and not sing in it. So I—"

Her gaze collided with Warren's. His breath stopped.

An eternity folded in on itself in that instant. Stars and galaxies collapsed and burst back into life. They were the only two people in the crowd, the town, the world. He would live forever, as long as he was with her.

Julia brought the microphone back to her lips, her eyes never leaving his. Her voice spun out like gold.

"It came upon a midnight clear, that glorious song of old…"

"…which now the angels sing."

Julia lowered the mic, her whole body pulsing with joy and light. Silence resounded in her ears for an instant before thunderous applause broke over her. Her chest tightened.

She searched the audience again, but Warren had disappeared into the sea of faces. She glanced to the side of the stage where there was a small area reserved for show volunteers.

Her nephews and niece stood there, all seven of them applauding. Hailey wiped her cheeks with a gloved hand. Evan put his arm around her. Tyler was grinning from ear to ear. Julia caught Luke's gaze. He nodded his approval, his own eyes glittering.

It wasn't enough, of course. A song, even one about angels and harps of gold, couldn't bridge the new distance between her and her family. But maybe now there was hope. Hope could still win the battle.

Julia's heart was a bird, fluttering and soaring over a crystal-blue sky. Her voice was imperfect, but her soul was not. From a child singing with her father to a barefoot gypsy girl traveling the country to a successful woman approaching the half-century mark…she was more than she had ever imagined she would be.

Her heart had been broken and then mended. Her confidence dented and then repaired. Her strength sapped and then restored. Her shine dulled and then polished.

She hadn't *missed* anything in life. Just the opposite. With Warren, the boys, Hailey, her life here in this town…she'd *found* everything.

CHAPTER 21

Christmas Eve night fell over Ocean Avenue. The multicolored lights continued to twinkle through the dark, but the shops and cafés closed up, and the seats emptied as people returned home to spend the rest of the evening with their families. The performers celebrated with a short backstage party of cookies, hot cocoa, and Sugar Rush treats before they, too, began heading back home.

"Thank you, Miss Julia!" The pig-tailed cherub threw her arms around Julia's waist.

Julia bent to embrace the little girl. "You did an awesome job, Maggie. All of you did. I hope you keep dancing."

She hugged all the other Wee Tinsel Dancers and waved as their parents carted them out to their cars. A petite, elderly woman wearing a bright red suit embellished with a holly-berry corsage came toward her from the front of the stage.

Julia's spine stiffened automatically. "Hello, Minnie."

"Julia, that was spectacular."

Julia blinked, not sure if she was more surprised by the compliment or the fact that Minnie had gotten her name right. "Thank you so much."

"The best Deck the Halls we've had." Minnie patted Julia's arm. "Everyone will be talking about it for months. And we have an opening on the Holiday Festival committee for next year, so I do hope you'll consider our nomination."

Julia demurred with a polite, "I'll think about it. Thank you for the vote of confidence."

Minnie patted her arm again and headed toward the stage doors.Julia collected her coat and handbag from a storage locker. If she'd pleased Minnie the Pitbull, then the event really had been a success.

"Nice work." Marco approached, his thick-lashed eyes fatigued but his smile as wide as ever. "You did it."

"We did it," Julia corrected. "I can't thank you enough for all you've done."

"Are you still mad at me?" he asked.

"No. In fact, you might find a surprise in your next paycheck. Don't tell anyone I said that."

"Never." Marco grinned at her and started toward the door.

"Marco."

He turned.

"Merry Christmas," Julia said. "Take the next week off. I'll see you in the new year."

"*This…*" he waved a hand around as if to encompass all of her, "…is a fabulous look on you, Miss Julia."

She smiled. He waved and did a little hop and a skip out the stage door.

Julia checked her phone, pleased to see a message from Gail that baby Emma Jane had been born an hour ago, a healthy seven pounds, ten ounces. Both mother and daughter were doing beautifully, and Grandma was over the moon.

Julia sent her congratulations and best wishes, then pulled on her coat and walked out to the dark, empty stage. An increasingly cold wind swept in from the ocean, and the fog had thickened to the point that it blurred the streetlights.

Exhilaration still sparkled like glitter in her blood. She stopped in the middle of the stage, her gaze sweeping over the empty seats and deserted sidewalks. A lone figure sat in the middle of the seats, his presence as welcome and comforting to her as a crackling fire on a snowy night.

Julia started down the stage steps. He stood and walked toward her. They met halfway. Warren's warm brown gaze seemed to drink her in, though he kept his hands in his coat pockets as if he weren't sure whether or not he should touch her.

"You're amazing," he said, his voice rough with emotion.

"I still can't believe I did that."

"I can."

Of course he could. He'd always believed in her, even when the world had tossed her around like a ship on the sea.

"Where are the kids?" she asked.

"They all went home. They knew you'd be tired and said they would see you tomorrow."

Tomorrow was Christmas Day. For the first time since she'd returned to Indigo Bay, there would be no big family celebration.

She and Warren returned to her house. Silence and darkness filled the room, unrelieved by any bright Christmas decorations. Julia stripped out of her gown and showered before putting on a cotton nightgown and crawling into bed beside Warren.

Though uncertainty still hung over them like a cloud, his body was so warm and solid that she drifted into an easy sleep. She woke still nestled against his side and shifted to look at him.

"Merry Christmas." He brushed his lips across her forehead.

I love you.

Still the words stuck in her throat. They wouldn't be her Christmas gift to him this year.

She pressed her face to his chest. Despite the success of Deck the Halls, a hollow feeling still opened inside her. "I wish it was the same as always."

"Things change, Jules. Life changes. Sometimes in bad ways, sometimes in good. This is good. *We're* good."

But they couldn't be *good* if there would always be a wedge between them and Warren's children. Warren and Rebecca's children.

"I'm going to New York tomorrow morning for my meeting with Evermore," Julia said. "I think the time apart will be good for us all. I guess we won't see each other until after the new year."

"I'm not going on the climb."

She looked up at him. "Not because of me. I refuse to be the one stopping you."

"No. Just bad circumstances." He ran his hand over her hair. "It's okay. There'll be another chance next year."

But would there? Wasn't that what life was about—grabbing what you could while it was there? Because there might not be *another chance*.

"What are the circumstances?" she asked.

His jaw tightened. He pulled away from her and sat on the edge of the bed, resting his elbows on his knees. "Bad attacks of vertigo. Ringing and pressure in my ears. No diagnosis, but the doctor ruled out any serious conditions. Unfortunately if I have an attack on the damned climb...I can't risk it. Not when there are four other guys with me. I won't."

Julia's heart squeezed painfully. Though she couldn't deny her relief that he wouldn't risk the arduous, dangerous expedition, she hated that he had to contend with the disappointment and, knowing him, the feeling that he'd somehow failed.

She rose to her knees and wrapped her arms around him from behind. "I'm so sorry."

He patted her arm. "Well, it's Christmas Day. Let's make eggnog waffles or something ridiculous like that."

Julia kissed the back of his neck before he stood and headed out of the room. She went to her computer at the desk in her bedroom and did some internet searching. She printed out a few pages and brought them to Warren, who was making a pot of coffee in the kitchen.

"Remember those acupressure classes you took to help with my migraines?" She spread the printouts on the counter. "Looks like acupressure can help treat vertigo and dizziness too. There's one point below your wrist called pericardium six."

Warren glanced at the papers, his eyebrows lifting. "But does the acupressure actually help your migraines?"

"To a degree, yes." She took his arm and found the pericardium six point. "Right here. There's also a point between your eyebrows and one at the back of your neck. The next time you have an attack, we'll try these and see if they help."

"Good idea. Thanks."

Pleased that she was able to offer a small suggestion considering all he'd done for her, Julia stacked the papers and set them by her handbag as a reminder to look around for an acupressure class she could take.

"Why don't I stay here for the next week instead of going to New York?" she suggested casually as he handed her a cup of coffee. The Matterhorn climb was scheduled for the week after Christmas, and she suspected the forthcoming days would be rough on him—being home while his friends completed the expedition.

"I can reschedule my appointment with Peck," she continued.

Warren sent her a mildly stern look. "You're going to New York. You've worked hard for this, and you're not giving it up for my sake."

"But I—"

"Ho ho ho!"

A male voice suddenly broke through the house. Sleigh bells jangled. A cacophony of voices burst into the kitchen as the front door opened.

Julia startled, her heart leaping. Her six nephews stomped into the foyer, all wearing Santa hats and red-and green striped scarves. They held green wreaths, boughs tied with ribbon, stockings stuffed with goodies, and—at the forefront—Tyler and Spencer carried a small decorated Christmas tree.

"What in the world…?" Julia stared at them.

"Since things got a little derailed this year, we figured we wouldn't have Christmas as usual," Luke said.

"And we've been feeling bad after Dad gave us that lecture about all the work you were doing," Carson explained. "So we decided to bring Christmas to you instead."

Julia's heart flooded with warmth. Beside her, she felt Warren smile.

"Thank you," she told the boys. "I love you all so much."

"And a good thing too," Tyler said. "But there's no way you're finding the pickle."

CHAPTER 22

I 'll see you when I get back.

Julia's text was still open on Warren's phone. After a Christmas of cinnamon rolls and cautious amends with the boys, she'd left the following day to catch her flight to New York. He'd wanted to drive her to the airport, but she'd said she needed to make a stop along the way and would drive herself.

With the exception of Hailey's continued distance from Julia and his lingering regret over the climb, things had settled down a bit. A short separation would be good for them all, but he couldn't help wishing Julia had given him the one gift he'd really wanted.

The words. The *I love you*.

He sat at the table in his workshop, studying the instructions for the half-completed model of a 1/24 scale Hawker Typhoon. He picked up the airplane, examining the frame structure, the cannon fairings, the roof panel.

"Man, you look like shit."

Warren glanced over the tops of his glasses. Justin, Dave, Peter, and Rick stood in the doorway of his office, looking at him like they couldn't reconcile their climbing buddy with the man he was now.

He didn't feel like the same man either, the one who'd spent the past year scaling rock faces and perfecting his scrabbling and icing techniques. The one who could run with a fifty-pound pack and bench press two-hundred pounds.

In addition, he was already missing his girl. Badly.

He straightened and scratched his unshaven jaw. "Feel like shit, too."

"That's why you gotta come with us," Justin said. "No way can you feel sorry for yourself on the mountain."

Warren shook his head, turning his gaze back to the model. "I told you I quit."

"Yeah, you quit, you feel like shit," Dave said. "You think there's a correlation? Come on, man. Hans and Amelie said it's a window of *perfect conditions*. If we don't leave now, we could miss out. Next week, it might be too late."

Miss out. Too late.

"There's a flight out tomorrow night," Peter said. "If we make it, we can start the acclimatization right away. I'm guessing you haven't unpacked any of your gear yet, right?"

"This vertigo thing hasn't gone away." Warren gestured to his ear. He hadn't ruled out Julia's suggestion of acupressure, but there wasn't enough time to try it before the climb started. "If a spell hits bad, I feel like I can't even keep my balance on level ground. What the fuck do I do if that happens on the ridge?"

The four younger men exchanged glances.

"*We'll* be there," Dave said.

"No way." Warren set the airplane down, his insides twisting at the thought of putting his friends in that kind of position. "I won't risk it."

They all looked at each other again, as if coming to an unspoken agreement.

"Look, you were the one who was there for Theo the most,"

Rick said. "You were at his bedside when he died. You called us with the Matterhorn idea—hell, you've been spearheading the whole damned thing. We've been training for a year because of you. And we're not going without you."

Wariness flickered inside him. "What does that mean?"

"What it means." Dave spread his hands out. "You're the boss. You don't go, we don't go."

Warren gave a hollow laugh. "Bastards. Go climb the fucking mountain."

They shook their heads simultaneously, their expressions grave.

"He won't submit to blackmail," said another voice from the great room.

They turned to see Adam coming into the office, his gaze on Warren.

"But if you remind him that throughout his entire life, he's always finished the game," Adam said, "and that he's always been the one to walk before us, the one we all follow, and that he taught us never to believe there are limits to what we can do... just ask Evan...then he'll realize that there's nothing he wants to do more than reach the summit of that mountain. And I'll put money on the fact that he gets there first."

Warren's vision blurred. He looked away from his son, out the window to the valley stretching all the way to the sea.

"Boss," Justin said. "We don't want to go without you."

"And we're not going to let anything happen to you," Dave said. "Just like you won't let anything happen to us."

"That's what we do, right?" Rick added. "We're Team Theo."

Theo. He'd been planning the climb in the midst of chemo. He'd have started training the second he was released from the hospital. If he'd made it.

Warren turned his head to meet his son's gaze. A current of understanding passed between them. He knew why Adam had always had a pull toward adventure and pushing his limits. He liked reminding himself that he was alive. That he had strength and endurance. That the world was full of challenges waiting to be met.

Warren looked at his model. He might not make it to the summit.

Then again, he just might.

CHAPTER 23

No, it hadn't been the Christmas they'd all expected. Certainly it hadn't been the Christmas Julia had planned down to the smallest detail with her Montblanc agenda and her excessive list-making.

But maybe that was okay. Not everything always had to be perfect. And maybe Whoville and the roast beast appeared in different ways for people who needed a little reminder...okay, a *big* reminder...of life's important things.

On her way to the airport for her flight to New York, Julia stopped alongside a narrow road just outside of Indigo Bay. She parked and walked through a small cemetery perched on the hillside overlooking the sea. Rows of headstones sat lined up like soldiers. She stopped at her sister's grave, her chest tightening with sorrow and love.

Rebecca Stone
Beloved mother, wife, sister

She would never forget the funeral—Warren and the boys, silent and gray, all of them watching Rebecca being lowered into the ground while, not ten miles away, Hailey lay unconscious in the hospital. Their shock and grief had been unspeakable.

Julia knelt beside the marble headstone and placed a small lantana plant at the base. In her other hand she held a red helium balloon tied with a string.

Fresh flowers—delivered and replaced every Sunday, per Warren's lifelong order—bloomed from vases on either side of the headstone. She brushed a coating of dust off Rebecca's name. She didn't often come here, not needing to see her sister's grave in order to remember her.

"I miss you," she finally said. "I'm sorry for what happened. I've tried to make it up to you. I hope I succeeded. But I...I don't know what to say about falling in love with your husband."

Saying the words aloud was like a breeze rushing through her, both a relief and a chill.

"I don't know when I fell in love with him," she admitted. "I tried to keep it a secret. Even to pretend like I didn't feel anything more than friendship for him. In fact, I told myself for a very long time that what I felt wasn't *love*, not really. Of course I was lying to myself because how could any woman not love him? Even thirty years ago, I could see why you loved him so much.

"He's so good. Honorable. Kind. Devoted. When you put your trust in him, you know he'll never break it. You just *know*. But I still tried not to love him. I failed miserably, I'm sorry to say. I do love him, Rebecca. With my whole heart, my whole being. I love your children. Warren, the boys, and Hailey have given me a life beyond anything I could have imagined for myself. A life I didn't even know I wanted."

She rose to her feet, still holding the balloon. She wished she knew how to hold on to this life.

But maybe the point wasn't to hold on too tightly. Maybe she also had to let go.

"Aunt Julia."

Her heart jumped. She turned to see Hailey approaching from

the crest of a hill, her slender body clad in jeans and a blue parka, her long ponytail whipped by the ocean wind.

"Hailey." Anxiety clenched her stomach. "Are you all right?"

Her niece shrugged, coming to a stop beside her. "I don't know. You?"

"I don't know either."

"Weird, considering you're usually such a know-it-all."

Julia managed to smile. "I'm so sorry."

Hailey let out a breath, her gaze resting on her mother's headstone. "I miss her."

"So do I."

"I think about her a lot, you know? What she'd say about my life, the things I'm doing."

"She'd be so proud of you."

Hailey acknowledged that with a tilt of her head. "It hasn't always been that easy, growing up with six brothers. I love them a ton, but even when I was a kid they could be pretty smothering. Annoying. Loud. Obnoxious."

"And they still are."

Hailey smiled faintly. "Dad was always so awesome, like he was some sort of lion tamer keeping them all under control. It seemed like there was nothing he couldn't handle. Nothing he couldn't do. Same with Mom. And things with her and me were different, of course, being that I was the only girl. I loved her so much."

Julia's chest ached. "I know you did."

"She was a tough act to follow, though." Hailey pushed her hands deep into her pockets. "She did everything so well. There were times I thought I'd never be as perfect as she was. And after the accident…"

Her voice cracked. Julia wanted desperately to reach for her niece, but she didn't dare. The wind picked up, seagulls squawking overhead.

"I mean, before that I always knew you as exotic Aunt Julia, traveling the world, you know?" Hailey continued. "But one of my first memories when I came to in the hospital was the sound of your voice reading *On the Banks of Plum Creek*. The chapter where Laura and Mary slide down the haystack and make a complete mess. You read that entire series to me."

"It was one of my favorites when I was a girl. It still is. I always wanted to be Laura, but I think I ended up more like Mary. Or maybe Nellie, god forbid."

Hailey gave a small laugh. "You're not a mean girl. Okay, maybe sometimes you *act* like a mean girl, but everyone who knows you knows the truth. Much as you try to hide it."

She turned to face Julia, her eyes bright and her face flushed with cold.

"I love you, Aunt Julia. I missed Mom so much, and to have had you all these years as not only my one female ally in a family of obnoxious boys, but as...as a *friend* is more than I could have wished for. I don't think I would have gotten better as fast as I did if it hadn't been for you. I definitely wouldn't know how to put on lipstick if it hadn't been for you."

Julia's mouth curved. "I love you too, Hailey. More than I can say."

"So the idea of you and Dad together is strange," Hailey admitted. "I mean, he and Mom were together for so long..."

"They were an incredible couple," Julia agreed. "Everyone thought so. Everyone was right, too."

For the first time, a kind of peace settled over her at the memory of Warren and Rebecca's marriage. Wasn't it nice to remember that love and devotion still existed in the world?

"People have thought that about you and Dad, too," Hailey said. "That you were a couple. Friends of mine have been surprised when I told them you weren't. I'm guessing a lot of people were surprised to learn that. You and Dad have been a pretty good team."

"I like to think we've all been a good team."

"We have," Hailey acknowledged. "I guess what I'm trying to say is I'm not going to get all freaked out and upset about you and Dad being together. Maybe I knew it was inevitable all along. And it wasn't that long ago that Evan and Carson were worried about Dad being alone so much of the time...so if you're the reason he's getting out into the world again, then we should be thanking you. You helped him the way you helped me."

Tears pricked Julia's eyes. "I'm not the reason. He'd already made plans before we...got together. I care deeply for him and never wanted to hurt you and your brothers, but I don't know what happens next."

"None of us ever do, Aunt Julia." Hailey stepped forward, pulling her hands from her pockets. "But I can tell you one thing that happens next."

"What's that?"

"I'm going to hug you."

Everything inside Julia gave way when her niece's arms wrapped around her. She let the tears spill over and held on to Hailey as if she were an anchor. When they parted, they were both red-eyed and sniffling.

"So what's with the balloon?" Hailey touched the string of the balloon still wrapped around Julia's hand. "Remember that movie *The Red Balloon*?"

Surprise flickered through Julia. "You've seen it?"

"Yeah, you showed it to me when I was back at home after rehab and watching a ton of movies," Hailey said. "You told me it used to be one of your and Mom's favorites. You both wanted to set a red balloon free."

Julia's heart felt as if it were filling with a thousand bright balloons. "I don't even remember telling you that."

"I do."

"I was going to..." Her throat tightened. She gestured to the ocean, spread out like a painting at the base of the hills. "Set it free."

Hailey smiled. Julia unwrapped the string from around her hand and let the balloon go. She and her niece stood beside each other, watching as the balloon drifted across the hillside, higher and higher, until it was flying over the white-capped waters of the sea toward the horizon.

CHAPTER 24

New York buzzed like a beehive. Julia had always loved it here—the electric energy, the intensity, the creative drive. She looked down at the city from the fifty-second floor of the Evermore corporate headquarters, her reflection blurred in the windows spanning the entire wall. Strange how, thirty years ago, she never would have imagined herself at this height. Now she thought—*well, of course. I've worked hard for this.*

"They're ready for you, Ms. Bennett." The executive assistant extended her hand to the open door of the boardroom.

Julia turned, smoothing her hands over the skirt of her Chanel suit. The ten male members of the Evermore board of directors sat in high-backed leather chairs around a huge oval table, the wood-paneled walls giving the room the air of a stately library. Vincent Peck—distinguished, gray-haired, smartly dressed in a tailored suit and cravat—rose from the head of the table and held out his hand.

"Julia, welcome. We've been looking forward to your visit."

"I appreciate the invitation." She shook his hand and took her seat at the opposite end of the table.

After a round of introductions, Julia gave her prepared

presentation about Queen Bee, explaining her vision for the line and showing them illustrations and photographs of her proposed designs.

Though the stakes were high, she wasn't nervous. She believed in her idea—maybe more than she'd believed in any of her ideas over the years—and if the Evermore board couldn't see how good it was, then they still weren't the right company for her. Even if their investment would put her in an entirely different sphere.

She distilled the extensive research she'd done about the buying processes and patterns of older women, and the fact that women over fifty were the most active, wealthy, and healthiest generation in history.

"In fact," she said, "women over fifty control a net worth of over twenty trillion dollars. They will control over two-thirds of consumer wealth in the next decade. They have enormous purchasing power. They are investors, professionals, business owners, executives. They are also mothers, grandmothers, wives, friends, sisters, and aunts. They are women who deserve to be both heard and spoken with. They represent a cultural shift in society to the recognition that age is a goal, a privilege, and an honor. Queen Bee is the fashion of that change."

The board members thanked her for the presentation, murmured among themselves, and perused again the written proposals she'd sent them last week. Vincent nodded at his assistant, who rose and distributed leather binders to each of them.

"We've had lengthy discussions about your line already," Vincent said. "We believe you've targeted a demographic that isn't just underserved, but has been outright ignored. We like your vision, your designs, your approach. I don't need to tell you that we're also very impressed with your company and your experience. We also find it refreshing that you've chosen to live in California when so many stylists and designers of your caliber prefer the East Coast."

Though Julia registered the oddity of that last comment—with increasing technology, successful designers could live anywhere they wanted—her attention snapped to the printed title on the binder. *Evermore Proposal to Purchase Queen Bee.*

Her heart started to pound harder.

"Let's have a look at our offer," Vincent suggested.

A rustle followed as everyone opened the binders. Vincent outlined the points one by one—an enormous amount of money, followed by details about stock options, assets, benefits, insurance, and the final point that Evermore wanted to retain Julia as the creative director of the Queen Bee line.

"It's your vision, after all." Vincent closed the binder and spread his hands out, a look of complacent satisfaction on his face. "We'd be honored to have you join the Evermore team as an in-house fashion designer of our department store chain, with Queen Bee eventually joining our curated brands. Exclusively, of course. You'd have your own office here in this building, with control over Queen Bee's design and retail development. We work with numerous factories in China who help keep our profit margins nice and high, but you'll direct the design teams and work with advertising to ensure your brand reflects your vision."

Julia's heart was now racing, but she managed to give a composed nod. "I appreciate the offer. As I'm sure you're aware, it's very important that I also continue to design the clothes, especially as we're still in such an early stage."

"Of course." Vincent waved his hand, as if that were a given. "We don't want to undermine your influence, though of course Queen Bee will belong to Evermore. We only want to help you grow, to see this concept reach its full potential. To exceed it, in fact. To make it more than you can imagine."

Beneath her concealed shock, Julia was tempted to respond to that remark with the Han Solo *Star Wars* line, *"I don't know, I can imagine quite a bit."*

Because she could—even if Vincent Peck thought her imagination had limits.

She took her time leafing through the proposal, scanning the clauses and the massive numbers that jumped out at her in bold print.

"As you know, I live in California," she said. "That's where my business is headquartered. My family lives there. Accepting your offer implies I'd move to New York."

"An apartment subsidy is included in clause sixteen," another man, who had introduced himself as a member of the legal team, pointed out. "We also work with a broker who will help you find a place to rent."

"I'm not willing to move to New York," Julia said.

Vincent smiled. "That's not a deal-breaker, Julia. Perhaps we can work out a bicoastal arrangement, or a situation where you'd come to New York a few months out of the year. That point is negotiable."

"Thank you." Julia rose gracefully from her chair and nodded. "This offer is quite…compelling. May I have a moment, please?"

"Take all the time you need. Agnes, show Ms. Bennett to one of the other conference rooms, if she'd like some privacy."

"Yes, sir."

Julia picked up the binder and her satchel and walked into the corridor, her spine straight and steps measured.

"Would you like anything to drink?" The assistant showed her into an empty conference room a few doors down from the boardroom.

"No, thank you. I won't be long."

Agnes nodded and left, closing the door behind her.

Only then did Julia sag against the door, her breath expelling in a huge rush. She sank to the floor and pressed her hands to her face, a trembling excitement rising in her like an earthquake.

She grabbed her cellphone from her satchel, her hands shaking.

Please answer. Please please please...

"You have reached the number for Warren Stone..."

Tears stung her eyes. She ended the call and tried to work through her tangled thoughts and excitement. Never in her career had she had this kind of offer. She needed to discuss it with Warren more than she could stand. Did she take the offer now or wait and see what else might come along?

She pushed to her feet, walked to the windows, and looked down at the city. Imagined herself working in this high-rise building, designing fashions for women.

For a company run by ten male board members. For the Evermore president who had once derided her for being "old" and "out of touch."

Her stomach twisted. She pressed her forehead against the glass.

Longevity is power.

She was no longer a nineteen-year-old who liked frilly dresses and strapless halter tops. She was an almost fifty-year-old woman who had worked, fought, guided, learned, and loved her way through a half-century. She'd established her own successful business. She was smart, sexy as hell, and took no prisoners. She'd made mistakes. She'd done her best. She had experience, knowledge, talent.

She'd carved her own path from the very start. Did she want to be under another company's control now? To sell them her phenomenal new idea?

Her phone rang with Coldplay's "Adventure of a Lifetime." Adam's ringtone.

Suppressing disappointment that it wasn't Warren, she answered the call. "Adam?"

"Aunt Julia."

"Yes." Faint alarm rose in her at his anxious tone. "Is everything all right?"

"Dad tried to reach you, but you must have been in the meeting."

"What's wrong?"

"His buddies stopped by yesterday to talk to him about the climb."

Julia pressed a hand to her chest. Her heart started to race. "But he...Warren said he wasn't going to do it."

"He changed his mind."

"What?"

"He's leaving for Switzerland tonight."

CHAPTER 25

D*on't go.*
The text popped up just as Warren was packing the last of his things from his desk at Sugar Rush. He'd been trying to get ahold of Julia for most of the day, but for whatever reason— meetings, bad connections, or she didn't want to talk to him—he hadn't been able to reach her.

But this…

He picked up his phone. His heart hammered.

Don't go.

She hadn't asked him not to climb the Matterhorn when he'd first told her of his plans. She hadn't liked it, but she hadn't asked him not to. So why was she asking him now?

"Hey, Dad." Luke stopped in the doorway, his keys in his hand. "We should leave now to make sure we get to the airport on time."

"Give me a second." Warren turned back to his phone. He called Julia's number, but the phone went to voicemail. *What the...?*

Frustrated, he put the phone in his pocket, grabbed his duffle, and headed for the door. All of his gear was already packed in his

SUV, but he didn't want to board the plane without talking to Julia first.

He left his office, vaguely noticing that the entire building was almost deserted. Post-Christmas lull. He took the stairs to the first floor and stepped outside. Applause and cheers burst like fireworks in front of him. Warren stopped in his tracks.

Dozens of Sugar Rush employees—his assistant, the VPs, the secretaries, the accountants, the managers—all stood on the winding paths of the garden, filling the air with noise. Handmade signs waved like flags: *Good luck, boss! We'll miss you! Enjoy the view! Keep climbing!*

His throat tightened. All seven of his children stood on the steps, clapping and smiling along with everyone else.

Carson approached to take his duffle. "Ready, Dad?"

Since he couldn't speak, Warren just nodded. *Onward.*

He started down the steps. The crowd continued cheering and applauding until a group near the parking lot quieted. Like a wave, a rustle suddenly passed through the throng of people, and the noise slowly stopped. Through the growing quiet, a woman's voice rang out.

"Warren!"

His heart slammed against his chest. He turned to the parking lot. The crowd parted. Julia was racing toward him, her hair flying behind her in a messy ponytail, her gorgeous figure clad in black pants and a T-shirt.

Everyone stared at her. Warren's hand tightened on the phone in his pocket.

Don't go.

"Warren." Julia ran up the pathway, seemingly heedless of the fact that almost the entire company was crowded around them. Panting, she came to a halt and bent double, resting her hands on her thighs as she struggled to catch her breath. "Shit. Don't...don't go."

Warren prided himself on knowing what the hell to do in

most situations. He knew how to handle a business meeting, negotiate, deal with employees, socialize. He usually had it down.

But now? He had no idea what to do. He knew he *wanted* to haul Julia against him and kiss her senseless, but…

"Jesus, I gotta get back to the gym." She straightened and held up a hand, her chest heaving. Her gaze collided with his. Her eyes burned with a thousand emotions—fear, worry, panic, hope.

Hope.

"I have to show you something," she gasped.

"Okay."

"I added something else to my *Before Fifty* list."

She fumbled in her pocket. Everyone was silent, people glancing at each other in bemusement. She pulled the crumpled list out and handed it to Warren. He unfolded it, his gaze going to the bottom where she'd written:

#51: Tell Warren Stone I love him

He looked at her. Bright, brilliant colors sparked right in the middle of his soul.

"I love you, Warren." Julia approached him, appearing finally to have caught her breath. "I…I had to tell you. I think I even fell a little bit in love with you when you came after me that night and told that guy you were my husband, then bought me bread-sticks. And I know I've spent the last thirteen years falling slowly in love with you because you've proven to be every inch the man I thought you were. I love your heart, your character, your sense of honor, your dedication to your family's company and your children. I love the way you make me feel. I love *you*."

He was already moving closer before she'd finished her little speech, his hands closing around her shoulders. He hauled her against him and brought his mouth down on hers, drinking in the taste and feel of her, the knowledge that she was his. He was vaguely aware of a renewed burst of applause, but all he cared about was the woman in his arms.

He lifted his head, stroking the side of her face. "I love you. I was trying to reach you, but you must have been on the plane. I got your text, though."

His wariness flickered back to life. *Don't go.*

"I *won't* go," he said hastily. "I don't need the mountain, not if I have you."

"Yes, you do."

"But your text…"

"I was talking about the airport. I didn't want you to leave before I got here." She smiled, her eyes warming to the color of bluebells. "You do need the mountain, Warren. And you need to finish what you started. If you don't, you'll regret it forever. Go climb the freaking Matterhorn, my love. When you come back down, I'll be waiting for you."

The colors intensified, spilling into his blood. "Wait. What about your meeting with Evermore?"

"I'm not taking the deal."

He frowned. "Why not?"

"Because I can launch Queen Bee on my own." Julia curled her hands into his lapels, her face glowing with expectation. "I thought about it the whole way home. I don't need a board of directors telling me what to do and limiting my options. I know exactly what I want for this line, for my business, and I'm the one who's going to do it. It's like my Matterhorn. Only less snowy."

Everyone had their own mountain to climb. He had no doubt Julia would reach the summit of hers. He kissed her again, everything inside him flooding with gratitude for her, for himself, for this universe that had given him so much.

Seven children who illuminated his world. The legacy of his family, a rich history to guide his path.

A love lost. A love found. The rest of his life to live.

EPILOGUE

Two weeks later

"Apparently you lost a toe to frostbite." Tyler peered at the screen of his laptop. "But you still managed to carry your buddy down the mountain when he was struck with altitude sickness."

"This one says you saved another climber who'd lost his way in a sudden blizzard," Carson remarked, scrolling on his phone. "You unfastened your safety line to reach him."

Julia met Warren's gaze from across the room, both of them amused by the enhancement of his legendary status. Social media had been awash in rumors of his alleged heroism since his return to Indigo Bay—the former president of the Sugar Rush Candy Company tackles the Matterhorn and wins.

But though Julia was aware that tragedies often took place on mountain climbs, there had been no frostbite or rescues this time. Warren and his friends had started the relentless climb in the dim light of dawn, picking their way up the rocky, path-less route. They'd balanced on precarious ledges to put on their spiked crampons, then ascended to the icy, almost vertical slopes leading to the summit.

They'd battled frigid wind, blinding snow, thousand-meter drop-offs. They'd roped themselves together and picked each other up when they fell. They'd climbed the last hundred yards to the highest point, where the edge of a cliff dropped off to Switzerland on one side and Italy on the other. Surrounded by majestic snowy peaks, they'd stood in awe on the summit, toasted Theo with protein bars, and began the precarious descent.

And when they'd entered the lodge, exhausted and battle-weary, Julia had been waiting for Warren. He'd been aching, wind-burned, freezing, and exhilarated. The light in his eyes would never die. They'd returned home a day later, ready to start the new year together.

Warren had fortunately not been plagued by vertigo during the climb, but upon their return another ENT specialist had concluded that the attacks were the symptom of an inner ear disorder that could be managed with treatments. Since he didn't plan to climb another mountain of the Matterhorn's magnitude, Warren had taken the news in stride—another life change like so many that had preceded it and the many that would follow.

"Man, this was the best idea ever." Tyler bit into a hot cinnamon roll, his gaze on the televised football game. "We should totally celebrate Christmas on January fifth every year."

Carson scoffed.

"What?" Tyler asked. "The lead-in is so much easier, right? No traffic, no crowded stores, no trouble finding groceries, no pressure. It's all good, man."

Julia smiled when Warren winked at her. It was *all good*. The Christmas tree, still fresh thanks to their late trimming, sparkled near the fireplace, and all of Julia's decorations were in place. Spencer and Adam were throwing a football in the backyard, the smell of baking ham drifted from the kitchen, and a stack of board games sat on the kitchen counter, awaiting post-dinner challenges.

It was more than *all good*, Julia thought. It was all perfect.

"Julia, what time is your show tomorrow night?" Carson was still on his phone. "Are we getting dinner beforehand?"

"It starts at eight, so yes, there's plenty of time." Julia was singing with the Jingle Belles the following night at the Indigo Bay Theater—to her surprised pleasure, her friends had asked her to join them for several upcoming performances.

"What about this?" Hailey turned a sketchpad toward her. "I don't think it should be too cutesy, but bees like buttercups and they can be rendered well for a logo."

Julia studied the sketch—a simple yet realistic illustration of a bee hovering over an open buttercup, laced with the words *Queen Bee* in a cursive font.

"I love it," Julia said. "It's very elegant."

"It might need to be even simpler." Hailey chewed on the end of her pencil with a frown. "Maybe a pollen-bearing sunflower would work better. I'll give you a few more options."

She turned back to her drawing. Julia patted her niece's knee and rose to head into the kitchen. She checked the ham, ensured that Tyler hadn't already dug into the apple pie and chocolate cake, and set various platters on the central island.

Two strong male arms came around her from behind. Julia relaxed back against Warren's chest, her heart and soul filling with warmth.

"I love you," she said.

"Excuse me? I didn't quite catch that."

She nudged him with her elbow. "*I love you.* How many times do I have to say it?"

"Countless." He turned her in his arms, his eyes crinkling at the corners with a smile. "Because I'll never get tired of hearing it."

He lowered his head at the same instant that she rose on her tiptoes. Their lips met in a kiss that contained a thousand promises and hopes. Whatever regrets or guilt they'd both carried had floated away like balloons, leaving only the knowledge that they had to make the most of the time they had together. Because at the end of the day, what was more of a gift than love and family?

"Hey, I had another idea for the list." Warren lifted his head, detaching himself from her to take a piece of paper out of his pocket. "I wrote it down."

He handed the paper to her. Julia unfolded it and scanned the items labelled #1 to #38. On the last line, Warren had written:

38. Get married.

Her heart stuttered. She lifted her gaze to his. "Really?"

"Really." He slid his arms around her waist, pulling their lower bodies together. "Be mine in every way there is. Let's have adventures, live on the edge, do things we've never done before. Let's do it all together. Marry me, Julia."

"Of course I'll marry you." She put her hand against his cheek, feeling as if she could burst into song. "But let's wait a little bit, okay? Maybe after we've crossed a few more things off our list."

"Whenever you're ready, I'll be here. We have all the time in the world."

Their lips met again in a kiss that felt like a homecoming. Julia had never before been so excited for the future, for all the years to come in which she and Warren could live, love, and check the action items off their new list:

Things To Do Before We Turn Eighty

ABOUT THE AUTHOR

New York Times & USA Today bestselling author Nina Lane
writes hot, sexy romances about professors, bad boys, candy
makers, and protective alpha males who find themselves
consumed with love for one woman alone. Originally from
California, Nina holds a PhD in Art History and an MA in
Library and Information Studies, which means she loves both
research and organization. She also enjoys traveling and thinks
St. Petersburg, Russia is a city everyone should visit at least once.
Although Nina would go back to college for another degree
because she's that much of a bookworm and a perpetual student,
she now lives the happy life of a full-time writer.

www.ninalane.com

THE SPIRAL OF BLISS SERIES

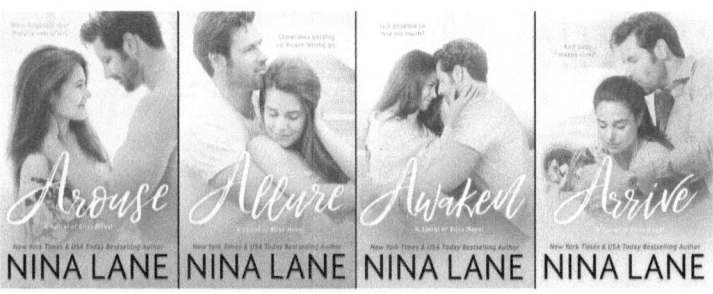

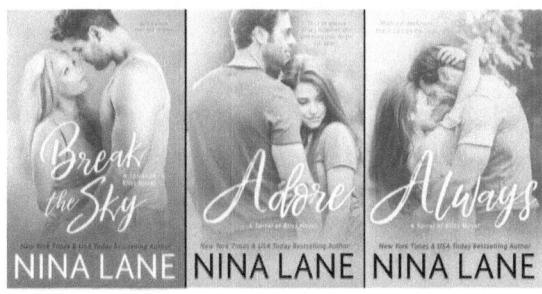

"Give me a kiss, beauty."

From an exhilarating crush to the intensities of marriage, Liv and Dean West embark on a passionate lifelong journey together. As the medieval history professor and his beloved wife face both personal challenges and painful battles, they never lose sight of the hope, humor, and devotion that belong only to them.

Liv and Dean's everlasting romance will melt your heart, turn you on, and enchant you with the power of a love to end all loves.

First we fell in love. Then we fell apart.

Shattered by tragedy a decade ago, two lovers fight the secrets that could destroy them.

"This book is a work of art."

A woman fleeing scandal. A town's mysterious recluse.

Lust and secrets collide in this provocative romance.